FLINGING ALL SPRING

BOOK 3 OF SAG HARBOR BLACK ROMANCES

LULA WHITE

CONTENT WARNING & DISCLAIMER

***This book contains strong language and medium-heat sex depictions.**

This is a work of fiction. Sag Harbor is a real place and the author has included some of its actual neighborhoods, streets and history. However, all of the characters and plot are fictionalized as products of the author's creation, as well as most of the small businesses. (I.e., please do not go to Sag Harbor expecting to visit Little Italy restaurant.) Names of real businesses may be included from time to time, for benign purposes, and to lend authenticity. Any resemblance to actual persons, living or deceased, is entirely coincidental.

All rights reserved. This book may not be reproduced, appropriated, or copied without express written permission from Lula White.

www.blackluxuryromances.com

THE SAG HARBOR COMMUNITY

The Sag Harbor world includes two book series- nine books and three novellas.

Each book contains a complete story with an HEA, and can be read out of order, but this simmering saga of love, rivalry, family and friendships is most immersive in order.

If you can't walk away from the Black Hamptons, here's the path to get acquainted with this world. The events do not occur based on order of the books:

Brown Sugar This Christmas

Hot Chocolate This Winter

Flinging All Spring

Overheated for Summer

One Tasty Night FREE Novella

Explore You

Rouse Family Christmas

Christmas Down Under (FREE Download- website only)

Taste You

Drink You

See Through You

Find You

www.lulawhitebooks.com

email: lula@lulawhitebooks.com www.blackluxuryromances.com

LULA'S FLINGING PLAYLIST

Hey Loves, I have a music playlist for all books in the series. These are the songs I listened to while writing this story, and am sharing with those who want Adella's soft vibe mixed with a little of Desmond's street. In my Loves Letter and on my web site, I'll share which songs go with which scene.

On Spotify it's free to set up an account. I will also send out the list of songs to my Loves, and will make the list available in the Books section of my web site.

Flinging All Spring on Spotify

PROLOGUE

THE DAY BEFORE THANKSGIVING

ADELLA

Dr. Adella English pulled off her bloody operating gloves and squeezed the arm of her eight-year-old patient, before she left the operating room. "I want to see him again in twelve hours. A little concerned about his stability, given his diabetes."

She released an exhausted sigh, unfurling her hair from the ponytail she'd worn the last two days. Her next to last shift before the Thanksgiving holiday brought a smile to her lips. One more round of twelve hours, and she'd be free for four days.

In the doctors' locker room, she showered and threw on her street clothes. Then, a pair of familiar arms circled her waist. Her bottom lip slid under her teeth, and she leaned her head back to savor her man's warm breath on her neck. And his lips.

"Good morning," Wes murmured, since it was 9:33 a.m.

"Good morning yourself," she twittered like the birds on the windowsill outside the locker room.

"How was surgery?" he asked.

"Successful for now. But I'm coming back early to watch the little guy, make sure he remains stable. When do you think you'll be out?"

"Probably midnight." He steered her to face him. "Then I'd like to take care of somebody else for Thanksgiving. My most special patient."

He kissed Del, and her rapid heartbeat might have propelled her from the floor.

After devouring her lips, he gave her a final peck, sweeping his finger over her brow. "And I'm hoping this holiday, we can finally…"

His gaze slid over her figure, a subtle reference to all he hadn't experienced yet.

A giddy heart surgeon gazed back at him, rubbing his shoulders and trying to forget the slight tension in hers.

She doubted how much longer she could hold him off. How many thirty-five-year-old men waited for a virgin?

"Have I not shown you how I feel about you?" Wes referenced the ring he'd bought her, that she couldn't wear at work. His eyes examined hers.

"Of course, you have." She stroked his cheek. "But how many times have we talked about my family?"

His head fell. "Adella, it's the twenty-first century. We're no longer delivering our mail by horse and buggy."

"Can we please not talk about this here at work?" She lifted his head and brought his gaze back to hers.

"Sure, I'm sorry, I was just hoping…"

"I know, and so do I. And we *will*. I can't tell you how much it means that you're so patient."

Wes's eyes flared. "I seriously can't wait to meet this family of yours that has such an iron grip on you. My family adores you, Del. They can't wait for us to marry and you to become their daughter. So when will you tell your folks?"

Her breaths became shallow.

"The next time we're all together. Everybody's headed to Cape Cod for Christmas. Come with me then, and that's when we'll tell everybody."

Wes kissed her hand, a smile returning and his eyes shining again. "Really?"

Del swallowed the anxiety clogging her throat about her family's reaction when they learned that Wes was white. But she wondered if that was her only fear.

Still, Del nodded. "Yes. Really."

At that moment, her phone buzzed in her purse. Her attention shot to the screen.

Solomon. Del's oldest brother. He rarely called her.

"I have to grab this."

A happy Wes put a final peck on her lips. "See you tonight then."

"Yes, tonight." She hurried to swipe on the phone so she didn't miss her brother's call.

"Solomon, hey! Happy Thanksgiving! It's been too long, big brother!"

His heavy voice greeted her. "I know, Adella, and I'm sorry to deliver bad news, but you will need to come to the Cape. Papa is sick. In the hospital, and they're not sure he'll make it. He woke up for a bit, and he wants to see… you."

Her beloved grandfather was one of her favorite people in the world. She plummeted to the changing bench and dropped her purse. "What happened to Papa?"

"He had a heart attack two nights ago. We're scared his condition may worsen. So the elders are rounding up the family."

"Two nights! Why am I just now getting a call?"

"The elders only called the grandchildren today." By the elders, he meant Papa French's eight children, including Del's mother.

Del blinked as if her eyelids were windshield wipers that could clear her confusion.

She'd just spoken to eighty-six-year-old Papa a few days before, and he'd sounded fine.

Del and Wes had intended to stay in town for Thanksgiving, dine with friends, and take in a couple of shows. Now, she strategized making the drive that would likely take three hours.

She tore out of the doctors' locker room with her purse and keys, hoping she could reach Papa's hospital by early afternoon. She made a pit stop by the cafeteria to inform Wes of the emergency.

A big smile crossed his lips. "One more goodbye kiss before you go? How did I get so lucky?"

"I'm so sorry."

"What do you mean? Sorry about what? You look like your dog just died, and you don't have a dog, my love."

Del reeled as she forced herself to say the words. "I just got a call from home, and it's my papa. He had a heart attack, and his condition is not stable."

"Whoa, oh wow, babe. You shouldn't go through that alone. I'll go with you and support you," Wes offered. "I can tell the chief to pull somebody else in here to cover me. I know how much your grandfather means to you. I'd like to meet him if I could."

Del looked into the eyes of the man she'd been dating the past year. Her insides screamed that that was not a good idea. She cleared her throat.

"You know what? For right now, let me feel out what's happening with my family."

Wes's shoulders slumped, but he sucked back his clear disappointment. "Alright then. Sure, whatever you say, Del. We'll wait."

Her worry for Papa was mounting inside her. She fretted over whether each moment of her delay might be the last that Papa breathed.

But even under the weight of her anxiety, she saw Wes's disappointment.

"Meet me there in a couple of days. I'll go first, be with my mother, and help her. And on Saturday, come and join me. How's that?"

A tender, grateful kiss was Del's send-off. Wes stroked her neck. "I love you. My prayers are with you and your family. Call me and tell me when you've made it safely."

She nodded and sucked his lips one last time, breathing in the familiar mixed scent of closeted doctor scrubs, latex, and medical-grade sanitizer. To the rest of the world, the scent might have been a horrendous reminder of a Halloween house of horrors. But to Wes and Del, it was the smell over which they'd bonded the past year.

"I love you too. I'll call you." Their fingers clasping a final time, their gazes held a few moments longer. Del forced herself to turn away, and she made a hasty dash for the doctors and nurses' exit.

The drive to the Cape gave her ample time to stress over how she would prepare her traditional family for a white country guy in the form of Wes.

It was the last thing Papa needed after a heart attack. Her grandfather had always made clear to his family that roots and heritage were everything. In fact, the *only* thing worth preserving.

While the Manuel family's wealth may have placed them among mostly whites in their professions, neighborhoods, and country clubs, they were to always remain committed to their Black-American ancestry. So for her to bring a white man to Papa's *dying* bedside... she cringed at the tornado of angst forming ahead.

Arriving in the Cape, she didn't stop by her grandparents' home but headed straight to Cape Cod General Hospital. After her cousin texted her the room number, seconds later, she was entering a parade. Cousins, aunts, uncles, and extended relatives filled the corridor outside her grandfather's room. Many who had flown into town overnight had not visited Cape Cod in years. She guessed they were waiting for his last breaths so they could get to the distributions of the estate.

Adella greeted her cousin, Afi. "Afi, how is he? Any changes?"

Afi shook her head. "He's awake but weak. Hooked up to a ventilator."

Mentally, Del took off her heart surgeon hat and settled into obscurity as the anxious granddaughter. Even if she possessed insight into her grandfather's condition, her mother, aunts, and uncles would likely dismiss it.

A long line of relatives waited to see him. Adella prepared to wait her turn, greeting relatives she had not seen in a while. Second and third cousins had flown in from colleges, graduate schools, and jobs across the country. Even her grandfather's long-lost brother appeared. And more relatives trickled in every few minutes.

"Del! I've been waiting forever. Get in here," her mother's frustrated voice called to her from Papa's room.

"But, Mom, I'm skipping the line. What is it? You have a medical question? His heart?"

"No. We are waiting for *you*. He has asked where you are," her mother replied, hands gripping Del and pulling her inside.

Confused, she followed her mother who maneuvered Adella past her grandfather's seven other children.

"Pa," her mother whispered into Mr. Manuel's ear. "She is here, Pa."

Del went to his bedside, where a frail man seemed stricken by a comet and eaten by its radiation, since she'd last seen him three weeks before. "Papa."

His eyes formed slits as their pupils rolled around in a dazed state. They found her. "Del... ba... by," his hoarse voice creaked.

She leaned closer, and his fingers shook to find hers.

Cracking a joke, she asked, "What are you doing in here? I thought we were going golfing this weekend?"

Hard as Del tried not to cry, tears slid down her cheeks for this tall, strong man now rendered so feeble.

A thin smile cracked around the corners of his lips. "The…" he slurred.

Del's surgical mind presumed his tongue was likely dry and its muscles impacted by heavy sedatives.

"The lllaww…"

"The law, Papa?" Del tried to clarify.

"Law… yer. Talk to… lawyer. K?" He managed to nod an inch. "I tr… tru… st… yyy…"

Del blinked numerous times. "Stop trying to talk. Preserve your energy for healing. You will get up in a couple of days and walk right out of here, and we will go hunting. Nothing else."

He smiled, a tear running down his face. "Proud." Another slight nod. "Pr…" His chest heaved up and down.

She started to check his vitals and heart monitor.

"Papa!" Del cried.

"Pa!" Her mother pushed Del out of the way.

As did each of his scurrying children, until Frenchie Manuel's granddaughter found herself the farthest from the man who might have been closer to her than her own father.

The guttural wails and cries that rang out around the room confirmed her fear.

She made her way back outside, and her cousins crowded around her.

"Well? Did he speak? What did he want?" Afi asked.

"Why you?" another relative asked.

A sea of faces surrounded Del, but she was still trying to decipher his strained last words. Talk to a lawyer about what? She wasn't one of his children, so why did she need to concern herself with his legal affairs? Her mother and Aunt Lizelle and Uncle Bryce could handle all that. She simply wanted to mourn that Papa's strong voice and stronger spirit were only a memory now.

"He's hooked up to monitors and could hardly breathe. I only made out that he said he was proud," she lied.

"Proud of what? Proud of who? Did he say anyone's name?" a flurry of voices asked, one after another, until they fused together.

"Excuse me. Doctor?" a single voice rose above them all.

Del ignored it, assuming someone called for a doctor and nursing staff to come and perform standard resuscitation protocols before pronouncement of the death.

Swirling in a windstorm of grief, she grabbed her forehead. Maybe Wes should have come with her, because her grandfather's loss was hitting her like a wrecking ball she hadn't expected when she'd driven in.

"Dr. English? Adella English?"

When she lifted her heavy head, a lone arm extended toward her. It offered her a sealed envelope.

"Yes?" she asked.

"For you, madam," a mail courier responded. "Would you sign here, please, confirming your receipt?"

All eyes fell on her.

Did she open this document in front of everyone?

Adella stood to trudge away, having no clue if this was private or something intended to be read in front of the family. She decided she would inspect it first.

"Where are you going?" Afi asked.

"This envelope is addressed to me alone."

After reaching a small chapel, she sat on a pew before opening it with shaking fingers.

Adella English, you have been named the sole heir to the estate of Charles Francis Manuel. With conditions. Please present yourself tomorrow, the day after your grandfather's death, November 24, at 9 a.m., at the office of Attorney Scott Walden, 90329 Bishop Street, Cape Cod, Massachusetts.

She sat back. On Thanksgiving Day? The man wasn't even cold yet.

No.

DESMOND

Seated in a plush leather seat of his mother's boardroom, an exhausted and hungover Desmond fought sleep.

"Did you hear a word I just said to you?" Mrs. McLain asked.

He opened his eyes. "You were speaking?"

"Take this seriously. This is real life. Our business needs you, and now is not the time to slack off and screw everything in here that has a hole! Grow up!" she hissed. "I brought you in and gave you a job. One job. You had one. Vice President of Public Relations. Get off your ass and do it."

"Did it ever occur to you that I have interests of my own? And construction isn't it?" he asked.

"Whoring and foam parties are not a legitimate business profession."

He longed for his football days, the only escape he'd ever had that allowed him to forget his family name, family business, and family commitments. Of him and his two siblings, he was stuck in the middle, and as such, it had allowed him to fly under the radar for most of his life.

"Now," his mother began, and set her hands on the conference table. "You have an opportunity to redeem yourself if you don't want me to cut your balls off financially."

Here it came. The point of this meeting.

"Finally." He closed his eyes again. Whatever she wanted, he would go out and do his normal routine where he half-assed it. Then, he'd come back and tell her at least it got done. Then she could shut up, and he would go on with his life.

"We need to elevate our presence in certain parts of the country, specifically the Hamptons. It's been one of our hardest markets to break into. Very exclusive communities that operate behind the scenes, and only based on name recognition. That crowd only trusts longtime friendships and reputations. Without increasing our client value, we will struggle by end of next year. We need richer accounts and we've found one inroad."

"Okay?"

He didn't bother opening his eyes, but his phone buzzed. He swiped the screen to smile at a nude photo of the girl he would, for sure, be pounding on that night.

"Manuel Realty and Company Owner is Frenchie Manuel," his mother continued, snatching his phone.

"Damn, Ma!"

Scrunching her face like she was twisting a tire onto a car, she continued, "He's a longtime Hamptons operator since the seventies, whose commercial properties have been on the ropes for a few years now. Vast real estate holdings throughout the Eastern and Southern parts of the United States. Maryland, Massachusetts, Virginia, Alabama, the Carolinas, Georgia. But he never fully recovered after the two-thousand-eight housing crash. Since then, his holdings have suffered, particularly as shopping malls and big-name physical stores go under."

Irritated he couldn't see what nudes the chick on his phone had just sent, he scratched his chin. "And?"

"We need his name brand and prestige, and he needs our money. There is one best way to achieve this." She moved to take the seat directly in front of him.

"What? Public relations tour? Photo ops? Shake some hands at a party? Ribbon cutting? Some new collab somewhere? Just tell me the date and time, and I'll put on the clown suit and show up."

He nestled his back in the seat, waiting for her to bore him with her next pointless assignment.

"Marriage."

Desmond's eyes popped open, his head reeling as if one of her bulldozers had hit him. Rarely had anything she'd said ever shocked him.

"Mm... *what?*"

"You will marry Mr. Manuel's granddaughter. Or I cut your lazy ass out of my will. You meet her in two days. Sober up and get shaved."

RENOUNCE IT

ADELLA

"Why are you doing this?" Adella's mother hissed from across the room. "Call it off. Immediately!"

"No," Adella muttered, nearly wringing the blood from her hands. She paced the floor, terror clanging her knees together.

"She is putting this family to shame," her Aunt Lizelle complained, the chopping blades of her eyes cutting into Adella. "No one else would have done this, only her."

Adella digested her aunt's condescension. "Aunt Liz, you all have no fewer than five lawyers already outside right now!"

"Yes, and all because of you!" her aunt bellowed back with tiger eyes and her long nails appearing ready to claw her niece. "To make sure you didn't influence Pa in some way. I think you put him under duress, or you did something with his medications."

Adella's mouth dropped at the suggestion she may have poisoned her grandfather. "Are you out of your mind?"

"Hardly! Everyone knows you were his favorite," Aunt Liz shot back.

"That's not true. He had no favorites," Adella insisted.

"Then, please, explain to us how *you* wound up with everything! You are not the eldest grandchild, not the youngest, not in the middle, nor the smartest! So then... how?" Aunt Lizzie raged.

"I don't know!" Adella rubbed her head. "If I could give it all back, I would!"

The tall, overbearing woman's eyes flared. "Then do it. Do it now. Renounce it all, and then no one inherits anything for years to come. And we're all equal."

At that, Adella shuddered.

"No," her mother replied, flashing a silent warning of her own at Adella. "She's not giving up anything."

Meanwhile, neither of Adella's siblings spoke up for her. Of her six siblings, two were present—Solomon, the eldest, and Constance, the second eldest. Rather, they sat in the corner, their eyes holding silent conversations with one another as Adella roasted on the grill.

"Solomon," Del began, "I could use a little help here. You're one of the vice presidents of Papa's company. Your mouth doesn't work?"

Solomon's stare could have been a shovel throwing dirt on his younger sister's grave. "Like you, I would prefer to wait for my attorney to arrive. Before we speak further."

Del turned to Constance, a partner at an accounting firm. The elder sister's stiff fingers clasped together to form a gun that she aimed at the younger sister.

"We all have the same question, Del. Until the lawyers sort all this out, is there really anything else to say? And besides, you could always just sign your rights over to Mom or Solomon, and they will manage the company for the family."

"She could also sign them to Bryce, who has worked very hard at Papa's side!" Lizzie demanded.

Sucking teeth, clenched hands, and jutting jaws were Adella's only comfort in the coming desert storm.

Two events were occurring today: Adella would meet the man

whom her grandfather had in mind for her to marry. And she would decide if she would accept.

But first, they awaited the arrival of her attorney. The reason for Aunt Lizzie's ire was how Del had the nerve to question the legality of her unexpected gift.

Two days after Thanksgiving, she paced the floor in her cream-colored Donatella Versace pantsuit.

"You should be wearing a skirt," her mother muttered.

"This isn't the year nineteen hundred, Mom. Whoever this person is, he should know I am a professional."

"You are presenting yourself for marriage, not a third college degree."

"Be grateful I'm standing here at all."

Her grandfather's funeral was that Sunday, the next day.

His will had insisted:

I bequeath to my granddaughter, Adella Francesca English, the entirety of my real estate holdings, personal property, businesses, and assign to her all accounts payable and receivable, provided that she marry a man with a demonstrable background in the construction industry within thirty days of her thirty-second birthday. Should she fail to do so, the estate passes to the first great-grandchild to create a profitable business by age twenty-one.

Adella's birthday would be on Valentine's Day, February 14th, and thirty days after that would be March 14! In four months, she would need to find a husband in the construction industry. That was impossible. The language had been written so cleverly as to limit her options and timeframe.

So Del had called in her own attorney, a former high school classmate and one of the top lawyers in Massachusetts. Del wanted to know for herself that these testamentary conditions were legal. It just seemed too archaic, too seventeen-hundreds, to require that someone marry to secure an inheritance.

Fine, if her grandfather insisted that she be the one to serve as steward of his estate, she would make it her priority because she loved him. What he had instilled in them meant everything for their family legacy and heritage. But for the past forty-eight hours, a ship anchor had been chained to her neck.

An hour later, her high school classmate, Attorney Warwick Hastings, turned to her after reviewing the conditions stated in the will.

"It's legitimate. Has the appropriate witness signatures. The testamentary condition precedent is dicey but could pass legal muster in court."

The anchor on Del's neck dropped her to the sea floor. "You're kidding."

Warwick explained to her, "He cannot require you to marry a specific person. But he may require anyone in the construction industry, so your freedom is not *that* limited. You can still choose anybody else with a proven background in, or connection to, construction."

Del plunked to a couch, right after her heart all but splattered on the floor. Hand flying to her mouth, she buried her shriek.

"The answer is simple. Renounce it," her Aunt Lizelle's voice grated over her ears.

Even if she were to go along with this madness, how would she find a spouse she preferred in such a short period of time? Papa Frenchie had boxed her into a decision that would chain her either way.

And then there was the separate issue of her agreeing to the marriage before her grandfather's body was laid to rest.

If not, his body would be held in the mortuary until she formally rejected.

If she refused to accept, the other terms of the will, for a trustee to manage the estate, would then go into effect.

Del would be free. To walk out of here. With Wes. That was the answer.

But why her? Papa Frenchie had so many grandchildren to choose from, all well-educated, accomplished, and just as worthy as she, if not more.

Confusion had choked her since she'd heard the words read to her and his children. She had been the only grandchild present in the lawyer's office. The only one invited.

"But why was it you?" Afi protested.

Adella would not repeat her grandfather's words, read aloud by his lawyer, that still reverberated through her.

"I trust you, Del Baby. Don't let us down."

So cryptic, it told her nothing, but this responsibility changed everything.

Adella had run as far from her family's money as reasonably possible, toward a life of her own. Her ten-year plan was to settle down on a quiet farm somewhere, away from society and the pressures of cliques, social circles, and clubs. And especially her family. Wes could give her that quietude. A simple life, in which she would do the one thing she loved—save people's lives— every day and go home to a garden, animals, and maybe a couple of kids.

Over the years, she'd picked up the necessary real estate knowledge her grandfather had required of them all. She'd become conversational in property holdings, investments, limited liability companies, and real estate structures. But aside from that, she'd buried her head in science and medical books so the family would never bother her about coming to work for the company.

Hiding from her family's business allowed Del to excel in school. She'd graduated magna cum laude from Massachusetts Institute of Technology, second in her class. And was now becoming one of the best heart surgeons in Boston, attending conferences, speaking at engagements across the nation, and lecturing at Harvard and Yale.

But most important, she had managed to create a small piece

of life she could call her own, one where she mattered and her colleagues and patients respected her as more than Frenchie Manuel's progeny.

How dare Papa punish her this way. He was indeed getting the last laugh. Even now, he would not let her run away.

"Do you need me to draft a marital contract?" Warwick asked.

Del blinked.

Her phone buzzed in her hand. Wes had sent a text.

Wes: *I'm here in Cape Cod, my love. Where should I meet you?*

Wes! In the shock of this situation with Papa, she'd forgotten Wes would arrive today, and the promise she'd made him.

A train seemed to be running over her.

"He is here," her cousin, Afi, said, entering the family living room.

Del's eyes bounced from her phone.

"Who's here?" Del's mother asked.

"The man Papa wants you to marry. With his family."

"Just give me a moment." Adella stole away to an upstairs bedroom and hugged a bedpost so her heart didn't explode.

Her grandparents' photos of her cousins, aunts, and uncles all surrounded her. Fishing trips, hunting excursions, horseback riding, yachting—in all the photos, her grandfather's boisterous joy could light up a city. His children and grandchildren clung to him and their grandmother, frolicking throughout every season.

But Adella was missing in most of the early childhood photos of her siblings and cousins.

Survival of the fittest, Papa had always insisted.

Don't pout, cry, or whine, his voice ricocheted between her ears just then. *Survive.*

A photo of him seated on his conference table faced Adella.

Del Baby, saddle up our horses. Show me you were paying attention, he would call out to her. She could not ride the horses with Papa and the other children, only prepare the horses for the others to enjoy.

Del Baby, make us crab cakes and salad. Let me see if you remember the ingredients.

Carry my briefcase. You remember what should go in it?

Go pick the crickets for trout... the bait for deer... cleat and hitch the yacht.

Meticulous and choosy in all he did, Papa never let a detail slide.

He prepared them as much as he could for every aspect of life, so they would be caught off guard by nothing. Yet he had prepared no one for this.

Burning through her was the question of what had led him to skip all his children. The sands of time were slipping away, and Del only had a matter of hours to decide her fate, so Papa's body could go into the ground.

"Adella! What are you doing? Come out of there," Constance spoke with a not-very-hushed tone through the door.

A terrified Adella let go of her grandparents' bedpost.

THE GIRL

DESMOND

Minutes after exiting his family's jet, Desmond, his mother, two siblings, and a host of lawyers and finance guys, all rode in an entourage of Cadillac Escalades proceeding through the illustrious Cape Cod community of South Yarmouth. The houses were spread so far apart on the properties that neighbors must've waved to each other using binoculars.

They finally arrived at a quaint, two-story clapboard house, spanning about twenty acres that must have been worth at least fifteen million dollars. A breathtaking view stretched before them, miles of endless coastline along the saltwater marshes and the turquoise waters of the Atlantic Ocean. It was a long plane ride away from eating SpaghettiOs and playing on the rough streets of Baltimore where the McLain's once struggled.

Desmond's heart had never pounded so much. He stepped down from the truck and tried to find his footing on solid ground. His sweaty palms holding the bouquet of pink roses, he reminded himself not to wipe his hands on his jacket. It was one of his mother's numerous etiquette admonishments he'd tried to forget but couldn't.

Once the door opened, there was no turning back. Looming before him, an older woman, beautiful and regally dressed, stretched out her hands. "Mrs. McLain."

"You must be Mrs. English, Mr. French's daughter," Desmond's mother said.

"Yes. Come on in and join us. So glad to have you."

So formal, and dry and stiff. All Desmond needed was a wooden pipe, tea and biscuits.

Just inside the entrance, stone-faced expressions signaled for him to cut and run. Desmond and his siblings, Chaitra and Keenan, stood in a circle of unsmiling people who all somewhat resembled one another.

"Dude," his brother, Keenan, muttered under his breath while scoping the tension, "if you marry this chick, I know one place I'll never be coming. I bet they've got a closet upstairs where they'll lock you up, on some *Flowers in the Attic* shit."

The quick thought crossed Desmond's mind that the door was right behind him. He could still leap through it.

The women made small talk that wasn't loud enough to surpass the beating in his eardrums. As he shook hands with each statue in the room, Desmond scanned to see if he was looking into the eyes of The One.

"So, Desmond, tell us about yourself while my daughter is still getting ready," Mrs. English said, inviting him to sit down.

In a scene that reminded him of the Wild West, the families separated to either side of the room in a sort of stand-off.

Himself? What about himself? If he was honest, he loved his whiskey straight from the bottle, riding his women barebacked, sometimes two at a time, enjoyed rough sex, slept until at least noon, inhaled junk food, and had little tolerance for spreadsheets and data crunching.

"I love the water. Love swimming, boating, jet skis, parasailing. Guess you could say I'm an outdoorsy guy, so it only makes sense that outdoor construction runs in my veins, huh?" he responded.

The woman's smile dripped with faux politeness. "Oh, how lovely, an outdoorsman. Ever hunt? Duck shooting and deer season are some of Del's favorites."

Hell yes, did he enjoy hunting. In fine hotels. All seasons of the year. And his meats were always Grade A. Never out of season. Oh, and cougars. How he loved a well-seasoned, fun and adventurous cat who clawed. It was usually the married ones.

"No, I can't say I've hunted much. But some of my former teammates down South who do, claim it's a lot of fun. It's on my to-do list."

Not.

Finally, a figure appeared in his peripheral vision, standing atop the stairs. His mother's hand nudged his leg, and everyone stood.

Desmond turned to see a vision in cream descending the stairs. A heavy thud accompanied each step, lips unsmiling, as if she were Pallas Athena wielding Zeus's thunderbolt. Long, wavy hair surrounded her round, heart-shaped face. A face that was part-angelic, part-warrior, complete with eyes that seemed scared and yet ready for battle.

"Ms. English," Desmond's mother called to the young woman, stretching out her hand, "I am Margaret McLain, and this is my son, Desmond. What a pleasure to meet you. We've heard so many wonderful things."

"Doctor."

Desmond wasn't sure who in the room had spoken, because the girl's face was so stiff and frozen it seemed her lips didn't move.

His mother's eyes batted in confusion. "I'm sorry?"

"Doctor." This time, the girl spoke louder. "It's *Doctor* Adella English. You called me miss."

Margaret McLain's eyes widened, as did her flaring nostrils, and Desmond almost expected them to blow fire. He thoroughly enjoyed his mother finally crossing someone who did not cringe in her presence.

Adella's mother, Mrs. English, threw back her head, clasped her hands together, and let out a fake laugh to fill the awkward silence in the room. "You say po-TA-to, I say po-TAH-to. It's all trivial. Who cares?"

The girl ignored her mother, and Desmond's, and moved to him directly. Her eyes narrowed, closing in on him. Why did he suddenly feel like he was the fly underneath a raised fly swatter and about to be smashed?

"You're the football player."

Up close, her face reminded him of a spring meadow in the fields of Norfolk, Virginia, where he'd gone to school—open, soft, and budding. Yet still frozen under winter ice and not fully blossomed.

"Speak," she said, doing that thing again where her lips barely moved, which kind of creeped him out.

"Uh, yeh, I did play at one point. In college and for a few years professionally. Now I work at my family's construction company—"

"Doing?"

Why was Desmond's throat clogging up? "Operations and securing new clients."

"So then, nothing."

The fly swatter of her glare smacked him. Desmond's mother's mouth fell open to protest.

"She didn't mean that," Mrs. English interrupted. "What she meant is you are probably still finding your place in the company. What would you like to do there in the future?"

"I meant it," the girl affirmed and addressed Desmond only. "I've read about you. Two DUIs. One car accident, under the influence. Three fights leading to arrest—one in a bar, another on a cruise, and another in a grocery store parking lot. Arrests for evading police. Subpar C and D student. No major accomplishments besides the lead role in a high school play."

Desmond chuckled to cover the weird pain that just shot through his chest cavity. Was it humiliation? "Wow. Don't forget the two Hollywood actresses I banged over the weekend. At the same time. I'd almost think you knew me better than my own mama."

The entire room gasped, mouths fell open, and he even caught a few men cracking up on the far side of the room.

The flower blossoms of her soft but penetrating eyes did not relent. "Will everyone please leave?"

"What?" her mother asked.

"You heard me, Mom. If you want me to even think of doing this, leave us, please."

Her mother cleared out all the relatives, including Desmond's. Before the older woman exited, mother and daughter exchanged tense stares that reminded Desmond of a scene out of *Mommy Dearest*. The woman's stern face contradicted all the tranquility of surrounding ocean and lands. She closed the sliding doors, leaving Desmond alone with this chocolate princess.

The girl carried herself as a queen. Shoulders back, silk suit falling over the right places at her breasts and clasping around her waist to hold in voluptuous curves. But her tender eyes read that she wasn't as tough as she made out.

"What do you want?" she asked him.

He shrugged. "Do you want the truth or the right answer?"

Silence was her response. He fidgeted.

This girl's gaze remained on him, waiting.

"A-a good wife, I guess," he finally managed.

"What do you want?" she asked again.

"What do *you* want?" Desmond insisted, since his first answer apparently wasn't good enough.

"My freedom. My life."

He blinked. That was the last answer he'd expected. She didn't have freedom already?

"Aren't you… grown? You don't feel free enough?" Desmond asked.

Maybe it was none of his business. Was he being too blunt? Hands shoved in his pockets, he stared around the spacious sitting room, complete with a Steinway grand piano, spaced apart from rich, worn leather furniture and deep mahogany tables that told of wealth and dated tastes.

"Yes, I am grown. But I am not free. And I'm trying to make that happen." Her voice barely lifted above a murmur.

Definitely some Mommy Dearest *shit*, he thought. *They probably hide her in the closet.*

Desmond peered out the window, at the Little Sippewissett saltwater marshes and dunes with speedboats racing. Yachts and sailboats left a stream in the water as they took their afternoon time. Even in the fall, water lovers still got in their favorite pleasure. The water was calming.

"You seem like a pretty smart lady. So if that's the case, just walk out the door then. And have a nice life."

"I can't. Not until I find out why my grandfather wanted this."

"Well, last I heard, your family business is struggling. And you need to make a move. Sooner than later, so…"

"That is true. So if I take my freedom, I'll never resolve my grandfather's issue."

"But you'll have your freedom. And I don't know too much of anything, but I do know about freedom. You really should try it out. Freedom is a sweet-ass thing. Doing whatever you want, with whoever you want, it's like a drug, and you don't even have to pay for it."

She squinted as she examined him. "But what do you want? Tell the truth."

Desmond swallowed. "Not to get kicked off my mother's nipple. Hmph." He chuckled, lowering his head. "Because as you so delicately put it, I am that lazy bum girls like you run from, on the way to get your high-end Ivy League degrees."

He wasn't staring at her, but he heard her weight shift.

Desmond continued, "Yeah, I read up too. I saw you were second in your class at M.I.T. Big time heart surgeon in Boston. Lecturer and all that. But you don't feel free? Isn't that why you did all the studying? To become free?"

He didn't land the plane of his eye contact on her, instead choosing to gaze at the boats outside, wishing he could be on one right now. Or anywhere besides this stuffy mausoleum of a house. From experience with his own sister, Chaitra, he thought it might not be best to make eye contact. So she wouldn't feel called out.

"If only it were that easy," she replied.

Desmond finally turned away from the boats and deigned to look at her. Adella wrung her hands and appeared like a trapped little girl. Her crisp winter white suit did nothing to gloss over the tight anxiety clamping her unsmiling jaws shut.

"It is. That easy." He shrugged. "We can make it easy. We don't..." His gaze darted around the room. He was unable to believe what he was about to say. "... have to stay married forever."

Her eyes fluttered. "You mean," she gulped, "deception?"

"No. I mean, we do what they want us to do. You settle your grandfather's affairs, I get my inheritance, and then we split."

"But they want us to have *kids*." She said it as if someone had poured vinegar—not the regular kind, but the nasty apple cider—directly on her tongue.

Desmond stopped himself from guiding her to sit down so she wouldn't wring the bones from her hands.

A hand on his chest, he ruminated on the idea. "Divorced people do it all the time. Pop out a couple of kids and then walk. You don't love me. I don't love you. The terms seem simple.

Shouldn't be too complicated or messy. For three years, we commit to getting our money."

The doorbell yanked them out of a conversation that was finally feeling normal.

Was she expecting somebody else?

The voice of a male emanated through the house. A white male. His accent hinted of someone who just jumped from a tractor trailer in Nebraska.

"Yeah, am I at the right house? Is, uh, Adella here?"

The girl's mouth dropped as if she'd forgotten something.

AM I CONFUSED?

ADELLA

With baby steps, Adella meandered through the path of relatives that parted. Out of the living room, and then the foyer, she finally reached the front door.

The sun streaming through his smile, Wes still stood at the threshold of where she'd grown up, oblivious to the fact that he hadn't been invited inside.

Wes held up flowers. "Hey, you. Hope I'm not too late." He leaned in for a kiss.

For the first time since they'd started dating, his lips felt numb. They were real, as in she felt them, but unreal in that they brought no comfort to her right now.

She took his hand, ignoring the stunned faces among her ocean of relatives, and led him some place where she saw no bodies—their sunbathed kitchen that did not brighten Del's dark day.

"Hello, how are you?" he said to the stony people they passed in the house.

Adella didn't stop to introduce him to her mother or aunts.

"Okay, I know I'm white and all, but I was totally not expecting that, Del," he said, shaking.

"I'm sorry," she whispered.

"You didn't tell them I was coming, did you?" His gaze could have been a scalpel sliding into her.

Adella stalled by placing his flowers in a vase with water and then went to stand before him, not in the intimate way they embraced after a particularly long shift. When he circled his arms around her in front of the lockers and planted what felt like a million slow kisses all over her neck and face, Del's muscles relaxed. All the other times, Wes's affection caused her bones to no longer feel like surgical knives under her tired skin.

Wes leaned against the kitchen counter and pulled Adella toward him so she couldn't avoid his green eyes that she'd welcomed every other time.

"You didn't introduce me to this powerful mother I've been waiting so long to meet. Nor to your grandfather. Nor to any of these aunts and uncles, and brilliant cousins I've been hearing of."

Her eyes fell.

The stranger in her front living room was right. She could walk out of here right now, renounce everything and live the country life she and Wes had talked about. Freedom.

"My grandfather has passed, Wes," Adella whispered, still staring at the floor. Tears crept to her eyes and dropped to the marble tiles.

"Oh, Del, I'm so sorry to hear that. You just saw him a few weeks ago, and the two of you hunted together."

His hand swept her hair, and he kissed her head. Again, real and close, but so unreal and distant in this moment, his comfort was so discomforting. Her insides shuddered.

"He wants me to marry, Wes."

He laughed, lifting her face toward his. "Well, that's wonderful. Perfect, right? I mean, his passing is awful. But he wants you to be happy!"

His face looked like a kid seeing Disneyland for the first time.

She shook her head, the tears continuing to splatter on the floor when her head sank again.

"He chose someone of his own. It's in his will. He has left me everything, but only if I marry and bear children."

The tremor through his body ran through Del's as would a flare of electricity.

"I thought you said you didn't want your family's money, and that's why you became a doctor. For your own identity. Your own place in the world. Your own... *life*." Wes's beautiful green eyes whipped around his head as if they flipped through the album of numerous conversations they'd shared in which she had bared her soul to him.

"I know."

"Then, am I confused? About the things you said. Our plans... breaking away from the city one day, moving to the countryside, opening our own practice, living quiet and anonymous. No fancy houses or clubs. Isn't that what you said?"

"Wes."

"You would do that? Give up your life for money? The very thing you said you would never do," he muttered, his gaze no longer meandering but landing firmly on her.

She started to repeat the stranger's words. "If I stick this out for just a few years—"

"A few years? *Years*, Del?" As if the words were electrons generating opposing magnetic force fields, they separated him from her. "Why?"

She wanted to explain her suspicions about Papa, but her lawyer had counseled her to keep her thoughts quiet for now. Del feared saying too much here in the family kitchen, with relatives likely straining to listen on the other side of the door.

Del clasped her hands, afraid to touch him now as he wandered about the kitchen. "I can't just turn away from it. This isn't about the money. It's his legacy."

"Are you sure? Because that's what everyone says. It's not

about money. Until it is." His green eyes might have darkened, the sun he'd carried inside with him completely clouded over.

Del licked the salty tears meeting her lips, tasting the anger on Wes's face.

"It's not about the money. My papa, I'm so sor..." Her voice trailed off into a dark tunnel of disbelief, of what she was doing. Strapping herself to her family's empire. In the worst way.

"No. You're not. But I am."

"Wes, if you just please wait—"

He was out the kitchen door, taking Del's insides with him.

His cowboy boots dragged across the spotless, buffed marble floors. And then onto the front patio. Down the stairs. No one stopped him.

Her feet jumped to run after him, toward the quiet sunrises, breezy sunsets, farm animals, and coffee at a worn wooden table with grits and thick slabs of bacon. But her brain stopped her.

His old Jeep rattled to life, and with it, Adella's girlhood dreams of throwing off the family chains.

The old gears shifted. Last chance.

Go, Adella. Leaving is what you always wanted. You have the perfect man to leave with. To finally be who you are. You don't need this.

Wes's loud engine blared, so near. And then farther. Until it was no more.

Her mother came to stand at the kitchen door. "So you have made up your mind, dear girl?"

Adella rushed past her, back to the sitting room where the stranger stood. She slammed the French doors shut, leaving just the two of them.

"This is an arrangement. Nothing more," Adella snapped at him. "You will stay in your mansion. I stay in mine. We'll use IVF for children so I never have to touch you."

The football player blinked as if he'd been hit by a dart gun. "Well, damn, nice meeting you too."

∼

TWENTY-FOUR HOURS LATER, Adella's eyes were puffy and red from more than seeing her grandfather's body laid to rest.

She'd cried as she'd signed off on the marital agreement in which she accepted the conditions set out in his will. An hour later, his body had been set in the ground.

"Afi, stop being so cold," she said to her favorite cousin.

Afi shifted in the car. "You should share it. Split it among everyone. Equally," she spat as they rode together in the car from the grave site.

"I don't know Papa's intentions. I have not inspected his books. How do I know what shape they're in or whether there is even any money?"

"Solomon knows. He has worked hard for a long time to take over," Afi countered, referencing Adella's elder brother, the head of her grandfather's company, who'd graduated from Tuskegee. Seven years Adella's senior, Solomon had spent all his time, since he was at Papa's knee, learning the business and inhaling the company records. "Why aren't you talking to him? He can help you understand what you clearly do not."

Del kept silent about her suspicions. If Solomon knew so much, why had Papa felt it necessary to take such drastic measures? Why would he merge with another company, out of the blue, without mention to anyone, if his business was so secure?

Papa knew how Del loved medicine. Why would he uproot her life for a scheme that would almost certainly take her away from her heart's desire?

How would she split her time between medicine and real estate? Whom could she hire to help her sort out Papa's affairs, search for problems in the bookkeeping, property values, and leases?

Papa's funeral had happened with Del in attendance but not

mentally present. What had the eulogy said? Who had delivered it? What color suit had Papa worn in his casket? What memory of this day could she cling to that would pull her through the feelings of him abandoning her here?

When they returned to the house for the wake, the room seemed to split into factions. Adella may as well have been doused in a toxic dump. If anyone dared approach her at all, it was to pour barrels of disparagement onto her. Like mosquitoes in the dark, so many voices attacked her that she could not tell from which direction they came.

"How dare you," her elder sister, Constance, griped. "Solomon has always looked out for the family and done right by us all. You need to meet with him, *tonight*, and work out a management plan."

"Give it back," her Aunt Lizzie insisted.

"Del," her elder sister, Rachel, started, in an effort to be a buffer between their older siblings and the younger. "You already have so much to handle with your amazing career. Why bother with all this? You've never even cared for real estate. Be reasonable."

Painful memories of her siblings leaving her behind as they left for skating parties, sledding, ice skating, and amusement parks, all flooded over her. Flashbacks crushed her lungs until she could not inhale, and she may as well have been in a casket.

"Don't you mean I should let you more able people take care of me, since you don't think I can care for myself?" Del slid her eyes away from Rachel, often the intermediary among the siblings.

"That's not what I meant, Adella," Rachel said.

Del's cold food stared at her from the plate.

By the time her eldest brother, Solomon, approached her, from the sea of suddenly foreign faces she'd known her entire life, she held on to a chaise lounge to avoid running away screaming.

"Solomon, what is it? Why are they being this way? Treating

me like I'm the one who wrote the will?" She sighed, wishing he would crack a joke and reassure her that this upset would soon pass.

"March fourteenth," he whispered.

"What?" she asked.

"The day you marry. That's the date we've negotiated that falls within Papa's deadline. And later tonight, we can talk about our family's portion of the money, yes?"

It was a good thing Del had not eaten. Nothing inside her was left to come out.

Then came her mother. Never truly a source of comfort, but a disciplinarian who saw that her children did as they were told, from preschool through the Ivy Leagues. Still, Adella searched her matriarch's face for traces of shared grief and reassurance. Especially in this storm.

"Mother, Papa's hunting guns, I wanted one to preserve."

"Never mind that. Your fiancé will move into your home within the next two weeks, and that way, you will continue practicing medicine while you make a transition," she said in a rushed voice, rambling out all the syllables in one long, uninterrupted sentence.

"Moving *where?*"

"With you. You have a full-time job as it is, and his schedule is more flexible. Desmond can come here while you transition out of your job over the next few months."

Del could have been swallowing her scalpel. "Out of my job… but we didn't discuss…"

"How else will you run the company, dear? It's a full-time commitment, and I expect you to carry it out well." Her mother leaned in, whispering, "Or the storm in this family would never end. No matter the condition you found the company in, they will always blame you for its failure."

Instead of solace from her mother, Del received a stern

memorandum, that even on this much-dreaded day, there were tasks to execute.

Sharp pains squeezed Adella's chest.

By the end of the repass meal, three attorneys had arrived at different times. Each one served her with legal papers, challenging her grandfather's will, and warning her to do nothing with the company until a judge had intervened. Flipping through the papers, she noticed that one set was from her brother, Solomon.

Adella stood in the house in which they'd all played and grown up, the house that was now hers alone. Rather than sharing memories or stories, as they had at their grandmother's wake years before, her cousins turned away from her, one by one. As well as five of her siblings.

Her brother, Martin, gave her shoulders a quick squeeze. "Good luck, girl. You'll need it."

"Don't pay them any attention. They're irritated, but it will pass," her mother murmured. "Come on."

Relatives had begun searching the house for items and keepsakes they could take.

"Everyone," Adella spoke. "Please, don't touch anything. We will have someone go through the items and inventory them so we can ensure everyone receives something."

In the middle of near chaos, a car arrived, and a well-dressed, messenger-like figure exited. He held flowers, and when the front door opened, he entered and set them down in the foyer with a note.

Terribly sorry for your loss. Please accept condolences from Desmond and our entire family. May this be the beginning of new bonds and generations.

— DESMOND

That was the football player's name.

So informal and impersonal. Had Wes been present, he would have played his guitar or at least turned up a country song on his truck. Her family would have loved him once they opened their minds under different circumstances.

Her mother received the bouquet and sent back a note of her own to the McLains.

"Be grateful, Adella. This is not the worst that could have happened for you."

"Oh, really, Mother, then what is?"

"Poverty. Destitution. Hard labor. Starvation. Certainly not crying in a mansion because you're a wealthy woman about to marry a wealthy man. Speaking of marriage, you should get rest. You've got your work cut out for you during the big move. All while we start the wedding planning."

In two days, this football player, Desmond, would begin the move into her home, since he lived in Maryland and had no residence in Massachusetts.

They would begin touring the headquarters of both companies in the next week and sit down to hash out details of operations and the company sharing structure with the lawyers. All the mundane tasks and minutiae Adella had deemed pointless through her life. Paperwork awaited her.

None of this would keep a single heart alive. It would never heal a child. Or revive a mother. Or reunite a family. Adella shuddered at the notion of this being her life now.

Days later, she stood atop the stairs of her home in Boston, watching with appall as Desmond's moving crew rolled in his things. To a separate bedroom, at the opposite end of the hallway, as far away from her as possible.

The families felt they should start getting to know one another, ahead of the quick marriage date.

Del's grandfather had bought her this home years before, as a gift for acceptance to medical school. For the past three months, she and Wes had lived here together.

But by the time she returned to her home from the family estate in Cape Cod, he had collected his things. All traces of him had vanished, as if they'd never breathed the same air. Now his absence was cutting off Adella's air.

At the end of the week, Adella stared at a stranger in her house.

Finally, the football player closed the door to the house, staring up the stairs at her.

"You want to go for a walk or something?" he asked. "It's not yet sunset. Maybe we can talk."

Everything in Adella's soul quaked. "About what?"

He shrugged. "Tuh. Um…let's start with your favorite color. What you like to eat. Your shoe size."

"I'm tired. I'll see you in the morning," she said, turning away from him. "The house staff have food ready in the kitchen."

"You want to join me and we eat outside? Since both of us like being outdoors?"

"I have no appetite. You enjoy."

The football player was trying his best to connect with her. But Adella's heart connected with someone else, somewhere else, and all she wanted was to get her heart back. It no longer dwelled here, in her own home.

NOBODY'S WHIPPING BOY

DESMOND

"I'm bored out of my mind. She's always working!" Desmond complained to his mother and sister, Chaitra. "And even when she's home, I may as well be in the house with my jailer! Why did you send me here? To be some houseboy?"

He stood at the offices of Manuel Real Estate, where Adella's staff and employees would not allow him to do anything besides water the plants. They'd placed him in an office with an empty desk, complete with a clean computer and basic phone. So Desmond had spent his mornings and afternoons at the bar, or the strip club, or sleeping.

"What time do you all leave?" his mother asked over the speakerphone.

Desmond ran his finger across the dusty windowsill of his office in the very back of the real estate holdings company. "In a few minutes. Now we're headed to The Hamptons, with her stuffy-ass friends. When will you all be you coming?"

"In a few days. Meanwhile, this is a time for you and her to bond."

"Bond? How can I bond with somebody who walks around carrying her surgical scissors, like she stays ready to slice me up if I walk too close to her?"

Chaitra's skin-crawling laugh was a little too much giddiness over his predicament. "So if she's carrying scissors, why don't you ask to borrow her stethoscope? Let her listen to your heart. If she slashes your ass, that could make for some really kinky sex, ya know?"

"Chaitra!" their mother admonished.

"You could call her Dr. Slasher in bed," Chaitra joked. "Have you guys done it yet?"

"Chaitra!" their mother said with a higher pitch and slight snarl.

"Paging Dr. Slasher. Or, you know, Dr. Blood Love. Do you know what kinds of things you and her could do in that hospital?"

Now Desmond pressed his head against the window overlooking downtown Boston.

"Ma, I'm not doing this." His body might have been depleted of a soul, if he ever had one. "I can*not*... do this. She'll have to find somebody else. I'm not a husband. Or some person who can deal with other people's baggage. She is heartbroken over this white boy. And I know she's in there crying every night over him."

"You know what I said." His mother's voice spoke from the valley of the shadow of death.

Staring at a city he did not know, loathing a future he did not want, Desmond gasped for air. "Don't do this to me."

"You've done it to yourself. Find a way to earn her trust so you can get into those books."

"Paging Dr. Blood Love." Chaitra's voice slinked into the mix before his mother hung up.

An hour later, he got into a chauffeured car in which Adella waited.

"How was the office today?" she asked.

"You would know better than me, since you've instructed your office staff not to let me even take out the trash." With that, Desmond took his flask from his inside jacket pocket and twisted off the cap.

Her deft hand stunned him, snatching his comfort drink and staring at him as if he were a petulant child.

"Put the cap back on and pay attention," the doctor ordered.

He sat back in the seat. These were the first words she'd spoken to him in days. He didn't know whether to be happy to finally hear her voice or pissed at her nerve to treat him like some student.

"Who the fuck do you think you're talking to? I'm going to be your husband, woman. I don't know what puppets you're used to playing with, but I saw you treat that white boy with a whole lot more respect than you've treated me, so don't think you'll—"

"That white boy, as you call him, saved three peoples' lives today." Adella's glare tightened. "And what did you do with your time?"

Well. When she put it that way…

The chauffeur continued maneuvering through the city to get them to the airport.

She shoved her tablet at him, with images of strangers visible on the screen.

"What am I supposed to do with this?"

Adella stared at the window as if she wanted to fling herself out of it. "Look at who they are, so you'll know before you meet them and you don't come across as an idiot. These are smart, fine people. Top of their game in everything. In medicine, politics, entertainment, investing. Even if you don't rise to their level, at least know their names."

"I've got important friends too," he shot back as they exited at the private airplane hangar.

"Oh, really? Where are they? The titty bar?" the doctor, who looked all of twelve years old, shot back.

Desmond put two and two together. "Is this the only reason you rode in the same car as me? So you could school me about your uppity friends and talk down to me?"

"Yes." With refined poise, she reached out for the railing to steady herself on the stairs.

Desmond made an effort and placed his hand at her lower back to support her.

"You don't have to touch me," she snapped.

Wishing he could toss her off the private plane and leave her, he took his seat at Adella's side.

Desmond's mother had been the one to suggest they go on a Christmas vacation, to thaw the glacier between them and grow accustomed to one another. Where Adella could relax in a place that was special to her, among her friends and family.

She chose Sag Harbor.

"Who is this?" he asked, pulling out the tablet and doing something that might gain him more than her wrath.

"Madison Page. A Capitol Hill staffer for a politician in Virginia Beach. On her way to the White House if her candidate wins next year."

"And this?" He pointed to another woman, curvy and sexy, who might have bathed in money every night.

"That is Chriselle, the wife of a Hollywood talent agent, and now she's becoming an agent herself after leaving her husband. We call her Chrissy."

"What does this guy here do? Sleep on a pile of cash and eats it for breakfast?"

"Kevin. I think he would eat his cash if he could, just for shits and giggles. A techie in Silicon Valley. Everybody hates him. But he's not the kind of man you want as an enemy, so people tolerate him."

Desmond smirked. It was the first time he'd ever heard the little girl curse.

The private flight stewardess arrived with potatoes and duck drenched in red wine sauce.

At least the stewardess offered the most pleasant atmosphere he'd received in weeks. While Adella dived into her dinner to avoid eye contact with him, Desmond's attention shifted up, to the stewardess.

He cut into his duck, but plump meat, round in the right spots, and juicy was how he would have described other hunting game in his sights. She pranced up and down the airplane, bringing more sauce, pouring more water for Adella and serving him another cognac. Her button-down shirt displayed a healthy bra size D of delectable goodies. Each time she bent forward reminded him of how he was being deprived while cooped up in Adella's house or her family's Boston-based office.

Desmond hadn't seen any action in the three weeks since he'd arrived. He was actually trying to respect the damn girl and give this marriage thing a shot. Do his part. But right now, the melted fudge that was the stewardess called on him to ditch his new diet.

"Would you like dessert now, ma'am? Sir?" the stewardess asked.

"No, thank you," Adella muttered.

"Sure."

Both answers emerged at the same time.

Adella lowered her eyes.

Desmond questioned why she did that. Why was it that sometimes she was so sure of herself, and other times, she withered?

The stewardess lingered a bit longer. "And what kind of dessert would you like, sir?"

"None," Desmond huffed, sitting back against the seat with a hard-on.

Not because he really didn't want any, but the little girl sadness in Adella's face had dampened his appetite.

He didn't need for the stewardess to make another trip and remind of the sex he craved but wasn't getting. Desmond wouldn't cheat on the girl during the plane ride she paid for. And he didn't want to think of those childlike eyes falling while he banged the shit out of her airline stewardess.

Instead, he twitched in his seat, wondering how the hell he would survive this way. Staring into Adella's red, puffy eyes. Every day. *And* no sex. That much she'd made clear.

Alas, several days before Christmas, they exited the chauffeured car in the Sag Harbor enclave of The Hamptons. The woman-child jumped through the doorway as if it were an escape hatch.

First, they went to her family's home where he encountered all the non-talking statues of her relatives again. She entered, not like a woman happy to see them all but a scorned sinner preparing to be stoned.

Desmond sucked in a big breath for another round of wooden funeral greetings.

"Adella, my sweet, you two made it," her mother greeted them. "Come on in, we have so much to discuss for the wedding. The guest list, we'll go over it and finalize, and then I've found the perfect gown for you." She turned to Desmond. "And, Desmond, welcome, please meet our family."

With well-moisturized and manicured hands that had no wrinkles and appeared not to have ever touched a day of hard labor, Mrs. English embraced him. First she introduced him to her five siblings, Adella's aunts and uncles. Their arms extended toward his with all the energy of a rusty car needing a boost.

They greeted Adella with less enthusiasm.

In Desmond's peripheral vision, she moved toward her siblings. With tiny steps that were not nearly as strident as her step inside her house, or when she was bolting away from him.

Instead, she took timid, uncertain motions. One by one, her siblings delivered respectful kisses to her cheek. Without lifting their arms to embrace her.

"You all remember Desmond." Adella's voice had fallen to forty decibels. She turned in his direction but did not meet his eyes.

"Desmond, this is Solomon, my eldest brother. Lonnie, my second eldest. Martin, my third brother. Rachel, my eldest sister. Constance, the sister before me. And then Ilyana, the baby of us."

Of all the siblings he'd just met, Ilyana was the only one who reached out to hug Desmond, and even that was stiff as if she questioned what she was doing.

"Drink, Desmond?" a lone voice finally rose in the room.

As if in shock, both Adella and Desmond spun around to see who it was.

Martin.

Adella's eyes fluttered, almost as if offering a silent thanks.

"Y-yes. Please," Desmond replied, stammering after deciding he would not bolt for the door.

With shaky hands, he accepted a shot of very expensive Scottish whisky. In one swig, like David Copperfield, he made it disappear.

Later, in the sea of Del's relatives talking and catching up, Mrs. English returned to Desmond and Adella with a lifted eyebrow.

"Since all the family is here, we don't have space for you to stay in separate rooms. So though you are not married yet, you will have to share a room. We will make an exception, this trip, only until you two are married. But when you are back at the family home in Boston where we all have our homes, same rules apply."

Desmond's whisky mixed a fiery cocktail with his blood that flamed to his face. He was a grown-ass man, and who was going to tell him who he could or could not sleep with? If he and Adella wanted to fuck, who was her mother to stop two grown individuals?

"Yes, ma'am," he answered in the most respectful tone.

"I'll get a hotel room, Mom. Desmond can stay here, and I'll come in the morning."

Thank you. Damn, girl, assert yourself with these people.

Desmond's liquor was kicking in. "I'll come, too, and rent a room of my own. Then we can respect the family rules of no sleeping together before marriage."

Hey, if there was an exit, he'd take it. Desmond had his own goddamn money. He didn't need these stuffy folks' whacky accommodations. In fact, he and Del could even room at different hotels, so he could find a "comfort" buddy without her being close enough to discover it. That would be perfect.

"You're not doing that," another male voice spoke. Solomon, the eldest brother. "You can stay here."

The fire-ready eyes of Adella's eldest brother shot right past his sister, to target Desmond. Almost as if daring him to speak again.

"Fine. We'll stay," Adella capitulated.

"You'll stay. I'll go." Desmond had had enough. He gave not two shits about this family having a name in The Hamptons. Their name didn't travel anywhere else that mattered in the real fucking world. "I'll come in the morning for breakfast." While his final last words torpedoed through his mouth, he aimed his own cannon at Solomon.

Desmond strutted outside to the residential street. There were no cabs around to hail, but he was only a couple of blocks away from a scene that appeared to have bars and restaurants. In the December Hamptons cold, he took off walking. Maybe the frigid air would refrigerate his disgust.

As he walked, he halfway expected his fiancée to come running for him. To call out and ask him to come back. Tell him they could make this work. Or at least he hoped.

But he passed more houses until he'd covered a whole block. And the only sound walking with him was that of music approaching from the dive bars ahead.

DESMOND HAD SHOWN up dutifully for breakfast. He didn't know what fool part of him thought he had some brownie points coming for that.

By that night, when they got to the home of Adella's childhood friend, Madison Page, he was ready to pull out the little hair he had left. Adella held up her left hand, wearing the engagement ring selected by his mother's private secretary. Her friends jumped up and down, screaming for her as if she'd just won a ticket to the moon. Inside him, he screamed from his own front row seat to Hell.

At least her friends, Maddy and Chrissy, attended an HBCU—Spelman—and not the Ivies. So the snobbish classism still existed but tamped down a bit to make them civil enough. In that I'm-better-than-you-but-I'll-speak-because-Adella-is-our-girl   sort of way.

Among them all, there was one. One chick who didn't project a holier-than-thou presence among these black-shoe-polish-and-silk-scarf types.

Drinking, laughing from deep in her gut, this strange woman strutted around the backyard fire pit, pouring more liquor and filling up cups. Unapologetically loud. A Southern drawl fell off her words like cooked collard greens too big for a loaded plate. Her jeans must have been a size ten, full, no wrinkles or spaces, as the ham hocks of her thighs crescendoed down into her knee-high red boots.

"Adella and Desmond," Maddy introduced them. "This is my co-worker, Lana Gilley. She's here visiting me from Capitol Hill. She couldn't make it to Texas with her folks this Christmas."

Lana. With Texas-sized lips. A Texas-sized personality. And a Texas-sized ass.

While Adella's friends discussed his sham wedding, and Adella sold it like a foreign car he knew would break down soon enough, he surveyed the Texas landscape. Biting his lip, he imagined just how much Texas cattle he could slaughter.

"So, Desmond," Maddy started, slicing through his thoughts with the blade of her sharply upper-crust English language enunciation. "Adella says your family is involved in construction in Maryland. I grew up in Virginia, and I don't believe we've crossed paths on the golf courses or country clubs."

Though her voice was airy and official, it carried a cool undercurrent, as did her eyes that needled him.

Hmph. How in the hell could a person as real as Lana be hanging out in The Hamptons with someone like this?

"Yes, our construction company has been around for about twenty years. Probably not long enough to enter the right circles yet. But we certainly hold our own."

He needed his boys. His family would arrive on Monday, and until then, he would have to suffer alone. Desmond longed to be around some real people whose convo wasn't stilted, before he lost his mind.

No. Actually, this engagement had to end.

His legs charged to rise from the chair. He would tell Adella he couldn't be the whipping boy of her friends and family for the rest of his life.

Just be a man and end this. Then, go home and face your mama like a man. Resign yourself to a shit job with shit pay for the rest of your life, the same as most other men.

Once he stood to face them all, a hand shoved him back down, squeezing his shoulder like she could break him.

"Honey, you look a little stressed. You want summa this?" the Texas belle that was Lana asked.

He held up his mug. "Oh, um…yeah."

She poured the liquor slow, her hand turned toward him and away from everyone else. Scribbled across the back of her hand holding the bottle was her phone number. Desmond quickly memorized it.

When he and Del left the gathering of Adella's friends, his fiancée started toward a family car they'd borrowed. He took off walking in the opposite direction, for the bars two blocks ahead.

"I need some fresh air," Desmond called, not expecting anything near a response.

"You can let your window down."

"It'll take more air than that for you and your folks not to suffocate me. I'll be back to your family's place in the morning." And with that, he took off from Maddy's house, in the direction of the *Oasis Cove* hotel where he'd rented his own room for this entire Christmas so-called vacation.

Lana met him in a corner of the hotel bar an hour later. This time she sipped water, the straw barely hanging from her burgundy lips as her head motioned for him to sit.

"So what the hell is your Baltimore ass doing here with all these counterfeit motherfuckers?"

Hard laughter couldn't come fast enough for them. Her relaxed aura, complete with the lazy don't-give-a-fuck smile so characteristic of where he came from, instantly placed him at ease.

Horny, and exhausted from boredom, he plunked onto a barstool in front of her. Her extra helpings of thighs and hips invited him back to the idea that had emerged in his head from the beginning. If he embarrassed his mother bad enough, she would cancel all this marriage crap and figure out how to elevate their family on her own.

YOU HAD ONE JOB

ADELLA

*A*fi would never lie to Adella.

Nor would her sisters, Rachel or Ilyana.

"Del, I've been meaning to ask you, how sure are you about your new man?" Afi asked.

Over brunch that Sunday afternoon, the question had come from nowhere. Rachel was especially shell-shocked, her head shaking so hard her jaws vibrated.

"Excuse me?" Del's eyes fluttered. "What in the devil are you talking about?"

Afi's dancing eyes stared across the table, with a tinge of vindictiveness in them, as if she savored what she was about to say. "Look, girl, I'm not trying to ruin your joy. But I've seen your man checking out other women right under your nose."

Del drew her hand back from across the table. Surely, Afi meant well, had intended no harm toward her.

How did she wade through the shame sliding around in her chest like grits? What else had they found out? And who else knew?

Did her friends know, with whom she'd yachted and partied over the weekend? Maddy, Chriselle and their other childhood playmates whose respect she'd always worked so hard for? Was everyone whispering, the way they had whispered about other poor souls? Did the other families in The Hamptons know she was lying? That she was only faking her joy? Did they know her three-carat Harry Winston ring was selected by his mother's assistant and delivered to her via the jeweler's private courier? Not the romantic proposal nestled next to a sparkling ocean and a sunrise that she had always fantasized about? Did the other families know she hadn't spent so much as five minutes alone with this man?

"And I hate to break the rest of the news," Afi added, sipping her coffee.

Why did Adella get the sense from her cousin's smug expression that Afi wasn't quite hating it as much she indicated? "Rest of what news?"

"He's sleeping with Maddy's co-worker. The one she brought with her from Capitol Hill."

"Maddy," Adella repeated.

No. That must have been a mistake. Maddy had always been the protective friend, shielding Del from taunts and insults on the docks and during yachting classes, when other children made fun of her knocked knees, her scoliosis condition, her slight stutter, and her super tightly coiled hair that her mother would not perm.

Maddy had forged part of her political persona by representing Adella in the sand dunes and salt marshes of unforgiving, upper-class childhood. Where the "brown paper bag" test excluded Del from the boys' invitations to dances, and one of Del's brothers always served as her escort. Where many girls received first kisses on the beach at sunset, and Del had stood on the docks serving as their lookout for any approaching parents. Where some of the hotel restaurant hosts seated her at the back of the dining room near the kitchen, if she was alone.

But Maddy had been one of the few people who hadn't

treated Del like she was invisible, a ghost, someone who existed but was not worth seeing.

"It's no big deal. So he sleeps around. That's married life with just about any guy," Afi chirped over brunch. "I'm sure you already knew. But just in case, what kind of cousin would I be if I didn't make sure you knew? Ya know?"

"And this is the reason I'll probably never get married," Ilyana added. She was normally quiet, and usually worked to avoid family drama so she could party and date without being noticed. "Who wants to be caught up in a pointless relationship? I'd rather just be by myself. Still, though, Afi, you didn't have to say it like that."

Adella turned to Rachel, who'd looked like a bunch of sour grapes jammed her throat. "You did not want her to tell me?"

"It's not that. It's just," Rachel started, tossing back a vodka cranberry, "you already have so much on your plate right now. Really, what can you do about it? It's not like you have a whole lot of options. You can't pull somebody else out of a Crackerjack box —if you don't like the first toy, you can't just open another box."

Still, Del didn't want to believe this fool would come to her vacation community, where all these people knew her, and hole up in a hotel with another woman. How stupid could he be? How stupid was she for not knowing he was that stupid?

This was perfect. She could leave his ass.

No, it wasn't.

The terms of her grandfather's will, and the marital agreement they'd signed, were clear. She had to marry a scion of the construction industry, and where would she find somebody so fast in less than three months? What should she do? Take out an ad on *craigslist*? In the *Boston Tribune* newspaper? An ad saying, *Desperate Boston Doctor Needs a Handsome, Non-Sleezy Construction Executive in Thirty Days?*

Adella was half tempted. Any scrub that rolled in would be a godsend compared to the little boy her grandfather had specified.

Her eyes wide as cue balls, cheeks shaking, that's how the ice was dumped on her humiliated head. Should she simply let the football player's whoring slide and accept that this was the way things would be? Del seethed. She didn't love this guy any more than she loved the guy who wrote out parking tickets. She was in love with another man, a damn decent and good man. And since this jerk didn't have her heart, he couldn't break it if he threw it off a cliff. So what was this hot humiliation boiling through her chest? This couldn't be all she had to look forward to for the rest of her life.

Rachel was right. Adella had no options.

Except one.

On Christmas Eve, she marched into the *Oasis Cove Hotel* to confirm it for herself.

"Suite sixteen hundred." Afi had gladly given her the hotel room number.

When Desmond opened the door, he was clearly expecting someone else.

Del blew right past him. "Where is she?"

"Where is who?"

"Don't play idiot with me," she replied, scanning the room. She found no woman, but instead, she pulled long strands of hair from the bed linens, which were also smeared with makeup and Christmas-ornament-red lipstick. The same bright red that Maddy's friend Lana had worn at the holiday soirees throughout the weekend, including when Lana had sailed on Adella's yacht.

Adella whipped around. "You had one job. Come to The Hamptons and breathe. That's all. How incompetent could you be?"

Desmond's eyebrows almost rose to his hairline. "Wow. You mean you give a damn?"

"No. Do you mean to shame me?"

Desmond's eyes flared. "How can you be ashamed if you don't care?"

Adella's eyes flared back. "I care for my reputation. Your mother cares for hers. If you're planning to use marriage to elevate your family, this doesn't help you at all."

"I don't care about my reputation. Or my mother's. And if you care about yours, you can end this." Standing back on his heels with a fierce grit of his own, he he spread his hands between them. "End the engagement. Problem solved."

Was he goading her into being the one responsible for breaking it off? So he could escape back to his cave in Maryland. He sought an excuse to back out of it, just as she did.

Her grandfather. His fortune. All he worked for. In her hands.

Adella pivoted toward the door just as suddenly as she'd come.

Her next stop, Maddy's house.

"Where is she?" Adella demanded when Maddy's father opened the door. "Tell me it isn't true. That you didn't know." Del stood in the foyer, like a lost stranger in the night, as Maddy ate dinner with several people at their long table, including Lana.

"Del, hey. You all right?" Maddy asked, shooting up and approaching her.

Del put up an index finger to silence Maddy, a longtime friend who had been closer to Del than her own blood sisters. "Tell me you didn't know."

Cracking across her friend's face was the instant recognition that shit was hitting the fan. Maddy understood. "I tried to st—"

The floor fell out from under Del. Her longest-standing friend and defender, and at many times over the years, her *only* friend. "How could you?"

"I didn't!" Maddy reached for her, and Adella jumped back. "She ignored me when I told her not to."

"When you told her…" Adella staggered. "You knew. And did not tell me."

Turning away from a stunned Maddy, Del faced Lana, still

seated at the Pages' dinner table. "If I see you out on the street, you'd better hope I don't catch you."

She walked out into the Christmas cold, back to her rented Mercedes, and headed to the docks. Not ready to go back to her family, unable to confide in the one friend she had, having deserted the man she kind of loved, Adella drove away.

She parked on a small lot next to two cars of groping holiday couples. Shutting the car off, she let the frigid air creep inside and wind its fingers of reality around her.

Papa, how could you? You knew I was happy.

How would she do this? For the rest of her *life?*

She had finally found joy with Wes. Or at the very least, they had contentment. His companionship worked for her. He was a decent person, and when they were together, it felt good. But they'd never been fully intimate, and she couldn't place her finger on the reason for her hesitation.

Still, his absence had left a hole. He had transferred to another hospital and cleared from her house three days later when she'd returned. Not a single one of her calls did he take and had even blocked her number. Since he had been living with her for months and given up his old apartment, Del had no idea to where he had moved. Her only companion now was the giant crater sitting in the middle of her.

The speed with which Wes erased her from his life had knocked the wind from Del. In a way, she could understand. He had expected to come meet her family and cement their relationship, and she'd body-slammed him with news she had to marry someone else.

But, damn. They'd shared so much. He had to have known she would never do something as wild as marry a stranger unless she had good reason. It startled her how he'd spit her out like hot soup.

She screamed all her despair throughout the car. There would be nothing for her now. Only a long, dark cave with no light. Just like the ocean stretching out before her, endless eternity, so dark ahead she could not see its beginning or its end, nor where the sky met its border. Only black night.

Her car sat mere feet from the harbor, which included a boating dock that made the ocean water accessible. A gate separated her from the icy waters of the ocean. Without her, her family would be happier. Their ugly duckling, the weakest link, would no longer be their worry. The money and company would be theirs to do with as they pleased.

Adella restarted the car. Facing the ocean, she placed her hand on the gear stick.

A wild bang against her window threw her from her seat.

"Adella!"

The passenger door swung open before she could reach the locks. She didn't understand why they were unlocked.

Throwing herself into the car, Maddy entered like a rescue worker. Along with their childhood friend, Chriselle.

"Adella, I'm so sorry." Maddy's tearful eyes reflected Adella's upset. "Girl, you know I would never hurt you. I didn't know what to do when I saw them out together. Lana is scandalous, and I didn't know just how much before I brought her here. I saw them at the hotel, and then I had separate words with Lana."

"But we got in that ass and put her out," Chrissy added from the backseat.

Minutes later, they all passed around a bottle of whiskey they'd brought.

"Men aren't worth it," Chrissy said. Newly separated from her husband and headed toward divorce, who knew about heartache better than she?

"No, they're not," Maddy added, before passing the bottle back to Del. For the past few days, she had been flirting and frolicking with an up-and-coming businessman who was new to Sag Harbor, Jerrell Rouse, a former Wall Street banker.

But something must have happened between them, because

right now, Maddy's swigs from the bottle were just as long as Del's.

"Remember how, when we were little girls, we talked about the castles we would live in when we grew up?" Chrissy asked, passing the whiskey bottle.

"Compared to a lot of people, we do have castles. Just not the ones we want," Maddy said.

"And ours are made of glass." Del then chugged a couple of swallows.

"But, Del, girl, it's best that you found out now and not later. So now you can leave his ass and move on." Chrissy's voice was firm and adamant as she squeezed Adella's shoulder.

"I can't."

They were her friends. Should she tell them her engagement was a farce?

The other two turned to her. "What?"

More tears slid down Del's cheeks. Her lips trembled, as did her shaking hands, so much the liquor splashed in the bottle she raised. She needed to vent about her lifetime punishment to someone. Or she might perform an act she couldn't undo.

"My grandfather has conditioned for me to marry him as the only way to get my inheritance."

The words were a casket closing over her. More snow cascaded from an empty place in the sky. The women's arms found one another in the dark.

"We'll help you," Chrissy whispered. "You won't go through this alone."

"Never," Maddy joined in.

THIS ROMANCE SHIT

DESMOND

Before the pre-wedding parties, Desmond's younger brother, Keenan, tied his bow tie.

"Straighten up your face. It is what it is now, man," his little brother muttered. "There's a whole lot worse that could be happening to you than marrying one of the wealthiest black girls on the East Coast."

Desmond wrestled the lump filling his throat. "There are also a hell of lot better things that could happen. I could be marrying a poor girl who lives in a trailer, who won't look at me like I've got leprosy, and she'll do me every morning and night until I can't walk straight. And she won't trip if I screw around."

His brother gave him a playful slap on the cheek. "Well, train her ass not to trip, and train her how to screw you until you can't walk straight."

"How can I do that when we don't even talk or breathe the same air because we don't stand in the same room?"

Desmond had always wondered if he had a heart. He was

confident that, since he'd never been in love, he did not. But whatever contraption that should have pounded in the center of him now hung outside his body and scraped around on the floor like a clock dragging its innards.

"Time for you to get out there and make this coin, man. Every time you look at her, just think of one-point-five *million.* Now go put in that work," Keenan said, giving Desmond a hard smack on the ass.

The celebration was held in The Hamptons, among the wealthy sets of both their families. At a secluded castle estate in an ornate house with picturesque views, lush gardens, essentially a Garden of Eden on Earth that made him feel a special, warm kind of fucked.

All this beauty and ambiance surrounding him was a juxtaposition from the cold, barren marital prison awaiting him.

He met Adella in a sitting room before they got ready to formally enter their pre-wedding party and meet their guests. Since the engagement had happened so fast, their parents had combined the engagement party and wedding festivities into one long weekend that started on Thursday and would end on Monday.

Surrounded by lilies of the valley and the peach and cream tulips, Desmond turned to a withering flower seated by the window. An early afternoon chill settled on Del's arms lined with goosebumps. He started his hard labor in the marital fields.

"How are you doing this morning?"

"I'm here, aren't I?"

Hmph. She had a little humor about her. Though she probably wasn't being funny.

"Yes, you are. You look nice." He was trying.

Today was Desmond's first time seeing Adella since Christmas Eve, when she'd barged into his hotel room and found Lana's strands of hair on his bed. He'd intended for word to get back to her, but not for her to actually give a damn enough to come and confront him. At the most, he figured the good doctor would have taken her stethoscope to her stiff, overdressed mother, slapped her with it, and then jetted.

But shock had hit him. That night, she'd had real emotion on her face, the only time he'd seen signs of humanity in her. He didn't get the sense that Adella's pain came from him, but that she was lashing out from another place of agony in her life.

Today, her baby-pink dress was a fantasy-like gown, with sheer poofs at the shoulders, its fabric floating outward in fairy-tale fashion. He supposed it was appropriate for the old castle they were standing in. Stale, old-fashioned, like something out of a *Titanic* movie frame.

Against her stomach, Adella's hands clasped tighter than Celie and her sister grabbing hold of each other in *Color Purple*. Desmond hated feeling like he was *Mistah*.

How did he put a smile on her face before they went out to the three hundred people who awaited?

"Look, I know this sucks. But it's three months later and we're both still here. Against our wishes, but here nevertheless. I haven't bolted. And despite my best efforts, you haven't either." Desmond paused, walking to her. He would have thought he truly did have leprosy as she flinched. "Let's at least get each other through this." He watched her tremble harder than a tiny puppy in the snow. Why did she have to do that? "I can be funny sometimes. Maybe I'll tell you some jokes, and one of them might actually make you laugh. Anything to see your beautiful smile."

He didn't know if her smile was beautiful since he'd never seen it, but his other lies sometimes worked, so this was worth a shot. Desmond held out his hand. "I promise, I washed it and moisturized it before I came down."

As if hesitating to pet a snake, Adella inched her arm toward his. Her head still turned away and, gaze still pacing the floor, she joined her shivering hand in his. He then moved it to the crook of his arm. Since her fingers were as frozen as chicken tenders, he covered hers with his.

"It'll be okay," he murmured, more to himself than the girl.

They walked outside, and once they emerged at the top of the balcony, peering down the circular stairs, their families and friends cheered them.

Desmond had no clue how to be a gentleman. His family's wealth was new, so all the etiquette training, horseback riding, and other trappings of wealth so familiar to his rich party buddies, his family had not given him. Not that he would have received it if they'd tried. But his mother had always been too busy working, so Desmond and his siblings had missed out on learning to be cultured.

Still, his unrefined street wisdom gave him the sense that he should do something romantic, to make this arranged shenanigan seem legit. He turned to the girl doctor, shivering in the princess dress her mother likely chose, and forced a smile. His hand still covering hers, he moved in for a kiss.

His eyes pleaded with Adella's: *Please don't drop dead.*

To her cultured credit, he sensed in her a desire to please her family, and from that place, she leaned forward to do what might make them all respect her more than they had at Christmas. Out of duty, she kissed him back.

Desmond let his lips linger on hers, sucking her bottom lip and tasting it. Sweet, plump, the kind of lips his tongue could spend hours tap dancing on. If she didn't hate him so much. The kind of lips he would enjoy feeling around his…

When he opened his eyes to see if she was enjoying it, a lone tear slid down her cheek. While they still locked lips, as discreetly as he could manage, he swept it away with his thumb, so when they turned to face the crowd again, it was gone.

They descended the imperial double stairs, while Adella clung to his arm like a circus trapeze artist hanging on to the bar. From the top balcony, Desmond could pick up on everyone. Particularly all those in the sea of faces who frowned, clapping as if their hands were magnets, or didn't bother clapping at all. All of them were from her side of the party.

At the time for the toast, Del's oldest friend, Madison Page, faced them. The last time Desmond had seen her was Christmas as he geared up to screw her co-worker.

Right then, the gun barrels of Maddy's eyes targeted him.

"Adella is the best of us. Determined, compassionate, with a heart as pure as gold, sweet, kind. Throughout our lives, whenever she got knocked down or was told no, she strived to be that much better than her doubters. Her fortitude is what we should all work our very best to try and emulate. She is an angel among us," Maddy said, slaying her words like a farmer reaping wheat.

When Maddy's eyes rose from her champagne glass, she sliced Desmond with them. "And if she is treated as any less, that person will wish they faced the wrath of Ramses instead of my wrath." Across Maddy's lips was the blade of a smile she must have spent years sharpening at cutthroat parties on Capitol Hill. "That said, go forth and be blessed."

Part of the room froze, wondering what to do with that. But several women's hands came together with energetic force, all wearing intense faces that matched Maddy's. Were they circling around Desmond ready to squabble? A high-society gang all planning to take him out?

Del's friends were making it clear they wanted to demolish him.

He seethed. How the hell could this be? Why didn't they address Adella's family? He'd never seen her siblings approach her to spit on her! What venomous warnings did they get?

"So tell us! How did you two meet?" Scott Gooden, one of Desmond's company co-workers and a superb marijuana grower, yelled out from the audience.

"Yeh!" several of his other beer buddies from the stocking and supply room at his family company cheered and hooted as if they were at the strip club.

Desmond and Adella made eye contact, finally connecting in their shared horror.

"Camping," he answered. *Camping?* Where had that come from?

"Camping?" Scott asked. "Dude, you've been holding out on us. I didn't know you camped. We should all totally go sometime."

Desmond gulped. This inner-city Baltimore kid never slept outside a day in his life, and sure as hell not in the woods. "Yeah, I like to use that time to just, uh, think. And be one with nature. So one night I was outside in my sleeping bag and tent, and..."

"I was out for a hunt," Adella finished as his voice tapered. "In the evening, I was hunting snow geese. First time hunting in Maryland. And I admit that I got kind of lost while finding my way back to my group. Then I accidentally bumped into Desmond's tent."

"Literally, she walked right into my tent," he said with a laugh. Nervously, he checked her out for whether she would smack him.

"I thought it was my friend's tent that's similar. Then, I said to him—"

"Standing with her hands on her hips, she caught a big atti-tude and said, 'This is my friend's tent. What are you doing in here? I'll call the police'. Very confident and bold, she stood like she knew what she was talking about." Desmond imitated her crisp, proper New England accent.

The room broke into laughter. Or at least his half of the party that didn't know the truth.

"When I finally realized that it was his tent, I apologized," Adella added, while shifting from one foot to another.

Picking up on her discomfort, Desmond slid his arm around her waist and squeezed. She stiffened. "I told her I would only forgive her for threatening me if she came to dinner with me. She accepted."

"And right there on the spot, I stepped out to his fire and cooked him his dinner—my goose I'd just shot."

More guffawing across the room. Desmond gazed at the audience, and a few of her relatives suppressed smiles, their stomachs shaking under their folded arms.

"And in classic Adella fashion, she said, 'Here's your dinner, and now you can go have a nice life.' Needless to say," he concluded, in the face of his fiancée's frostiness, "I wouldn't let her dismiss me that easily."

Clapping and applause followed with well-wishers raising their glasses. He breathed a sigh of relief, and next to him, he felt her take a deep breath of her own.

In her tart-and-sweet, Loretta Devine sort of way, Adella's covert feistiness might have been a smidge tantalizing.

THE ASSES around Desmond were popping, no doubt about that. Women from Adella's side of the family were blessed. Thick, meaty, with rounded lips, grab-worthy waists, all stuffed inside expensive designer suits. Their outfits, appearance, and jewels sang money.

There must've been a hundred different aunts, uncles, and cousins in Adella's family. And Desmond got the distinct impression those females were ready to cut her up in any way possible, for whatever her grandfather had done.

Her female relatives leaned in his face, displaying their lace bras and thong lines. When they brushed against him by "accident," size double Ds spilled over like oatmeal. Weaves and wigs flipped against his neck, and phone numbers found their way into his plate.

He couldn't help wondering what kind of relatives would stab

Del in the back this way. His family may have been a lot of things —'hood, loud, conniving, and definitely non-Europeanized. But one thing no one tolerated was backstabbing.

Even though her family was wrong, and their menacing conduct disgusted him, Desmond was still a man.

And the expensive, high-dollar asses throwing themselves at him that afternoon kept his attention. He only tried his best to ensure he wasn't surveying the options in front of Adella or her parents. He was already calculating the schedule in his mind, for how he would make this situation work in his favor. He could spend some days back in Boston, a couple of days in The Hamptons, and still make it to Maryland three times a month to check in with his mom's company and pretend he was doing real work.

One big girl worked out, as was clear from the drumsticks sticking from under her short skirt suit. Meat and muscle. Damn. She bent over the table to reach for croissants, just enough that he could see the outline of her panties through the satin fabric. She got up and left for the next room, throwing Desmond an inviting glance over her shoulder. To *not* pursue this would be foolish.

Hell, he deserved this. He'd been a good boy for over three months since he'd moved north.

Now, he and this chick could find some place quiet. In this big-ass mansion, there were plenty enough nooks and crevices.

His wood getting hard already, he took off. And this would be exactly what Desmond needed, because he hadn't had any action since Christmas with that Texas chick, Lana. She had turned him out with her Texas moves. For now, these high-priced city girls would have to do.

Rounding the corner, he exited the main ballroom and followed the ass. Already, she was lifting her skirt, and her twitching motions were like syrup pouring over biscuits. His tongue hanging out, mouth wet, ready for an excellent adventure, he walked faster.

But out of nowhere, a body taller than his appeared, and Desmond slammed into it.

"Damn, man, watch your step," Desmond admonished before he'd gotten a good view of the person's face.

It was Jerrell Rouse, the boyfriend of Madison Page.

Desmond knew little about him other than he had been a banker on Wall Street and was running some bakery business now. Another Ivy League Negro from Louisiana who had made it and now thought his shit didn't stink.

"Where are you going, man? Aren't you supposed to be on that side of the party? What are you doing way over here?" Jerrell asked, his chastising eyes peeling all the leaves off his birch switch that he held in front of Desmond.

Desmond had to give it to him. The man seemed ready to yank those hands out and throw down at the drop of a hat. Okay. So he might've been a real Negro.

"I'm headed to the bathroom. What are you doing? I don't know you. You checking up on me? Hello. My name is Desmond. And you are Jerrell? Maddy's dude?"

The tall, athletic man, who could've been a professional basketball player, scanned behind him, in the direction where the female had just strutted off. "You weren't chasing that, were you?"

The Baltimore native seethed a bit. "I'm a grown-ass man. So whatever I'm doing, really doesn't have shit to do with you. I am now asking you, politely, to back up off me."

Desmond really hated to throw down in The Hamptons, especially not at his own engagement party.

Hands still in his pockets, Jerrell stepped aside and cleared the way for Desmond. "My bad, man. We're cool." But Jerrell's eyes narrowed. "Just remember, your ass isn't in Baltimore anymore. You're in The Hamptons now, player. And one little mistake can go a long way. I would think twice about that, if I were you, and head back into the party without embarrassing yourself."

Jerrell's sternness almost dared Desmond to proceed and

chase tail right here at his own engagement party, with one of his fiancée's relatives.

It bothered Desmond. He was getting tired of these bougie Negroes turning their noses up at him and casting judgment as if they had never done anything wrong in their lives.

"Man, don't be judging me. You don't know shit about me, okay? You don't have a clue about my situation. So don't be acting all holier than thou," Desmond complained.

Now that he had been called out, the thrill of a good piece of cat had dissipated like ash into the air.

Jerrell remained relaxed. "I'm not your judge. But I am an outsider, just like you. And I know how these folks can be. It's not easy. And once you fuck up, you *are* fucked. Is that what you really want for yourself? If it is, hey, by all means, have a good time."

Desmond rubbed his forehead as a headache developed. "But my situation is not yours. You found Maddy of your own free will. When Maddy stares at you, roses must fall from the sky in Heaven or something. But every time I touch that damn girl, she breaks down crying. I don't know anything about this Hamptons high-class shit. My language is Baltimore. I know street life. I know what's real. I can't handle this."

Desmond didn't mean to vent, but he had nobody to talk to, not even his own siblings who were too busy dueling each other for the biggest piece of his mother's pie. That left him alone to deal with this Adella situation. For the first time in over three months, he actually found an ear that might relate to him. Even though Jerrell was a complete stranger, this guy seemed to have a few more drops of blackness in him than most of the room. And since Maddy and Adella were close childhood friends, Desmond and Jerrell would likely be crossing paths a lot.

Jerrell gazed through the stairway and into the main entryway where Maddy stood. "You're right. My situation is definitely a far cry from yours."

Just then, Maddy peered back at him, and they shared a loving glance across the mansion.

"Maddy is my diamond. If you want Adella to start looking at you that way, you need to treat her like yours."

"But how?" Desmond's frustration was knotted up inside the tie Keenan had made too tight. "I've never been good at this romance shit. When I want ass, I get ass. When I want to be held, I bang, and I might let a chick lie in my arms for a minute. Then she's got to go. But no long-term love. Dude, nah."

When Desmond's father had been around, he'd never taught them about the art of romance. And after watching his parents' devastating breakup, Desmond had decided he never wanted to be in love and hurt that way. So he had never taken a woman out for a full-scale meal.

The whole notion was foreign to him. From college parties to tailgating, foam parties, strip clubs, and hotel orgies, Desmond's life had been one long scene in *Hangover*. He didn't have the slightest idea where to begin for an actual relationship.

This had never truly dawned on him until now.

Jerrell's lips rolled in, and he let out a sigh. "I'll tell you what. If you need anything, holler at me. I'm in New York City and in The Hamptons. I'll be at your wedding. We are catering some of it. If you need a couple of pointers, we can hook up. But just remember what I said, okay? One stupid move…"

A distracted Desmond took his card. "Yeah, man, yeah."

"Maybe you, me, Adella, and Maddy can all go out or something, see if we can help you out."

With that, Jerrell excused himself and rejoined Maddy.

Hours later, Desmond and his buddies were sick of seafood. They had eaten all the shrimp, crab, lobster, and scallops, every form of shellfish, and they just wanted some regular food. So they ordered up pizzas. Adella and some of her friends had disappeared somewhere. Because he was so relieved not to deal with her and those innocent eyes that tugged at him, he was grateful. When the delivery guy called and said he was outside, Desmond took the stairs two at a time, eager to get some solid victuals in his stomach.

But upon hearing voices, he stopped in his tracks.

Who else was still in the mansion beside him and his crew? Many of his relatives had gone sightseeing and partying on the town.

"I don't care, Jerrell, no," a shrill voice snapped. It sounded like Maddy. "We will not associate with him and his ilk. It's already bad enough that Adella's hands are tied to this... dump truck. We will not force her to endure even more torment than she's suffering. Poor thing."

"Maddy, you can't say stuff like that," a male voice responded, obviously Jerrell. "He may not have come from your stock, but he is a human being. He is a man, and he is marrying your childhood friend whether you like it or not, so why don't you help her... I don't know... adjust? That's all I'm saying."

"But I thought you said you were all on board with them having one or two babies, and then we help Adella find somebody worth her while later? What happened?" Maddy asked.

Where Jerrell stood under the skylight in the main entryway, the top of his shoulders shrugged.

"I met the guy. Talked to him. I heard the pathetic in his voice." Jerrell laughed. "I actually feel sorry for him now. I remember what that's like."

"Baby, you are not *him*. Your parents worked their butts off for you to learn how to be a gentleman and to elevate you in New York."

"But when I first got to New York as a kid, though, *I* was the outsider. The country boy with a country accent who didn't belong and who didn't know shit. That was lonely as hell. So, baby, yes, a part of me can relate to getting dumped in this situation that's been thrown on him. And being left to sink or swim by himself. I get it. So alls I'm saying is," he assumed a Southern drawl while continuing, "give the man a chance to learn. After that, if he still fucks up, then okay, you have a right to hate him. But don't rush to chop off his head and you haven't extended him grace yet."

"Are we talking about the same guy who fucked Lana, my co-worker? He had his shot and he blew it! If he had his way, he would fuck her again."

A big sigh came from Jerrell. "He's in our circle now. He wasn't then."

At that moment they hugged, and Desmond knew that he was standing at such an angle that if he didn't go down, they would discover him. He descended the stairs to make his presence known, to avoid them finding him lurking.

"How much of our conversation did you just listen in on?" Maddy asked in her trademark lawyer-in-the-courtroom cross-examination.

"I heard enough," Desmond answered. He moved to the opposite side of the marble fountain, in which a white angel pissed water into its basin. "And you know what? You're right. I shouldn't be here. But I am. And since neither Adella *nor* I—yes, I can speak European English correctly—have not run away screaming yet, I'm going to be around quite a lot. You should probably start getting used to that."

Desmond exited to get his pizza.

ME. A WOMAN.

ADELLA

Adella freed herself from the stupid dress and flung it to the floor.

It had been her mother's silly idea to dress her up like some black fairy. She wanted to wear a more chic, sophisticated bandage dress. But her mother, Rachel, and Aunt Lizzie insisted on soft, girly, more inviting that did not scream "trying too hard."

She needed a strong drink, but did not want to be seen. Her cousins and siblings had gone off and left her, and Del was fine with that. Ilyana asked her to come out on the town and take the edge off, but Adella needed solo time.

Not a night had gone by that she didn't think of Wes. She should not have waited so long to give herself to him. Maybe he would've at least listened and had more patience with her. If they had been intimate, perhaps he would have felt their relationship was worth at least hearing her out. He might have helped her figure out this situation. Yes, the news would be upsetting to anybody, but why had he been lightning-fast to bounce?

Now she was so overwhelmed with all the expectations—wedding planning, document review, lawyers, executives, and then there was still her job—she could not think straight to get herself out of this.

Surely, there must have been some loophole. Even Maddy, fabulous Maddy, had tried to help her figure a way out. But once Maddy and her lawyers had reviewed everything alongside Adella and her lawyers, they could find nothing. Her grandfather's will and stipulations were airtight.

Unable to go to sleep, tossing and turning, Del rose from bed, threw on her robe, and gently turned her doorknob. Tiptoeing into the hallway in her bare feet, she didn't see any lingering relatives or friends. Along the dark, dimly lit halls, the house was mostly empty, and she could venture to the kitchen to steal a bottle of gin.

Two minutes into the trip, she was successful, padding across the floor, scooping up a big bottle and a red cup. Then she pivoted for her bedroom where she'd sip in misery. In the distance, a noise approached, and she rushed up the central stairway to escape before being seen.

"Good evening. I thought you were out with..." a familiar voice surprised her at the bottom of the stairs. "Somebody. Any one of your army of relatives."

Adella eased around to see Desmond, still in his dress pants, his button-down shirt half tucked in, half out. Standing in his bare feet with a pizza box, his shirt was partially open, displaying a respectable beefy, sculpted chest. His football-playing days were clearly long over, though his stocky frame still held much of its muscular form. Maybe it was the late night hour and her exhaustion had overtaken her right mind, or she was subconsciously psyching herself out so her situation wouldn't seem so bad, but the football player actually appeared...handsome.

"I thought everyone was gone." It was all she could think to say.

He shook his head. "Not everyone. Nice story you came up with today."

"You didn't do too bad either." Adella clutched her robe across her chest while managing to balance the bottle of gin and her cup.

"So you're actually a real person. Capable of lying, like everybody else." He moved up the stairs, heading toward her.

He kept coming closer, and she panicked. Desmond's hand reached out.

"Stay away from me. What are you d—"

He touched the silk scarf on top of her head. Adella jerked back as his fingers gripped it, but she pulled herself right out of the wrap. Her puff of kinky, tight hair sprang from underneath the cloth.

"Give me that!" she snapped, swiping the air for her scarf.

"Why do you wear wigs when you have all that?" Desmond stared, completely unbothered with how embarrassed she was that he'd seen her hidden crop of natural hair.

"*Give*. It. To me," Adella demanded now.

Leaning forward to retrieve it, she was hit with the aroma of liquor on him.

"No." Ignoring her request, Desmond held the scarf over the stair banister.

Adella's eyes flapped in horror as it left his fingers. The scarf sailed away from them to the first floor below.

Her nappy hair, unkempt and wild, was exposed. And now she felt naked, even though her fist clinched her robe across her throat.

Desmond's pupils became airplane engines flying toward her. "Aside from lying about how you meet men and concealing your natural hair, what else do you hide from the rest of the world?"

"None of your business. You had no right to do that."

"In three days, you're going to be my wife. You don't think I have a right to know what's really under there?"

Her fist still clutching her silk robe against the hollow of her throat, she glared at him. "No."

His gaze fell to her chest, and then her hips, thighs, until they dropped to her feet. Del now felt self-conscious, questioning what he thought of them, even though she went for a pedicure every two weeks.

His gaze rose again, and Desmond reached forward, his movements quicker than she expected. Was he about to cop a feel? Before she could swing away, he took the gin from her arms. She'd been so worried about protecting her body from his touch that her grip on the big bottle had loosened.

"Why don't you let me make you a cocktail? I mix pretty good drinks," he murmured.

While she was still in shock, he held out his hand to lead her back down the stairs. But she refused.

Instead, she finally found the wherewithal to uproot herself, spinning around to flee up the rest of the stairs until she stood safely on the balcony again. As if walking faster now might erase this exchange, Del scurried back to her room.

"I'm the last person you should be running from," Desmond called out behind her. "Maybe the real people you should be escaping are your family."

Those were his last words right before she shut her bedroom door and fell against it. Her mind replayed how he'd scanned her body with all its imperfections, her weight shifting and jiggling in ways Del had always swept to the back of her mind. Since she'd been sick in her early childhood, she'd always concerned herself more with her intellectual speed to clap back at bullies than on her appearance, She'd also been grateful to simply walk at all, and join the other kids for festivities. But now...

As a football player, Desmond must have slept with truck-loads of toned women and appreciated their more Europeanized, skinny-girl physiques. Adella tried not to imagine the explicit acts he'd likely performed on them. Before she could stop it, her mind sprinted off to what he may have done with Lana.

Now, the top-rated heart surgeon found herself staring in the mirror, faced with what she may have always deliberately ignored. Would anyone ever perform illicit—dare she think it—*nasty* acts on her?

As her childhood tormentor, Kevin Middleton, had made so clear, too many times throughout her life. *Who would want to touch you, let alone kiss you?* Kevin's taunting still rang through Del's mind, decades later.

Moments before, she'd seen the same questions in Desmond's eyes. Had he been disgusted? Had he been so repelled by what he'd seen that he needed a drink to digest the sight?

Tears springing to her eyes, she slid to the floor, still leaning against the door. She didn't have the strength to make it to the chaise.

Inches from her ear, on the other side of the doorway, a clink tapped the wood.

Dropping her face to the floor, she kneeled on all fours and peered through the space under the door. The base of a cocktail glass awaited her, its cone filled with lime-green liquid. Then came another glass. And finally, a third.

"Sleep tight, Doctor Good Liar."

ADELLA, Maddy, and Chrissy enjoyed brunch on the heated terrace of the castle the next day. Surrounded by peach ranunculus flowers on the tables, crystal goblets, and walkways through gardens, the mood was anything but flowery.

"He is a brute, undeserving of you. And you need to end this. We'll figure out the situation with your grandfather's company. There has to be a loophole and we just haven't found it yet," Maddy insisted to Adella. "You don't need money. You're not poor. You make enough money just from your doctor salary."

"But I'm not doing it for the money, Maddy. Or the inheritance. I'm doing it because I think there's an issue Papa never brought up and I need to learn what it is. I need to know why he did this, and I still haven't found out yet," Adella replied. "Without that answer, I won't just walk away and leave it all behind. No matter how badly I want to. He worked so hard to protect his legacy."

"Then I'll help you. We'll get to the bottom of this."

The early spring cold still bit their faces.

Del was jealous of her friends and how happy they were. Maddy had found love over Christmas with Jerrell. Chrissy had begun seeing Jerrell's brother, Sheldon, although the relationship was being kept under wraps while she finalized her divorce. Still, the smile on Chrissy's face, the way she gazed at her phone and giggled occasionally, pricked at Adella's heart. It reminded her of Wes and their secret moments in the hospital cafeteria, gazing at one another while sitting in meetings or conferences, stealing a glance here, a hand touch there.

"I was seeing someone before this," Adella blurted. "He asked me to marry him."

Chrissy and Maddy exchanged looks.

"What?" Chrissy asked.

"Yes." Adella lowered her voice.

Her friends' hands shot out to squeeze her arms, their heads diving in closer.

"Is it someone we know?" Maddy asked. "We can go and find him, see how we can make this work for you, so you're not stuck in this prison you're entering."

Chrissy's matter-of-fact face cosigned on the forced marriage concerns. "Yeah, girl, we'll find your dude. Because trust me, nobody deserves to do time in marriage jail. I'd rather somebody beat me on my feet with canes and make me walk across hot coals," Chrissy said.

Maddy burst into laughter. "I think it's wonderful, Del. You shouldn't give that up for anything."

"Isn't it strange? How just six weeks ago we were lamenting

about how awful men are? And how we would be single for the rest of our lives?" Chrissy turned to Adella. "And that entire time, you were hiding the *real* hot tea from us. You little sneak!"

Adella smiled at the thought of Wes. "He sees me. Not a doctor. Not a money bag. Not someone who can give medical answers or show up as window dressing when it's convenient, or," she paused and wiped her eyes, "to be some kind of chess piece everyone can play."

"Oh, honey," Maddy cooed.

The aftershocks of breaking the news to Wes still flowed through Del. "He didn't look through me, the way everybody else did. As the sickly or… ugly girl." She sniffed.

Chrissy handed her tissues.

"You were never that. No matter what *Kevin Middleton* said. You truly are the most beautiful of us," Maddy told her.

"But I know what people think. Even my own family. And Wes saw me. *Me*. A woman."

She removed his engagement ring from a small handkerchief in the side pocket of her purse. A pair of sweet dolphins inter-twined, encircled Adella's birth stone. Wes had left her home so suddenly she hadn't had a chance to offer it back to him.

She continued, "We planned to live on a farm and quit city life in a few years, once he paid off his student loans. I never told him that I was intending to pay them off for him."

Chrissy's eyes watered.

Adella continued, "We were going to practice medicine in the countryside. Open our own office. He introduced me to his family, and he wanted me to introduce him to mine. But I was scared. You know how my parents are. My brothers. My grandfa-ther. But still, I was going to do it and face the consequences. We both just wanted peace and quiet. That's all I still want. And instead of peace, now there's this. Crazy. And loneliness."

"Oh my God, that sounds terrible," Maddy muttered.

"And you know what?" Adella rubbed the spot over her heart.

"If my family had cut me off, it would not have mattered, because they don't love me. They didn't even know I existed until that day Papa left me everything. Now I'm not sure which is worse, being invisible or hated."

Maddy's hand flew to her mouth. The old friends hadn't had one of these talks in years. They'd all been too busy and scattered, first attending college and then, building their careers. In Chrissy's case, she'd been supporting her husband and taking care of her kids.

"We're going to take care of you this afternoon," Chrissy determined right then. "Let's get rid of those hideous engagement and wedding clothes your mother picked out for you." Chrissy wiped Adella's tears.

"That's right," Maddy joined in. "Let's make today a girls' day. And we will plot how to get you out of this and to your true love who puts that grin on you."

"Who you deserve!" Chrissy chimed.

Within an hour, they were at a high-end boutique along The Hamptons shoreline. They started with the black-owned stores.

Maddy was a mastermind at building public images and personas and spinning narratives and soundbites that fit into her political schemes. Though she was a Capitol Hill operator, her more appropriate calling in life was as a publicist.

With determination on her face and a march in her step, Maddy set to work on Adella. She selected smooth and crisp fabrics, with tight wraps and gathers, all designed to accentuate Adella's thick hips, breasts, and thighs. Rather than recreating Little Bo Peep, Maddy validated Adella's desire to be a professional. Feminine but strong.

As they stared at one another's reflections in the mirror, Maddy yanked on Adella's hips. "Hold your head up. You are one of the most accomplished doctors on the East Coast. Hell, in the United States. Own it."

Adella stared at her childhood friend.

That was Maddy—stronger than a cup of coffee, no cream, always willing to go to war for the people and causes she loved. Right then, Del's guardian angel peered down at her phone.

"It's Jerrell. They want us to join them for a late lunch."

"They?" Chrissy asked.

"Yes. With *him*." Maddy rolled her eyes. "Desmond. Before we all head out on the evening cruise."

"Why is Jerrell helping him?" Chrissy asked.

"Also what I'd like to know," Adella added.

Maddy sucked the back of her teeth. "He sympathizes with the guy. Jerrell is an outsider who struggled when he moved to the East Coast from the South, and he feels bad."

Adella's sigh was an objection. "Since the two of you will be with us, fine. I'll do it."

"But first, your hair," Chrissy noted.

Adella stared. "What about it?" Defensively, she adjusted her wig. For a split second, Desmond's hand brushing her scalp the night before crossed her mind. Her flesh burned hot at the thought of him touching her. *Why are you wearing a wig when you have all this?* His voice still echoed between her ears, pissing her off all over again.

"Girl, whomever you marry, whichever guy you wind up with, that wig cannot stay on at all times," Honest Chrissy pointed out. "You'll have to take it off at *some* point. May as well be now."

Maddy also examined Adella's head. "She's right, girl. You don't have bad hair, Adella. No matter what Kevin Middleton said."

Kevin had tortured all of them as kids, and right then, the women bonded in their shared disgust. Their faces all shriveled up like prunes at their mutual disdain for His Pompousness.

Especially Maddy who'd had a teenage crush on him and tried to win his affections for the longest time.

"I'm so glad you didn't choose him over Jerrell. I really wanted to strangle you at Christmastime for even letting the thought cross your mind." Chrissy scoffed.

Maddy chuckled along with her. "We all have our brief moments of lunacy."

They made their way to the salon and sat with the black stylist, Coral, with whom Maddy already had a relationship.

Adella studied her crop of natural hair springing everywhere. Thick, coarse, and unruly. It had been years since she'd sat in the beautician's chair. Instead, she kept her hair flat braided against her scalp, over which she wore wigs.

Coral slid her fingers under Adella's chin, tilting her face up. "Let's do a blowout. With a soft, wavy bob that frames these incredible cheekbones and beautiful lips. You have eclectic beauty. Let's accentuate that."

The last time Del visited a salon, the experience had been one she'd tried hard to forget. She was in college, and the stylist used a wide-toothed comb to try get through her coarse locks, placing Adella in tears. But the tears had not come from pain but rather the woman's words. "I feel like I'm combing the Amazon jungle," the stylist had said as she'd rammed its teeth through Adella's crown like it was untamed bramble weed.

Coral must've now sensed Adella's fear of the stylist chair, because her hand gently squeezed Adella's shoulder. "You are already perfect. I'm only setting you on a pedestal so the world knows."

"Well, hello there, ladies!" another female voice called out.

They all swiveled around, their jaws dropping.

Lana Gilley.

"Lana, what are you doing here?" Maddy asked.

She held out her arms. "Last I checked, we live in a free country. Am I wrong?"

"You know what she means." Chrissy's statement could have been a snarl. "Why are you in *this here* part of the free country?"

"I've got a hair appointment, just like you." Lana took a seat in one of the waiting chairs. Then she focused her attention on Adella. "I hear somebody's getting married tomorrow. Congratulations. I wish you well. Especially on your wedding night. I can say from personal experience," she paused for effect, licking her lips, "Desmond is quite a wild ride."

"Lana, you need to shut your mouth," Chrissy warned, her fist clenching.

Lana's eyes flared. "Or you'll do what? Whoop my ass here in this fancy establishment with all these nice people? Don't be upset, Chrissy… just because I'm taking the *Ivory* away from you. And Kevin and I are working together, after you failed."

"You don't have the *Ivory*, and you won't get it," Maddy replied.

"*Yet*. But I will. And I will teach all of you uppity women not to fuck with a Texas real one." She leaned in Adella's direction. "In fact, I've already started teaching class. Tell me, have you and Dezzy done it yet? Have you figured out his favorite position? I have. You want me to show you what he does with his tongue when you speed up real fast?"

"That's enough!" Chrissy bellowed.

"It'll be enough when I say it's enough," Lana snapped back.

"*I* say it's enough," Coral intervened. "For disrupting the peace, you can see yourself out, Miss Gilley. Your appointment with me this afternoon is now cancelled. Or I can call police. Your choice."

"And I hope you'll be returning my one-hundred-dollar deposit," Lana replied.

"Since the cancellation is your own fault, I don't have to. Sue me," Coral replied.

Adella's insides cooked in the flames of Lana's wildfire. Her words had cut deep.

It wasn't that Adella loved Desmond or wanted him.

It was that Lana had touched something that belonged to her and, whether Adella wanted it or not, Lana could now use her unpermitted access as a source of power.

Now Del would go and break bread with a man who had done the same, her future husband.

MOMENT OF TRUTH

DESMOND

Desmond entered the barbershop with a huge lump in his throat. He wished he could be anywhere else right now. Jerrell had convinced him to leave his boys behind and come alone.

"That's your first problem," Jerrell chastised. "Thinking everything is some kind of damn party."

"It's not?"

Jerrell ignored him and stared at the barber. "Get all that shit off his neck too."

"That's my beard. It's my sophisticated, grown-man flex. Women go for that!" Desmond complained.

"No, it screams that you're a man-child who hasn't grown up yet, and you're *hoping* you look sophisticated," Jerrell rebuffed him. "How are you going to caress her face with yours, and kiss her, if you're running a Brillo pad over her cheeks and shit?"

Desmond rolled his eyes. "I don't normally need to kiss them. They're too busy enjoying other hairy spots." Sitting in the barber's seat, he sulked.

"That's your second problem. You don't get a woman to fall in love with you by shoving her face between your nuts."

"I've never needed a woman to fall in love with me. That was never the point."

Jerrell leaned forward in his own barber's seat. "But it's the point now. So focus." He sized him up. "And get rid of that stupid bracelet and the chain around your neck. Replace it with a Swiss timepiece that's worth something. Makes you look like you've actually got some place to go."

Desmond rubbed his forehead. But he had no place to go, because his mother did not trust him enough to run anything. Nor did Adella.

When Jerrell was finished with him that afternoon, Desmond had ditched his cargo pants and yacht shoes, as well as the button-down shirt that screamed *fuck me*. They had decked him in slacks, loafers, and a thick cable-knit sweater. Stiff and stuffy as all the fake Astroturf that Desmond swore he'd never touch again once he left the football field in heartache.

It had been Jerrell's idea to reach out to Maddy and Adella for an impromptu afternoon lunch, to thaw the North Pole between everyone. But Adella and Desmond had been hoping to spend their final hours as far away from each other as possible. Desmond in The Hampton bars, holding tits and ass, and Adella doing... whatever she did. Instead, at Jerrell's urging, they all arrived at the Sag Harbor Yacht Club at three o'clock for a late bite.

"Hey, baby," Jerrell said before a slow kiss on Maddy, his arm settling around her waist, his hand cupping her butt cheek.

Desmond watched Maddy gaze at her man, all that tough Capitol Hill shark ego evaporating by the millisecond. In Jerrell's arms, she became rose-petal soft, as if she would follow him to the ends of the earth. Then her eyes slid to Desmond, and her horns suddenly reappeared.

"Good afternoon, Maddy. Thank you for joining us on such short notice. I realize you're busy." Desmond attempted to charm

Adella's oldest friend. And a powerful one at that, whom even his mother had warned him not to piss off.

His preliminary, please-don't-cut-me-up greeting seemed to deescalate a coming attack she was preparing for him. He caught sight of Jerrell's face just in time to see him giving Maddy a warning glance. Begrudgingly, she acknowledged Desmond.

"Desmond."

He'd take it. It was better than her calling him a dump truck.

He stared around the foyer, hands in his pockets since he did not know what else to do with them.

"Where is Adella?" Jerrell asked what Desmond wanted to know.

"She's coming. Needed to take a call first, but in the meantime." She returned her cannons toward Desmond. "You'll never believe who we ran into today."

Jerrell smirked knowingly at his woman. "Do we *want* to know who you ran into today?" Between the two of them, they held their own silent conversation, as if Jerrell were admonishing her again to go easy.

"I'm sure one of you does," she replied. Clearly, Jerrell's warnings only went so far. "Lana!"

At the mention of the name, Desmond's body experienced multiple chain reactions—first, extreme horniness as his penis remembered those glorious nights at the *Oasis Cove Hotel*. That had been some of the best sex he'd had in a long time, and Lana had whipped him from one end of the room to the other. Buck wild, unabashedly proud of her skills, Lana had put it on him good. Just thinking about it, he could've come in his pants now, where he stood.

Then he was reminded of where he stood. Followed by the appropriate amount of shame as Maddy's glare nailed him to the floor.

Desmond inhaled. "Say, Maddy, I understand that's your co-worker and Adella is your close friend, but we did not know each other at the time."

"You were *engaged*. You had made public appearances as Adella's fiancé." She enunciated each word as if it were a key banging on a typewriter. *Click. Click. Click. Click.* "To all intents and purposes, it didn't matter whether you knew us or not."

Desmond shrugged. "I hope over the next few months, I don't know, maybe…"

"Maybe what?" Maddy wielded her purse like it was a sickle and she was the Grim Reaper.

"That I'll earn your trust," Desmond finished.

"I doubt that. But the least you can do is stop embarrassing us all," she muttered through her curled lips.

Jerrell gave her arm a squeeze.

Desmond was too relieved when Adella finally entered the door.

Only this afternoon she floated in different, a grown woman.

The girlie wig of ringlets had disappeared, and in its place, a soft crop of natural waves fell around her shoulders. She flipped it out of her face. For her outfit, instead of puffs and pastels turning her into an over-frosted cupcake, her buxom figure was draped in an elegant off-shoulder, wide-legged jumpsuit. Appropriate for the chilly weather, it hinted at the undisclosed locations on her body, and whispered promises of untold adventures at each stop on her.

But the stop sign for Desmond was how Del's gaze met every face in the group, until it finally landed on his.

He might have lost a few of his breaths when she breezed in. "That suit on you is—"

"Let's eat. I'm starving," she said.

He exchanged his silent irritation with Jerrell, as if to say in silence: *I told you so.*

Jerrell threw him a glance that replied: *Give her some time. She'll come around.*

Once they were seated for salad and drinks, Maddy and Jerrell worked to bring some warmth to the table. This was the engaged couple's first meal together, since Adella had refused to join Desmond for any others. She turned to Jerrell just then.

"Jerrell, my family could not stop talking about your incredible pastries you served yesterday. Thank you so much for catering some of the food. We can't wait to have you and your grandmother at the wedding," Adella said, offering him a sweet smile.

Maddy gazed at her man with all the pride of a girlfriend who served him all the action he wanted, on the regular.

Must be nice.

But keenly aware of the situation, Jerrell cleared his throat and steered the conversation back to Adella and Desmond's big day. "So where are you two going for the honeymoon?"

Both of them hid in their plates, neither bothering to make eye contact. They had avoided one another the entire conversation.

Adella scraped her utensils across her plate. "There will not be a honeymoon."

Desmond hated salad—fucking rabbit food—so he dipped his spoon into his tomato bisque soup. "I'm sure there's someplace nice where we can escape for at least the weekend. The Bahamas, Jamaica, Montego Bay. Places where you can… have a little fun. For a change."

"I have to get back to work." Adella sniffed. "Some of us *do* work."

Desmond had had enough. The nerve of this woman! He hadn't seen any sex in over three months.

"Is that what you have to do?" he pressed back against his fiancée. "Or do you really need to get back to that white boy? The one who showed up at your house the day we met, with flowers in his hands and his face all hopeful and shit. Is that who you got your hair all done up for today? Because I know it sure as hell wasn't for me."

Jerrell's foot found Desmond's under the table, applying pressure until Desmond winced.

"Man, calm down, all right? We are in public. A very white public at that," Jerrell warned as his eyes picked cotton around the tables of white diners eyeballing their group.

But the teeth-like spindles on Desmond's cotton-harvesting machine were ready to rip apart this entire overpriced cotton field.

"No. I asked her a question. And since they're so good at interrogating people," Desmond paused, sneering at Maddy, "I want them to answer some questions of their own. Let's all be honest here since she is going to be my wife in… what, twenty-four hours?" He continued dressing down Miss Maddy. "I'll go first. Yes. I fucked Lana over Christmas. I was pissed, and felt some kind of way about being forced into a marriage with a woman who does not want me. And I tried to sabotage the engagement in a fuck-fest with somebody you people clearly didn't like. My mother doesn't trust me. I don't hold any legit responsibility in her company. I have a sham title. And I keep up sham appearances." He wrapped up his moment of truth in a wave of cathartic relief he hadn't felt in… never. "Now. Your turn, Adella."

He sat back in his chair with enough heated energy to fuel a rocket for blastoff.

Adella's closed eyes and tiny shakes of her head indicated she was ready to blow. Through clenched teeth, she muttered, "Stop acting like a child."

"Don't dodge the question. Are you, or are you not, in love with that white boy?"

Squirmy restaurant guests seemed about to shit in their seats. Desmond cared not one iota.

The waiter popped up at the table right then, with his pitcher of water between the two of them and a faux politeness that transported Desmond back to his grade school English teachers standing over his desk and forcing him to speak properly.

"Is everything okay over here?" the twig-skinny waiter pretended to ask what was more of a school principal statement, frosted with a singsong lilt.

"Do I look like everything is okay? Does she?" Desmond snapped.

"Everything is fine. We're just having a little spirited debate right now is all," Jerrell explained. With a glare at Desmond, he stated firmly, "Everything. Is just. Fine."

"Adella, is everything fine?" Desmond insisted.

She served him her side-eye as if he were a sickly dog. "All you do is whine. What have you lost? Nothing. I've lost everything. But you have everything to gain. By marrying me, you not only get your mother's money, you will also get some of mine. And as for me, what do I get? *You.* Spare me your attitude and your ungrateful tantrums. Just shut up."

Maddy reached across the table and gripped her friend's arm, massaging Adella's heart with her eyes.

Jumping as if the dumpster fire had landed in his lap, a flaming Desmond crowed, "Oh, yeh, that's it! Everybody feel sorry for poor little Adella. The powerful doctor. Ivy League graduate. Who spent every summer in The Hamptons and hasn't known a day of struggle or hard work in her *life.* Yeh, yeh, let's pity this poor little rich girl."

Jerrell straight kicked him in the shin now. "Man, pipe down. Let's everybody hit pause for a minute. Waiter! Can you bring us a round of shots?"

"That won't be necessary." Desmond removed the $11,000 watch he'd just bought, yanked the sweater from off his back, and threw them both on the table.

Maddy sprang forward in her seat. "Where do you think you're going?"

"Someplace where I can safely get the stick out of my ass," Desmond shot back. "But don't you worry, I'll show up tonight and be your house monkey. If for no other reason than to claim *my* money, to which I am rightfully entitled, for putting up with this shit."

~

ON THE WAY to the evening wedding cruise, Desmond settled into the limousine with his sister, Chaitra, Keenan, and his mother.

His siblings held their stomachs while laughing.

"Did you see that dress she was wearing yesterday? Why didn't you come kick it with us last night?" Chaitra asked Desmond.

"I was too tired and just wanted to chill at the house. All these hoops you've got me jumping through. All these fittings, and tuxedo shops, I'm drowning in fakeness."

Chaitra continued guffawing. "She was a giant cream puff, like somebody squirted her out of a doughnut."

Desmond did not laugh with her.

Any other time, he might've. But he was too irritated. For some reason, Chaitra's laughter bothered him. He didn't know why. He couldn't stand Adella—how condescendingly she'd spoken to him that afternoon, the repulsion squelching her eyebrows together when she'd stared at him.

"Oh, come on, you know it's funny," Keenan chimed in.

"And her aunts. What exact species are they?" Desmond's mother joined the roast.

"Tomorrow, we should feed them some peanuts and see if those trunks they have for noses will pick them up," Chaitra joked.

Desmond squirmed. "Enough."

"Wow! Now he wants to get all hot about his new in-laws?" Chaitra challenged. "What happened? Did the doctor actually give you some? Last night when we were all out? How long did it take you to dive in there?"

"I can't wait to hear this. Did you need a diving suit to go down under?" his brother teased.

"It's none of your damn business," Desmond muttered, agitated in a way that he did not understand.

"Oooh," His brother and sister chimed nudged each other. "He's getting defensive over this girl now. Damn. Something did go down. It must've been good. Look at him."

"Forget ya'll, man. Let's just get this over with. When is everybody else coming? And how long after the wedding do I get my first installment?" he asked his mother.

"The first installment of one-point-five million enters your account after the vows, as promised. Second installment is in six months. And then no additional installments until your first child arrives," his mother answered. "And you will not pull any tricks on me. You can't borrow a kid. Can't rent a kid, can't go to adoption, only to drop it off at the state office later. You must conceive, give birth to, and start raising an actual child."

His siblings cracked up at the meltdown on Desmond's face.

"I don't understand why you fucking treat me like this." He removed his flask from the inner jacket of his pocket, and swallowed liquid ire.

"Because you fucking get the treatment you earned," his mother clapped back with no apologies. "This could be good for you, Des. She is not a bad lady. In fact, I admire her. Maybe she could be the catalyst that finally gets you off your ass. Though she does have my sympathy."

They exited the limousine and joined up with their other family members, all walking down the boardwalk toward the boat.

In lieu of bachelors and bachelorettes parties—where people are actually happy to be marrying—their handlers had decided on a family cruise instead, for the two sides to mingle and get to know one another further. Really, this gathering was for Desmond's mother to cozy up to the wealthy elitists of The Hamptons. Margaret McLain was squeezing every moment out of this chance to pry into Adella's network, make connections, and parade herself around as the future mother-in-law of one of Boston's most prominent doctors. Every event and photo was about status and moving ahead.

Right then, his mother threw her arms wide open with a broad and welcoming smile for Adella's mother, father, aunts, and uncles, as if she had not just likened them to wild beasts.

"Mrs. McLain, what a pleasure," Adella's mother greeted her, not returning the love. It was clear from Mrs. English's expression that the only reason she was marrying off her daughter to Desmond was so their family company could survive.

Mrs. English held out her arm, as if she truly were royalty having to trouble herself with the lesser subjects beneath her, who possessed just the money and resources she needed.

"Mrs. English, come on over here! This wedding soiree is about to be one for the books!" Desmond's mother said with disgusting fraudulence.

Adella was nowhere in sight, and a fraction of Desmond was relieved, hoping she had finally found the good sense to cancel all this nonsense and spare them both. A part of him was starting not to care about the inheritance. He just might have been happier working a nine-to-five at a regular, miserable day job with regular people who didn't fake smile at each other, fake hug, or fake talk with exaggerated consonants that were long enough to wrap around his throat and strangle him.

On the boat, within five minutes he downed two shots of whiskey, for his own sanity. A hand slapped his shoulder, and already on edge, he balled up his fist, instantly ready to throw a blow.

"Eh, man. Calm your ass down. It's me. Checking in to make sure you're straight," Jerrell said.

Heart rate lessening a little, Desmond released Jerrell's wrist.

"I showed up. Let's just leave it at that."

"Listen, I know Maddy can be tough. It's just, she really cares about Adella. That's been her girl since… their whole lives." He shrugged. "Don't make anything of it. Just hang in there. Stick with your plan."

Desmond wiped a hand down his face. "There is no plan. I don't belong here with these people. This is not my life. I'm not trying to become something I'm not, for some people who are not going to accept me anyway. It's a waste of time."

Some of his clueless relatives approached him with hugs and handshakes, offering gifts. Desmond plastered on the best smile he could manage and accepted them graciously. Their kindness came in the form of envelopes filled with cash, checks, gift certificates and huge boxes from people he hadn't seen in years.

"I'm not far away. I have to see to my business here, but before you blow up or go off on anybody, just come find me. Especially if you get the urge to… You know. Don't do anything stupid tonight, of all nights." Jerrell delivered a final chastisement through his narrowed eyes and then disappeared.

Desmond busied himself with friends from work and some of his cousins who had come in from Baltimore. Adella had still not shown her face by late evening, so Desmond was almost home free.

Chaitra noted her absence. "Where is your beloved fiancée, bruh? Is she swimming underneath the boat and pushing it with her fin?"

"Chaitra, quiet," he warned. "Why don't you get under there and push it with your shark snout?" Since when did he start caring what anybody said about Adella? But even while he defended her, he chanted over and over in his head for her not to show. If he willed it hard enough, the universe might answer and his wish would come true.

No sooner had she asked than a murmur fell across the gathering of about a hundred people.

Desmond's focus shifted over his shoulder to find the object of all the curiosity. There Del stood, at the entrance of the boat, Maddy and Chrissy at her side.

The complete opposite of the little girl who'd appeared yesterday. A satisfied Maddy removed a cape from around Adella's shoulders.

The surprise underneath was a strapless dress that projected Adella's ample cleavage, a nice-sized rack that Desmond could bury his face in. They jutted out from her sculpted waistline, diving into the arcs of her curvaceous hips. A slim, A-line, simple dress cascaded over her ass. Graceful around her neck was a diamond necklace cresting her collarbone. And her skin seemed to shine as if she had been dipped in diamonds. Someone clapped, and the clap became a roar, spreading across the boat like wildfire. All faces turned to Desmond in expectation.

Panic and anxiety and fear suddenly caught in the in his throat, reminding him of the moments before he would run out onto the football field. Only worse this time. He'd trained for game day, had put in thousands of hours and workouts and two-a-day practices. But for this? Being somebody's husband? Even a fake husband. Was he truly prepared to go assume that position?

Since he didn't know what else to do, he forced his legs toward her.

On his way over, he felt something shoved into his hand. He peered down to see a small bracelet of flowers and pearls that miraculously matched Adella's makeup. Desmond quickly glanced for who had helped him out, and he caught Jerrell's annoyed eyes rolling at him. Jerrell's eyes slightly tilted in Adella's direction, subtly urging Desmond to keep walking.

"Right." Desmond swallowed.

When Desmond reached Del, no angry glint her eye blinded him this time. Rather, once again, she was nervous and anxious.

He slid the floral bracelet over her wrist before taking her hand and kissing it.

"Thank you," she murmured, with that way she had of speaking so low he was unsure if she'd spoken.

"You're welcome," he whispered. Feeling the eyes on them, hearing camera clicks, Desmond gave her a warning look to let her know he was going in. The good doctor returned a tiny nod as if she understood what they needed to do.

What they needed to accomplish in the next twenty-four hours: Not killing each other.

He kissed her lips, to which the guests and attendees went wild again. He tasted strawberry lip gloss. Her lips puckered inside he is, and she tilted her head, surprising him, so he opened his mouth. Thank God. She was relaxing some. In a reflexive move that Desmond did not control, his hand graced her neck, his thumb exploring her jawline.

They pulled away far slower than he expected them to, his rib cage vibrating from inner functions he wasn't accustomed to. His only felt his blood thrash through his veins when he was about to get the best head ever. Only now, this exhilaration hit different.

Awkwardness filled the space between them again. They did not know what to do next. Not hating each other had gone quite well for a moment.

"A toast!" someone called out.

"I'll do it!" Keenan offered before someone from Adella's side of the family could take the floor.

Keenan's toast was far kinder and gentler than Maddy's had been, and it actually sounded genuine. It was a good way to start a full night of partying, which Keenan knew was Desmond's comfort zone.

Desmond took Adella's hand. "You're actually giving grown-up vibes. I'm guessing your mother didn't pick this outfit."

"No, she did not."

"I see why you take such a liking to Maddy. She seems to have your back always, and puts the right amount of fear in everybody else."

Adella's smile was so tiny it was nearly undetectable. "But there's no better friend to have."

They began to talk at the same time.

"I'm sorry—"

"How did you—?"

Desmond paused. "My bad. You go."

Her eyes fluttered. "No, I didn't mean to interrupt."

"I just wanted to know how you liked the drinks last night."

"You're right. You do make pretty good drinks." This time, her smile broadened. For the first time ever, it wasn't a stingy one. "All three of them."

"I can make you another one now," he said.

"That probably wouldn't be a good idea with all these people here."

"It's a perfect idea. It's the night before our wedding." Pulling her to the bar area, he got behind it and grabbed bottles of liquor and glasses. "What did you want to say?"

"I'm sorry, for earlier today, telling you to shut up. It was disrespectful."

"I deserved it. I probably was throwing a tantrum. You don't have anything to be sorry for. I was definitely in the wrong for hooking up with…"

A flamethrower of a warning flared from her face, hitting him across the bar, communicating that he should not dare speak Lana's name on this boat. Desmond got the message, bright and blinding.

"… you know," he finished. Because, of course, she knew. "I apologize also. No matter how I was feeling about the situation, I was wrong. Aside from that, you made a good point. I don't know what it's like to be in love. I've never loved anybody. Not like *that.* Wouldn't have the slightest clue how it feels. Shit must burn like hell inside you. Sorry you had to go through that." He mixed and shook the ingredients of her cocktail.

"It does. And you are correct. Since we're being honest, I do love him. A lot."

And Desmond could see it on her face, from the way she sucked in her bottom lip to how her misted eyes darted to avoid focusing on her pain. But still, he wanted clarification.

"You love him? Or you're *in* love with him?"

At hearing the question, her face froze, like she'd been chased onto an emotional ice pond. Five seconds later, she still hadn't answered.

Desmond suspected if she'd truly loved the guy—the way a couple of women had felt about him despite his whoring and despite his not returning the sentiment—Adella would not be standing here.

"Here," Desmond said, sliding her three cocktails. "Drink. Maybe it won't hurt so much in a few minutes."

He watched her down her first, gratefully, licking her lips as she swallowed. But he also observed her self-consciousness evaporate, replaced by what may have been a desperate need to not feel. That despair apparently negated whatever etiquette and high-society training that taught her to sip slowly.

Before Adella downed another one, this time, they toasted. Him with his shot glass, her with her Midori Sour.

"To making it through the night alive," she said.

"I'll drink to that."

They tossed the drinks back. Others had already hit the dance floor, and started playing games, gambling at the casino tables, and betting at blackjack.

"Oh my God!" somebody cried, somewhere on the boat.

Adella and Desmond spun around to find a crowd forming at the blackjack table.

"Somebody, call a doctor!" a person screamed.

Desmond stared at her. "That's you."

IS THERE ANYBODY?

DESMOND

A fracas unfolded in the gambling area of the boat where attendees swarmed around the blackjack table.

Both Adella and Desmond pushed through the crowd with increasing worry and intensity, wondering which of their relatives had fallen ill.

"Adella!" Maddy yelped. "Hurry!"

They still could not see past all the bodies for who needed help.

"Get away from them! Move away and give them oxygen to breathe!" Adella cried.

People repeated the instructions before she could arrive on the scene. Finally, Desmond pressed ahead of her, parting the sea of people with his bulky arms.

"Come on now, folks, she said move."

Once they cleared the gathering and reached the body lying on the floor, he found his mother's favorite cousin, Furonda. Her adult daughter, Fretonia, leaned over her, crying and pleading for help.

"We need a doctor!" she screamed, her head swinging left and right. "A nurse! Somebody!"

"I am a heart surgeon. She may be suffering a heart attack." Adella kneeled and performed a preliminary analysis while listening to the chest of Desmond's unconscious relative. "Very difficult to hear the heart. Not good. Can one of your doctors bring me a stethoscope?"

Once a general practitioner provided her a stethoscope, Desmond and the entire room watched as she listened.

Adella's eyes darted up. "Muffled sounds, like the heart is underwater. Very likely pericardial effusion. Sounds like S3 heart failure, a tamponade." But before she could touch the woman to do anything further, yet another person yanked Adella back.

"Not you!" Chaitra declared.

"Chaitra!" Desmond snapped at his sister. "She's a surgeon!"

"We need a *real* one." Fretonia's eyes assessed Adella's worth the way one would a car at an auction. "This girl is too young."

The boat's waitstaff joined in. "The lady's correct! We require proof. That you really are a doctor."

The head waiter stared at Adella, conveying with his eyes that she did not fit his expectations of what a doctor should look like.

The waiter held out his arms over Furonda as if protecting her. "This is a liability for the boat, and if she cannot produce proof of her medical license and specialty, the boat could be sued. We cannot take that risk."

Fretonia swung around, as if Adella were not there. "Is there anybody who can help us?"

Maddy called out from the crowd, "What do you mean, 'is there anybody'? There *is*. Her. Adella English. All you have to do is Google her. She's one of the top doc—"

Maddy quieted as if Beetlejuice's metal had clamped across her mouth.

Jerrell pulled Maddy's hand behind his back, drawing her from between Desmond and Adella. Then, he tossed Desmond a hard stare. Yet again, Jerrell tilted his head in Adella's direction, as if to say: *Get your ass over there and defend your woman.*

A wide-eyed Maddy batted her stunned eyes, but Jerrell kept her at his side.

Picking up the cue, Desmond then went to stand by Del.

"Do you want death to be on your hands?" he asked, putting an exclamation point on what Maddy had just said. "Come on. Let her help."

"I'm a nurse," one of the white guys spoke, producing a wrinkled copy of a license from his wallet. "I can take a peek."

The waiter allowed him to check Furonda's vital signs.

"She's having a heart attack, sounds like a tamponade." The nurse stared around at everyone after repeating exactly what Adella had just informed them of. "We need to get her off this boat. Now."

"Not an option," the head waiter reported. "We've already called nine-one-one, and they're sending out a chopper to airlift her."

"By then, it may be too late," Adella replied.

"So what are you saying?" the waiter asked.

Fretonia cradled her mother's head. "I don't want my mother to die." She then glared at Adella. "But I also don't want this botched."

Desmond's anger crashed into their lack of respect for a black woman doctor.

"I would have to open her up here," Adella said, the wheels of her mind turning as Desmond watched a plan unfold behind her eyes. "Or she will die if we don't relieve that effusion."

Among Adella's sea of relatives, none of them uttered a word. Desmond tossed a glare at them all.

"She is one of the most well-known doctors in the country. You know that. Let her do her job."

His mother offered him a boost, and turned to Fretonia. "Ignore that she seems young."

Desmond stared down the waiter. "And ignore that she is black."

The begrudging way Fretonia motioned her approval to Desmond's mother, he would have thought his cousin would rather throw her mother off the boat than give this permission for Adella to operate.

As for the waiter, he lingered, his arm a railroad crossing that barricaded Furonda's body. "You are giving the boat permission to allow this stranger to proceed, and you are releasing this boat, its owners, and operators from any and all liability. You authorize a passenger, who has not produced a license, to perform medical procedures on this woman."

A distraught Fretonia coddled her mother. "Permission given." But the girl's eyes laid into Adella, as if to say: *You will be held personally responsible if you screw this up.*

Brushing it all off, Adella dropped to her knees and checked Furonda's vital signs. "Everyone, back up. Please get me alcohol for sterilization, a sewing kit, a straw, a medium plastic bag, and every size of knife you have. We don't have much time." She turned to the waiter. "Do you have emergency ventilators, oxygen, and cardiac monitoring?"

"This is not a large cruise ship. We've got emergency oxygen, but that's all."

"Get it." She had already begun unzipping Furonda's dress to get access.

Adella slid into a mental zone that Desmond had never seen. To help her work in peace and give Furonda the appropriate respect, Desmond stretched out his arms, pushing relatives, friends, and nosy people back. Jerrell took off his jacket and helped put distance between the unconscious woman and guests.

Adella took a paring blade to Furonda's chest, in which sharp-edged metal parted flesh and ignited wails of agony in relatives' souls.

Desmond's coworkers joined him and Jerrell in forming a human blockade around the woman.

"Come on, everyone, get back!"

The waitstaff now came to assist.

Out of sheer curiosity, Desmond peeked over his shoulder at what Adella was doing, just in time to see her push apart slimy organs inside his cousin's chest. The nurse assisted, his teeth clamping a flashlight while he inserted a set of tongs to pry back Furonda's bloody organs and tissue. Blood squirted onto Adella's face and splattered her gown.

The crowd gasped, groaning, and one woman fainted. Even Desmond's insides bubbled.

"Come on, everybody, get back. Have some respect." Desmond flipped his head away, but not before he caught the intense concentration etched across Adella's eyebrows and pursed mouth. As if she were doing what she was born to do.

Gone was the lost, doubtful woman whose family infantilized her, replaced by a hyper-focused general who could march across a body with her eyes closed, with fingers that were deft, arms steady, and none of the shaking or trembling Desmond had seen in her mere minutes before.

Adjusting lots of cloth napkins, she slid a spoon into the incision, as if moving an organ.

More blood spatter.

"Urgh," the crowd shuddered in unison.

Inside Furonda, Adella seemed to prop one slimy, pink body tissue against another, and then dragged the knife in deeper. Cries and emotion brought the gambling tables to a halt as Adella rolled the dice of life.

INSIDE A CHASM OF CHAOS, Adella's fingers switched from one piece of kitchen cutlery to the next.

"Where's that sewing kit?" she called out commands. "I need to close her up. Nurse, that straw and bag to drain out excess blood."

The human barricade formed by Jerrell, Desmond, waitstaff, and Desmond's friends stood between Furonda's open body and upset relatives.

Unfazed by the blood spatter all over her, or the vulnerable flesh into which she had dived her hands, Adella began sewing the woman up as best she could with standard mini thread that was more appropriate for sewing buttons. She removed the spoon, which sent pink body tissues smooshing back together again. Averting their eyes, Desmond and Jerrell swapped disgusted glances.

"Clots were inside the effusion. They're cleared. Blood is relieved. We need to get a heart rhythm."

While Adella performed CPR, the nurse checked for a pulse with an iWatch.

Small, subdued murmurs fluttered from a determined Adella. "Come on. Come on. Beat for me." She talked to the heart, leaning in as if waiting for it to talk back.

The nurse checked for a pulse. Then her eyes bounced like a slingshot around them all.

"Oh my God," Fretonia cried. "You killed her!"

Ignoring the noise, Adella did not let up, continuing resuscitation efforts.

Finally, the nurse's eyes enlarged. "I can hear a small pulse."

Applause and whistles rose among Desmond's co-workers. But his relatives still held their collective breath, as if it they were reserving their missile fire.

Adella remained unfazed. "Defibrillator," she called.

For the next three minutes, Adella charged up the electric pads to electrocute his cousin's heart to a stronger beat. Every time Furonda's chest leaped half a foot from the floor, the room wailed.

Desmond glimpsed behind him again. Furonda's eyelids now flitted while still closed.

"She's alive," his mother declared.

"Of course she is," Maddy snapped.

"She's unconscious but displaying slight movement. Vital signs still weak." Adella kept working. "In need of a heart monitor. Effusion removed, but she has high blood pressure, so she remains at risk," she reported into a radio transmitter as she called out the situation to EMTs who were en route via helicopter.

She addressed the nurse. "For right now, she is stable. Keep the oxygen supply over her nose and mouth. Monitor her pulse. Keep the straw and bag attached, for leakage."

But as Fretonia returned to her mother's side, she was still skeptical. "We will wait and see how this goes." She stared at Adella as if the doctor was a killer instead of the savior that she was.

"Fre, cut it," Desmond interceded. "You should be thanking her."

"I will thank her when I have actual confirmation that this was done correctly and my mother will be okay."

Desmond seethed at the lack of gratitude for the risk Adella had just taken with her career. And during her wedding weekend! They all could've just waited for the paramedics, and Furonda likely would have died during that time.

As if she were used to this, a relieved Adella slunk back against the blackjack table. Her gaze finally rolled over all the blood on her dress and hands, like she was now seeing it for the first time.

Again, Jerrell delivered a subtle glance at Desmond before his eyes dropped to a slightly dazed Adella.

"Adella!" Maddy and Chrissy rushed to ensure their friend was okay.

But Jerrell's arm shot out.

He barred both Maddy and Chrissy from reaching her, and he continued to silently admonish Desmond. This time his stern glance wasn't so subtle. From behind Jerrell's arm, Maddy glared at Desmond in a silent threat, her eyes about as encouraging as Japanese ninja shurikens.

Pulling himself together, Desmond grabbed wet paper towels and kneeled to wipe Adella off.

But she focused beyond him, *still* monitoring her patient, *still* concerned for a woman whose daughter *still* questioned her capability.

The helicopter arrived and lowered a gurney onto the deck before EMTs rushed to collect Furonda. Adella explained the situation and what procedures she had followed. Maddy had retrieved her medical license from her room and produced it, displaying it for everyone, which pissed Desmond off. He wished she wouldn't have conceded that way. The woman was still alive, and that should have been proof enough.

The EMTs carried her gurney away, and one of them stopped to shake Adella's hand. "I've read about you before. Don't you give talks at Harvard? I attended a conference where you spoke to emergency workers. It was inspiring. You told us about the surgery you had as a kid. Very good work you've done here today. She looks like she's going to be okay because of you."

Upon his saying the words, a a happy roar rose among Furonda's relatives. Finally.

But Desmond was not impressed at the late-coming acknowledgement. Why had they only celebrated after a white paramedic validated what Adella had already told them?

"I'm glad you enjoyed the talk," Adella replied. "You can contact me if you have any questions about the procedure, but I think I've provided all you need."

"Not bad for somebody who had to operate on the spot with kitchen cutlery," the paramedic said with a smile.

For a moment Desmond could have sworn this dude was flirting with her.

"Do you mind signing my EMT shirt?" The medic grinned. "I don't have any other keepsakes on hand at the moment."

A hint of jealousy nagging at him, Desmond started to speak up, but he refrained and let her have her moment. Adella damn sure deserved it.

With all the grace of a mourning dove, Adella replied, "I think your main priority right now is getting her to life-saving treatment as soon as possible. No?"

"Of course! Certainly! Nice to meet you in person, though," he said, offering her a final handshake before they rushed back to the helicopter for airlift to the nearest hospital.

Once they were gone, the doctor's head swung around at everyone as her mind seemed to finally rejoin the party. "Is everybody okay?"

An astounded Desmond reached toward her with more wet paper towels, wiping her arms. All the ass, tits, and sex on Earth didn't amount to what he'd just seen.

"Are *you* okay?" he whispered. "Because that was a hell of a thing you just did."

A BUSINESS DEAL. NOTHING MORE.

ADELLA

"You should go and take that dress off. Where did that come from? It's not the one I picked."

Adella shriveled like a dying heart as Flora English leaned over her, continuing, "You already had a dress. We spent a lot of money shipping it over from Europe, custom-made. And you come out with this? Piece of sh—"

"It was me, Mrs. English," Maddy piped up and cleared her throat. "Chrissy and I took Adella shopping. For something she would feel more comfortable in."

"Yes, well, Maddy, you know how I adore you, but Adella arrived here with her set wardrobe that we had already selected."

"*You* selected." Adella opened her mouth for the first time since performing the surgery. Stretching out to her was Desmond's hand to help her up. "We should get this boat back to shore so Desmond's family can go see about Furonda at the hospital."

"Foolishness! We can carry on. We will check on her tomorrow," Desmond's mother insisted, clearly more concerned with high-dollar hobnobbing, under the pretense of her son's wedding, than her cousin. "The EMTs said she would be just fine."

"It's up to you," Desmond said to Adella, still holding on to her hand.

"Fine. We can continue the cruise. She's not my family. And my job here is done."

Letting go of him, Adella scurried from the scene before her own mother could find something else to nitpick about. After showering and changing to one of the outfits she and Maddy had selected that afternoon, she took narrow service corridors to avoid the guests. Instead of the grand stairway, she used the workers' stairwell, heading to the back deck and then climbing to the top private view that was reserved for her and Desmond.

She hadn't intended to actually use it, but now, she hoped he had meandered off to gamble with his buddies, and that he'd get too drunk to remember this perk.

The boat was timed to dock around sunrise. It was now eight o'clock in the evening, so they had another ten hours of sailing. Heaters were provided throughout the boat, since it was mid-March. Falling against the cushions, she pulled a weighted blanket over her, curled up in front of a heater, and enjoyed the rolling waters. She loved the outdoors. The sky was clear, and the stars painted a masterpiece over her head. A perfect night to begin an imperfect life.

Moments later, she jumped at the touch of cold against her neck. Behind her, Desmond stood, having changed clothes. He held another tray of freshly made drinks.

She accepted the tray, her hands sliding over his to take it. In that moment, their eyes met and the ocean tides seemed to switch their direction. Unsure how to interpret a slight shift between her and the man in front of her, she focused on setting down the tray so their gazes didn't connect for too long. "You probably think I'm an alcoholic at this point."

"If you are, I won't judge. You've more than earned the right." As he said it, he opened up his own big bottle of gin, tucked under his other arm.

"Alcohol is a dangerous way to treat stress." But even as she said it, her lips slurped and she savored the fruity liquor chilling her throat, washing away a raft of issues she'd dealt with in the last two hours alone.

As if he could read her mind, Desmond sighed. "Why do you let them treat you that way?"

"I don't let anybody treat me that way. You would not understand."

"Please. I'm trying to understand. I really don't want to pop your mama," he said.

Adella wanted to speak up in defense of her mom, but instead of a smart-aleck reply, a big laugh burst from her chest.

The thought of her mother being slapped was one she'd fantasized about for a long time. Stunned at her reaction, Desmond joined her laughter. He had expected her to fuss.

"Do it," she said. "I might not stop you."

They continued chuckling and sipping.

"As far as this guy you love…" he started.

At the mention of the subject, Adella stiffened, and her humor condensed in the chilly night. "What about him?"

"If you want to keep seeing him on the low, after we take our vows, I won't be mad at you. I get. We had our own lives before all this, and our families shouldn't be allowed to ruin that. It can be an arrangement between us, for right now. A business deal. That's it."

Adella no longer needed the heat as her body generated enough heat for its own nuclear reactor. "And what will you expect from me in return? That you can carry on with Lana?"

She could see that question had stumped him.

"That wasn't on my mind. But now that you mention it,

would it be so bad? We can make ourselves happy while we get through this?"

Del's headshake was a stern admonishment. "You clearly don't know how The Hamptons operate. How high society operates. There are eyes everywhere. My job. Our community. When people read in all the papers that I am marrying, and they go on social media to see your face, there will be no privacy or maneuvering behind closed doors. Every time you step out, you risk humiliating us. Humiliating me."

"Why do you care so much what these people think about you? They hardly respect you."

"My reputation is all I have. Nothing else. Medicine. Saving lives. It's all I know. With scandal and gossip, you can taint my ability to thrive. I don't work hard for people. I work hard to thrive."

"Damn. You always have a way of making shit sound all apocalyptic, like it's going to be the end of the world." Desmond let out another huff. "Well, if I can't step out, and you won't step out, who else can we have?" He sat back and stared at her while he drank straight from a bottle.

To that, she was now at a loss for what to say.

Voices approached, coming closer.

On the deck below them, Adella recognized a familiar voice. Maddy.

"I need to find her so we can discuss what happened tonight. They shouldn't have treated her that way. It's wrong, and we will address it. She should go to the media."

"Maddy Cakes, no," a second voice spoke, Jerrell. "Let Adella decide how she wants to handle things. She is a grown woman."

"But you don't understand. She doesn't really speak up for herself. Never. It's always been me. She's wonderful when it comes to medicine and science but not when it comes to fighting back. She needs me to do this."

"Baby, slow your roll. Okay?" Shuffling came from below, as if

Jerrell and Maddy were in an embrace. "It might be time for you to accept that Adella will always be your friend, but she is no longer yours to protect."

Adella and Desmond exchanged glances, holding their own silent conversation about whether they should make their presence known. She did not feel comfortable eavesdropping, so Adella cleared her throat, loud enough for them to hear her below.

Maddy's eyes shot up. "Adella! Girl! Are you okay? Do you want us to come up there and join you?" She started to climb the stairs leading to the top observation deck.

Jerrell gently drew her back to him, and he did not move a muscle. "She looks fine, baby."

Adella noticed how Jerrell and Desmond exchanged glances.

"Do you know what she just went through?" Maddy asked.

Adella certainly wanted Maddy's comfort and concern, but she also needed quiet. To just stare into the open ocean and dread the vows that would soon hang around her neck, before sinking her in its watery grave.

For now, she blew her friend a kiss. "Yes, I'm okay. Love you, girl. Thanks for always having my back."

"I love you too, Adella, and you know I'll always have your back. No matter what. Are you sure you don't need me to—"

Without further delay, keeping Maddy's hand behind *his* back, Jerrell saluted Desmond and Adella. Then, he cleared the area, tugging a silenced Maddy with him.

"Wow, how did anybody ever get near you when y'all were kids? Did you have any other friends?" Desmond cracked.

But Adella reflected on the question seriously as she downed another fruity cocktail. "Not many. It's why she's so protective."

Upon hearing that response, Desmond's laughter faded. "Sorry."

"Not your fault," she replied, staring into the nothingness that reflected so much of her social life as a kid and teenager.

He passed his bottle to her and she drank. Then, they sat silent, taking the occasional swigs from his bottle, and she actually didn't mind his presence so much. After all, her future husband was the one person alive tonight who could walk in her shoes.

A LITTLE... HELP

DESMOND

*L*ater that night, after Adella excused herself to return to her room alone, or rather dismissed him the way she always did, Desmond fled to the food section of the boat.

Fortunately, Jerrell had not returned to his room yet. He oversaw his workers as they arranged the tables and dishes for the outgoing breakfast the next morning.

"Hey, man, what's up? What are you doing out here? How come you're not... in *there*?" Jerrell's smile was sneaky. "After all that hard labor your fiancée did tonight, I'm sure she could use some relaxation."

Desmond's gaze hit the floor, bashful embarrassment spreading over him.

Jerrell's amusement turned a tad impatient. "Come on, dude. Spit it out."

Desmond rolled his shoulders around a bit, preparing what he had to say. "I might need a little... help."

Jerrell's eyebrows stacked together with a big "confused" sign hanging from them. "Like, what kind of help?"

"Your boy is clueless on what to do... for somebody like Del."

There. He'd said it. He hoped the guy would figure out what he was trying to say without Desmond having to actually admit it.

Jerrell's head still bobbled. "I'm not understanding. You don't know… what to do… when… where?"

Jamming his thumbs through his belt loops, shifting from one leg to the other, Desmond squinted his eyes. "Tomorrow night?"

Excitement glistened in Jerrell's eyes, and he held up his hand for a grip. "Tomorrow night is your *wedding* night!" Then he jumped back, finally realizing Desmond's predicament. "Whoa. Dude, are you playing with me?"

"No! All right? Don't make this harder than it already is." Desmond pursed his lips, his eyes hardening. This could not have been more embarrassing. "This… *romance* shit. I've never had to set the mood first, just so I could… slice it up."

"Ohhh," Jerrell replied, rocking back on his heels.

"Yeah. That. These women are… different. I can't just unzip my dick and expect them to do what I want."

Jerrell rubbed his chin. "No, you definitely can't do that. I'll tell you what. Meet me here, first thing in the morning, and we'll go over some things. But keep this quiet." Jerrell snickered. "I mean *real* fucking quiet."

"Yeah, yeah."

Before the two of them departed, they surveyed the area to ensure they hadn't been seen or that no one had overheard.

At sunrise on his wedding day, Desmond's nerves jangled harder than broken wheels on the metal food carts the waitstaff pushed through the hallways. Leaving the bedroom where he'd tossed and turned alone, he wore warm vacation clothes to the dining room where Jerrell already waited. He stood proudly in front of a full spread of pastries set out for people to grab once the boat docked, party wedding favors laid alongside them. It impressed Desmond.

"This entire business right here? All this food… this is you?" Desmond asked him.

"Yep, all me." Jerrell inhaled, taking it all in and directing one of his servers to rearrange some of the setup.

"Wow, when I first met you over Christmas, you were just starting out, and already you're killing it," Desmond gushed in disbelief. "So you really left your job on Wall Street to start this up? Doesn't your whole family work in finance?"

Jerrell nodded. "That's right. My folks tripped hard when I did it. But I had to break off and do my own thing. It's been as hard as making bricks out of mud, but the payoffs are worth it."

Desmond admired such a big undertaking and wanted to try it himself. "Now you're serving your product on boats and at weddings. You've got these people eating out of the palm of your hand. Mad props to you." He meant every word of it. For a dude from Louisiana, this guy had really come up. Desmond did not exactly feel jealousy. But he did feel a lot of envy and had a ton of questions about the hard process of breaking away from his family and getting started.

Jerrell took a seat. "Come on, let's get this done before people start coming down."

They ordered a three-course meal from the kitchen to be delivered, since they didn't have time for a five-course.

"How much etiquette do you know?" Jerrell asked simply.

"What the fork, the spoon and the knife look like."

Jerrell nodded. So they ate and chatted, wherein Jerrell subtly demonstrated how Desmond should handle himself at the table, both with the silverware *and* with Adella. The way the napkin should lay over his lap, how he should sit back, relaxed, in his chair. How to rest his hands easily in his lap, at times even crossing his legs, lacing his fingers together, like he didn't have a care in the world.

"You want her to wonder what's on your mind, if you like her, what you are thinking of her. And to whet her curiosity, you should give off mystery and intrigue. Don't overdo it to the point of being shady or cocky. Just be calm."

As he spoke, he motioned for Desmond to try it and just sit back in the chair, which he did. Desmond sniffed, sitting back, legs wide open.

"Close your legs some, man. Your dick isn't supposed to be out telegraphing messages and shit." At that, they both chuckled, and Jerrell continued, "The key is to put her at ease, long before you hit the bedroom. You want her wet while she's still at the dinner table.

Desmond nodded.

"You pour her wine. Let the waiter pour the first glass, and after that, you take control and *you* pour from the bottle. Don't forget the toast. Get her food order in advance, and then you place it with yours. Makes you look thoughtful and considerate. When it comes to dessert, you order *one* and split it. Offer her the first bite. Save the last bite for her. During your meal, offer for her to try some of yours, you ask to try some of hers, you feed it to her. She feeds you." Glancing around to ensure nobody watched, Jerrell held out his fork across the table but not so far as to expect Desmond to eat from his fork. "You try it. Let's make sure you do it smoothly, without appearing shaky and shit."

So Desmond proceeded scooping up some of his eggs and extending them.

Jerrell's eyes entered the *Twilight Zone.* "You look uncomfortable as fuck. You're not feeding a pit bull. You are feeding your wife, the woman whom you will, presumably, spend the rest of your life with. Relax. It's no different than feeding yourself."

The rest of his life.

A certain ring to those words dragged Desmond along the bottom of the boat as if he were its keel. Even though he and Adella had agreed to divorce after two children, that was the equivalent of saying he'd only swim half the English Channel and then swim back.

Jerrell shifted positions slightly, and leaned in closer. "Now, occasionally you want to reach across the dinner table and very lightly, with your pinky finger, or your index finger, but with one finger, stroke her hand while you stare into her eyes, like every word that comes out of her mouth is gold. Try it now."

Desmond swallowed his rattling nerves, reaching his hand across the table where Jerrell's hand still lay, stuck out his pinky finger, and slid it across the back of Jerrell's hand. At the appall snatching Jerrell's features, Desmond immediately yanked his hand back.

"*Not on me!*" Jerrell muttered, fighting to keep his voice low as his head whipped from one direction to the other, checking for witnesses.

Desmond jumped in his seat. "My bad, man. My bad! I wasn't thinking. My head is somewhere else! It's a lot to fucking think about right now, okay?"

"All right, all right. It's cool. But I don't mean on me. Practice on the napkin. Caress the *fabric*, gently." Jerrell massaged the temple of his own forehead. "And when you do this to her for real, make sure you moisturize your hands so you don't cut the shit out of her the way you just did to me."

YOU THOUGHT WRONG

ADELLA

The wedding dress fell over Adella as if it were a straitjacket.

Her body as lifeless as a tranquilized patient, she stared into space after the makeup artist finished painting her into a happy portrait depicting all she was not.

Standing in the foyer of the massive cathedral now, she looped her arm through her father's.

Adella examined him now, Mr. Orlando English, whose mouth rarely moved when she saw him. Her parents had lived separately for over a decade, since she and Ilyana had left their parents' home for college. While her mother and father were still legally married, he now stayed in his native North Carolina. With his girlfriend.

"You are our blessing," he said, his voice hardly rising above the flower girls' chattering voices. "You confirmed it last night. And I wouldn't have expected anything less."

"Dad…"

He hadn't attended Papa's funeral, so her wedding was the first time Del had seen him in a year.

"I know. Your mother and I were arranged as well. It's how we grow wealth, dear. You find your happiness where you can. There is no perfect life."

His hand held hers, and he leaned over her. She inhaled the scent of cigar mingled with his favorite Eau Sauvage cologne that shot into her nostrils with notes of spicy basil, rosemary, and lemon over wood. His having worn it for decades reminded her of forced dinners in which he mentally checked out so her mother could dictate orders to Adella's older siblings.

Her throat clogged up at her realization of the life awaiting her and Desmond.

Her father planted the kiss on her temple the way survivors of a deceased threw the last dirt on that person's grave.

Maddy, Chrissy, Ilyana, and two of Adella's college friends appeared as her bridesmaids. Of course, a concerned Maddy threw her arms around her childhood friend's neck, in a seeming goodbye.

"You don't have to do this, girl."

Adella's arms encircled her friend, but she was determined to see this through. "Yes, I do."

Then, they formed the line for the procession at the cathedral threshold. At last, four months after Francis Manuel had sent a shockwave over her life, Adella and her father marched down the long aisle. Staring back at her were some of the wealthiest black elites in America. Every step took her deeper into the trenches, until she finally arrived at a stricken Desmond.

Stiff, wooden, nursing terror of his own, he reached for her hand. But her father's grip lingered for a surprisingly long time. Mr. English's glare put a surgical knife of his own into Desmond's eyes.

That's how Adella learned the football player wasn't so dull. Desmond gave her father a slight bow, indicating he'd received the not-so-subtle warning.

Mr. English leaned forward, kissed her forehead again, and finally, released her hand. Which Desmond then placed over his own. She was surprised to feel his hands trembling harder than hers.

Face to face now, intimately, nervously, Desmond lifted Adella's sheer chiffon veil that separated them. The veil's disappearance also seemed to reintroduce her to him, maybe to another side of him, to his subtly spicy and woodsy scent that entered her head, reminding her of a coming sultry adventure in the outdoors.

Slight tremors from more than the cold cathedral skipped down her spine when he locked his eyes into hers. Did the jock took this seriously? A nervous, cinnamon-scented breath fled from his mouth and tickled her face.

"You look... exquisite."

The nerve impulses in her brain experienced multiple shutdowns. How did she handle his nervousness that transformed him into more human than jerk? Where was the guy from yesterday afternoon? Why was this new person putting forth effort to smooth things over? Her head spun at his dueling personalities, making it harder for her to hate him.

"Thank you." What did she say to him without sounding fraudulent? "You smell nice."

Ugh. What kind of compliment was that?

A corner of his lips rose, offering a tiny break from their shared nervousness. "Good to know I got that part right."

They shifted to the reverend. For the next few minutes, like Mattel dolls posed in the proper position, they repeated every action the reverend commanded. The exchange of rings felt more like the filming of a soap opera—*and stay tuned for next week's episode of Will Her New Husband Drive Her Off a Cliff!*—to be recorded and displayed later for high society's viewing pleasure.

For the ring, Del reached for Maddy, whose eyes belted out every girl-you-need-to-leave-his-ass song they'd ever heard. Her childhood protector handed over Desmond's band that Adella had never seen before, since she hadn't selected it.

Desmond turned to his younger brother, who placed her wedding band in his shaky palm that displayed beads of sweat.

"Do you take this woman to be your lawfully wedded wife?"

The muscles of his jaw rippled, his chest heaved, and it seemed for a moment that he just might run away, which would have been perfect. His fleeing wouldn't be Del's fault. Yet she would be free.

Was Desmond staring at her? Were they having a staring contest? A game of chicken?

Since she was busy fighting to stay on her feet and not faint, she couldn't tell.

"I do."

Damn.

"And do you take this man to be your lawfully wedded husband?"

A storm tossed the ocean of blood pumping through her veins. With that, and the sudden blurring of her vision, she might have seen two or three Desmonds.

"I do."

In twenty minutes, the entire reality show they had plotted for months, lifted the curtain for the real drama.

Yet again that weekend, Desmond's face closed in on hers. She could not decide if his expression was one of tenderness or angst as he tilted his head and closed his mouth over hers. So that the photos would not look awkward, she pushed in and accepted his fake affection.

But under the gentleness of his warm, moist mouth, and his lips easing against hers, Del's heart performed an unexpected backflip.

She was stunned when he pulled back, and an unprepared part of her actually missed the sensation.

His fingertips on her neck set off a few chain reactions inside her bodice.

He took her hand, walking her down the aisle and out of the

cathedral that may as well be a dungeon. They stopped for cathedral photos. In tormented positions, they cranked their heads, pushed their lips together, held one another's hands, and laughed on cue. Photographers spun around them, snapping for all the society pages in fashion magazines.

"Maybe once we get through this, if our photos pass muster, I'll buy that guy a new pair of high-water pants," Desmond joked.

Adella was shocked at the guffaw that escaped her lips.

He continued, "And his assistant could use a shirt that covers the other half of his body."

Once again, Adella broke out with chortling. So he had a sense of humor. Which helped them get through the photo shoot, and they had managed to provide some sufficiently happy shots. Being swept away to the gardens of the castle, they arrived to a mixed crowd of stoic relatives on Adella's side versus rowdy, hooting co-workers and relatives in Desmond's group.

And when she peeped Desmond's half of the soirée, the faces of gratitude warmed her heart as his people reached out to her with open arms that shocked her.

Fretonia actually approached her with a bouquet and a long box. "Cousin, I cannot thank you enough for saving my mother's life."

Adella shook her head. "It's my job."

"And we were giving you hell about doing it. I'm an accountant, and I know how it feels to have someone question your capabilities on the job. I apologize for my behavior last night. Especially on your wedding weekend. I hope one day we'll get to know each other better," Fretonia said.

Desmond's co-workers and associates formed a line to introduce themselves and greet her.

A guy named Scott Gooden approached Adella. "I don't know if I could've done what you did last night, even if I were a doctor. Especially not after how those people talked to you. Good on you for your grace under fire." He addressed Desmond with a wink. "You'd better not screw this up."

Furonda's relatives also embraced Adella, squeezing her in a way that only Maddy and her grandparents had throughout her life.

She then turned to her own family members but expected little warmth. And they did not disappoint. Del had followed through on her grandfather's condition and removed their last hope for the inheritance skipping to the rest of the family.

"We need to discuss the disbursements you'll be receiving," Solomon muttered to her, the first words he'd spoken since her grandfather had been buried.

"What does that have to do with you?" Adella asked.

His eyes flared. "Surely, you don't intend to leave out your siblings and the other rightful heirs."

"The company needs help, Solly. We shouldn't be thinking of ourselves, but how to save Papa's business. You've already taken me to court. Have your attorneys discuss it with mine." An exhausted Adella lifted her gown and marched toward the cake.

After they cut it, Desmond was too happy to shove it in her mouth, unable to hide his pleasure. He was so damn giddy about it that Adella had to laugh at the icing he smeared over her lips. So caught up in the moment, and no longer self-aware, he leaned toward her to suck the frosting off, throwing her from her game of loathing him. His mouth was slow and intentional, and so was the way he stared at her when he pulled away.

He did not seem quite so repulsive. In his bow tie and tuxedo, dressed to the nines, he seemed less college beer keg frat house and more... civilized.

Then came time for him to pull the garter from around her thigh. She had wanted to skip this part, and Maddy fought to remove it from the itinerary, but the mothers of the bride and groom insisted on this entire shenanigan appearing as real as Rudolph's fake nose.

Adella's heart conducted a surprise somersault when Desmond kneeled on one knee before her.

His tongue waved at her. Del's jaw dropped. He was feeling bold. With her eyes, she chastised him not to test her.

He started at her ankle, moving up her stockinged leg, while Del's heart ventricles played hopscotch in the spaces of her rib cage.

Shaking her head, suppressing her amusement at his juvenile antics, she jumped at his fingers curling under her knees, unleashing a storm of fluids in her panties.

The game of hopscotch ended, and she wasn't laughing anymore.

Even through her pantyhose, his hands blazed a trail along her skin. Desmond's eyes stayed locked on hers, forcing the air from her lungs.

But upon reaching her garter, Desmond did not stop. His hands rose higher. Adella's eyes mushroomed. She had placed the garter low on her leg, purposely, to avoid him touching her any higher than was necessary. But Desmond's hands kept rising past her knee, exploring under her dress.

Adella's blood boiled now.

Her new husband's eyes hungry, his mouth parted, displaying a moist tongue, he tapped his fingers along her inner thigh. And lifted her dress!

He broke into a grin before his face leaned against the knee of an aghast Adella.

Beasts in the Amazonian jungles couldn't have screamed wilder than his friends, co-workers, and relatives.

Desmond's teeth clenched her garter. His lips at the top of her calf, his eyes gripped hers.

His wife clenched the edge of her velvet seat.

With a wink, he sent her into a conniption. His eyes never leaving hers, her groom's head moved tauntingly down her leg, peeling off the garter, no hands, from under her dress.

Sheer intrigue prevented her from darting away in shame.

He held it in the air to the exhilarating cheers of all his family and friends.

With her eyes, Adella swore to him that she would punish him for it later.

"You took a big risk out there," Adella snapped at him, taking their first stroll around the dance floor as husband and wife. "I should've hit you."

A self-satisfied Desmond was audacious enough to kiss her.

"But I knew you wouldn't. Not in front of all these people. I was just playing around. Having a little fun, trying to get you to relax," he said, his hand sneaking beneath her waist to palm her ass.

Damn. She couldn't yank his hand back up or they would get curious looks. He was taking advantage of her inability to push him off.

"I didn't want to lose my medical license for an assault charge."

He cracked up. "Your sense of humor isn't too dusty. I hope I get to hear more of it."

Del had been stupid to believe he might be showing signs of maturity and adulthood. She did not want him getting comfortable, or thinking she actually enjoyed his company, or that this seeming goodwill between them might last. So after the photographers took a fair amount of pictures, she let him go and took off faster than Cinderella escaping before midnight.

She and Maddy had plans. A private jet was waiting.

"Where are you going?" A stunned husband stared after her.

Adella hoisted up her dress. "That's enough. The stage play is over. The next time you hear from me, we'll be discussing the IVF arrangements, so you can get your next round of funding and I get my voting rights."

"What?"

"My voting rights against my brother, my authority inside my grandfather's company, increases once I have at least one child. You can have your representatives call mine and we can discuss when to proceed."

The lightning bolts of disbelief striking across his face kind of pleased Adella. But she had no time to bask in it and needed to jet, literally.

"And where will you be?" he asked.

"Boston. Where else?"

Adella hurried before her parents or siblings could notice she was slipping out.

She'd done what she was supposed to do: fulfilled the first condition of her grandfather's will and gotten married.

This would allow her to see his books, from the beginning of the company to how it was being handled now. She could not enter them previously, and her authority was limited during the interim transition time. But now, her elder cousin and brother Solomon had to turn over more documents for previous shareholder meetings, directors' meeting minutes, and emails to staff and administrators. Her team of lawyers would meet her at the offices in Boston that night, so they could all begin poring over why the real estate holdings had failed over the past ten years. Was there any mishandling of the affairs? Some reason beyond staggering commercial property rates?

Changing clothes, she packed up her room as fast as she could.

But a banging sound hit her door, startling her. Desmond's hulking frame nearly filled the doorway.

"Tonight is our wedding night."

"And?" Adella asked, sweeping from one luggage bag to another. "We've done everything. We fulfilled the terms of the agreement. Now I have to go. I'm sure you won't say anything to my family, since you don't talk to them anyway. And feel free to do whatever you want. Just be careful how you do it. Like we talked about."

His body seemed to sway, as if her words formed a baseball bat swinging at him. "You know what? I could have sworn, for a moment out there, that we might have had—I don't know— maybe a teeny, infinitesimal, fraction of a connection."

Focused on reaching the private hangar as soon as possible, she kept moving. "Well, you thought wrong."

He walked toward her.

Adella backed up.

He closed in, his hands jammed in his pockets, his eyes piercing and intentional.

Her insides performed new stunts she was starting to feel more often.

Half of Adella found him to be handsome in this concerned mode. But another part of her fretted at his unflinching gaze that seemed to ask her for openness she didn't want to surrender to him. His expectant eyes were throwing her off. Her body didn't know how to respond to the closeness of a man who was still very much a stranger and yet somehow, now, was not.

Desmond stopped a foot from her. "I am asking you politely, as your husband, not to go. Stay, and let's have a fun. We shouldn't begin even this mirage of a marriage on the wrong foot. The least we could do is try and be friends. I don't want to wake up in the morning resenting you."

He sounded sincere.

"Don't start throwing this formality around like it means something. You said it yourself last night. This is an arrangement. We got married for one reason. I gave up the only love of my life for that. And I'm finally about to learn what this reason is. If you had hoped for more, it's your own fault. But we agreed."

She picked up her purse, rang for the service staff, and stepped around him. But her nostrils were invaded by another whiff of his woodsy fragrance.

It was time for her to finally get the answers she'd wanted for months, now that the family house in Cape Cod was hers and hers alone.

Maddy arrived at the door. "Adella? You ready?"

As Adella walked out, her chest felt as if it hauled extra luggage. What was this new weight on her? Longing? Curiosity?

"What were you two talking about?" Maddy asked.

Adella shook her head, trying to clear it of that last conversation, and to erase Desmond's questioning eyes that still lingered in her mind.

"We were discussing living arrangements," she lied. But the entire ride to the hangar, no matter how hard she rubbed her chest, she could not soothe the vague gnawing that had begun eating the inside of her.

Minutes later, the wheels to the airplane lifted up. But a new storm inside her was touching down.

"GIRL, it won't be long now. I located Wes for you," Maddy reported on the jet.

The news sent twinges of joy and anxiety through Adella. Wes had not called her once in almost four months.

Maddy continued, "I know which hospital he's at. All you have to do is tell him this is a technicality. And you're only doing it to investigate possible fraud or malpractice at your grandfather's company, and as soon as you find the answers you need, this will be over and done." Maddy rubbed Del's arm. "We will get you away from that freak show as soon as possible."

Adella tried to settle back against the leather cushions.

The waitress came to take their drink orders and offer them appetizers, but Adella was not hungry. Maddy, on the other hand, ordered up a serving of shrimp pasta, Caesar salad, cheese dip, and chocolate mousse cake.

"And what to drink for you, Ms. Page? Your favorite—vodka

cranberry?" the waitress asked, familiar with both of them, since they had made several private flights over the last few months.

Maddy raised her hand. "No liquor. Just a Sprite, please. Thanks."

That shocked Adella. "No liquor? You know, you didn't drink yesterday at lunch either, and when you toasted, I saw you had the waiter bring you juice. What's up with you? Everything all right?"

Though it was pitch-black outside, the sun must've dawned on Maddy's face, as her eyes fell to her midriff, where she rubbed.

Adella's jaw dropped at the sight of her near-sister who had long sworn she would never marry or have children, unless she married the perfect man. And most certainly not out of wedlock. Maddy was the independent career woman who had burned through two failed marital engagements and decided she did not need a man in her life.

Adella's brain synapses clashed into one another, shooting off sparks as they tried to process this news.

"You're *pregnant*? But you and Jerrell have barely been dating two months."

Maddy displayed a giddy grin full of treasures that Adella jealously wished she could behold. "I know."

"Does Jerrell know?"

Her childhood friend beamed. "Girl, *does* he? He's over the moon. And so am I. It's not happening like the storybook fantasies we talked about when we were kids, and I'm making peace with that."

Like they'd summoned him, Maddy's phone rang with Jerrell, and she answered.

Jerrell's irritation was loud enough that it reverberated through the speaker. "Did you just take that man's wife away from him?"

"Baby, first, she is not really his wife. Second, Del is grown. This has to happen. It's what she wants. They've had an understanding from the beginning. Dump Truck shouldn't act like he's bothered. I'll see you in a few days."

"Baby, this is wrong. You can't keep getting involved. They took vows to each other, not with you," Jerrell replied.

"Babe, what's wrong is how he screwed around on Del and humiliated her in her own backyard. I'm going to be there for my friend in any way she needs, regardless of how it makes that guy feel. Del will not go through this alone. I love you," she said and ended the call.

Adella could only sink against the seat cushion. She was happy for her friend, but if Maddy was breaking The Hamptons' rules, why couldn't she?

Del had been so terrified to bring Wesley to her family, to The Hamptons, cowering at the threat of judgment and being ostracized.

"What's wrong?" Maddy faced Adella. "You look like I took your puppy. Adella? What?"

Disappointment cascaded in a stream of tears from Adella's eyes. Why hadn't she charted her own course? Made her own life? Been brave and bold enough to claim Wes for all the world?

"Wes. I'm happy for you, but I thought you of all the people would've waited for the fairy tale. You were the standard-bearer for us all. We girls all followed you as the model of who we should be."

Maddy's eyes clouded over, as if she were unsure how to process that statement. "But I'm *still* a model. We can redefine what a model woman is. I can be a mother and a career woman on Capitol Hill." Her sister-friend chewed her lip. For a moment she seemed to question what she'd said. "I fell in love. I didn't murder somebody."

Adella shook her head once she felt her friend growing defensive. "No. That's not what I'm saying, and I'm certainly not judging you. It's just… I admired you. I still do. And every time I ever thought of stepping out of line or doing anything that my family would disapprove of, I did not care about them. I thought of you. How Maddy is so perfect, and she is the gold standard for all of us, so I must absolutely be like Maddy." A flood of regret landed Adella's internal plane amid her thoughts of Wes. "And now you're going to lead us in a different way, and I'm proud of you. I'm just upset at myself. At why I wasn't so brave, as you always are, to bust up the rules myself."

"Oh, Adella, we need to make the world stop judging us. And holding us to its rules. You know all I've ever wanted is your happiness. I never meant to hurt you or to mislead you."

Adella stared out the tiny window of her new world, at the dark-gray clouds floating against a navy night. "I know. I just…" Adella didn't know what else to say. She had been stupid for allowing her family to bar her in its jail cell.

Maddy drew toward her, squeezing Adella's leg. "We're going to go get Wes. And you follow your heart, girl. I want you to feel every bit of what I'm feeling with Jerrell right now, times infinity," Maddy said with a laugh.

The two friends held hands as the plane flew them both to an uncharted future.

WHAT PAPA KNEW

ADELLA

lready seated in the living room of her grandparents' Cape Cod home were French Manuel's lawyers. His lead attorney brought forward an old wooden cedar lockbox that he passed to Del's attorney, Warwick.

As was agreed between Warwick and her grandfather's lawyers, Del's attorney had already presented proof of the marriage license, the wedding photos already circulating in the papers, and Desmond's things in her official residence. That finalized the evidence she needed to complete the transition paperwork making her the new CEO and chairwoman of the board of Manuel Realty and Company.

For the past few months, Solomon, her Uncle Bryce, and Aunt Lizzie had only granted her limited access to files, cabinets, computer hard drives, and offices. Now her access had been increased, and she owned thirty percent of shares with voting power greater than her brother's ten percent. Ten percent would go to Desmond's mother, and the other fifty percent divided between her numerous aunts, uncles and their children in smaller shares that irritated them.

Upon the birth of her first child, Del's voting shares would increase as well.

For now, with her family still back in New York, she and Maddy had only the few precious hours remaining in the night to work quickly.

As far as her family knew, she was still with Desmond back at the castle. They had expected him and her to depart on Tuesday. Del knew Desmond would not tell them she'd left, because he hated talking to her family.

"Miss Adella!" Franny, the maid entered, who'd been with her grandfather for a long time, since Adella was a child. "What are you doing here, my dear? Was today not your wedding day?"

"Franny, show me where my grandfather spent his last days. I want to know who he met with. And did he keep private recordings or memoranda?"

Her grandfather had been a meticulous man. From the way he'd carefully hooked his worms, grasshoppers, or cheese, selecting his bait based on which fish he was seeking that day, or what fishing rods he picked, and where he placed bait for quality types of deer, he'd always pondered his moves thoroughly. That had not changed when he had been at the office. At restaurants, he'd counted every penny and dime, to ensure his change was always accurate.

Franny leaped, and even at night, the woman's aged eyes lit up for Adella. "Oh, of course. There was something I wanted you to see. I have to tell you, now that nobody is here and we are finally alone."

Adella and Maddy exchanged looks.

"What is that?" Del asked. "Why didn't you tell me before?"

"Mr. English directed me not to," she said as her sixty-plus-year-old legs carried her to a corner of the library. "Your aunts, uncles and mother came in here, one after the other, the night of his heart attack, tearing the place apart while he was on his deathbed at the hospital."

Del's chest could have imploded, as would a sinkhole, from the weight of Franny's words. "The same night? No."

Months before, when Solomon called her with the news, she had asked why two days had passed before the rest of the family had been informed. Now it made sense.

"Oh, they did all right. They took turns, pawing and clawing everything. I almost died of a stroke at how they went through here and nearly uprooted the place."

"Do you know what they were hunting for?" Maddy asked.

"Yes, I do. But he did well to keep it all from them. Here." Franny poked at one of the floorboards of the first floor, which then slid back a panel inside the family's coat closet.

A set of descending stairs unfolded and slanted in front of them. Maddy's and Adella's eyes widened. Franny cut on a flashlight and led the way down, one creaky metal stair at a time, through a narrow hallway leading to a stalwart door.

"Open that there box you're carrying," Franny instructed and shined the bright-yellow light on the aged wood.

With the key she'd been given, the lock on the wooden box opened, and inside it was another key. They entered the metal door that must have been at least three inches thick. Inside was a tiny vault her grandfather had installed underground, where the flower bed was likely located over their heads.

The maid continued, "He did not want me to show you this until he was gone, and you had actually done as he wished."

"You mean," Adella's head cocked back, "me?"

"You and only you. Solomon is an able and willing businessman, very smart. Of that, your grandfather had no doubt. But your grandfather suspected that Solomon was making a secret deal with the others to break the company into pieces and sell it, so they could each take their wealth rather than running the company once he was gone."

Adella shuddered at the thought. "How do you know?"

"These are secret files he kept on all his children. His most personal belongings and business effects, dating back to when his family in Alabama got their slave manumission papers. Like I said, he knew Solomon to be very capable, but your brother has always been about profit and cash flow, not necessarily ownership and legacy. And for your grandfather, the legacy was more important."

Adella touched the shelves with boxes and leather-bound journals stretching decades. "But there are so many cousins, and brothers and sisters in our family."

Franny turned to Adella. "When you were a little girl, stricken with scoliosis, your grandfather told me he would ensure you were special. He saw how the world treated you and cast you aside. It's why he always took you with him. Check that there box for the letter he left you. I was there when he wrote it, and I signed as a witness. He did not want you to read it in front of the others. Frenchie knew there would be a huge fallout when he died. He preferred that you be alone."

Maddy hugged herself in a sort of awed silence. "And now you are."

"My dear, sweet Adella. If you are reading this, then it is your wedding day. And you have done as I asked. Thank you. You are the only one of my children and grandchildren who followed my wishes, not for profit, but because of your heart. It was not at all surprising to me that you chose to heal hearts for your living."

Her stomach churned with sorrow and longing. His voice rang through her mind as clear as if he sat there.

"I am proud of all my children. How each of you pursued amazing paths. Please let them know that. But what I'm certain of, if anyone will serve as a steward of our family's interests, it will be you. You will be the love and the heart that beats for this family's survival. You will be fair. And whatever direction you take our family legacy, I trust it. I cannot

say that for everyone. But since you were a child, I've trusted you. It's why you carried my worms. I knew you would not drop them. With your little legs, you struggled so hard to make Papa proud. When you carried my briefcase, you never dropped it. You never sat it down in public. Or forgot it."

Sniffling, she sucked in her bottom lip.

"When I asked you to crush the crackers for salmon croquettes or whip the eggs, you always tried your best. You never half-assed, never got bored, never ran off to play. You wanted so much for the meal to be thorough, perfect. You never wanted to let any of us down.

Yet, you were always last. Often forgotten. And more times than made me comfortable, mocked and pushed aside."

An ocean of memories rolled over Adella, pulling her under its current until her emotions flailed, cutting off her air. The paper floated out of her hands. She never knew he'd noticed. He'd never said anything.

Survival of the fittest.

That's what he'd always told them. All of them.

Maddy picked it up. And resumed reading it aloud.

"But I never wanted you to be a victim. Only a conqueror.

Now, you are the fittest, baby girl. The pinnacle among mountains. The tie that binds us all. Strong, and unbreaking. And now you shall be first. Now strongest. Now lauded. Whatever you choose, I have no doubt you will honor what we have built and make your grandmother and me proud. I realize you had your own plans. And you can still live them out. But not before you give the painstaking thought and delibera-tion I am certain you will give to the state of our family. That is all I ask.

"You may not like my rules and stipulations, but I know of the young man you married. I wish his mother was one of my own. But I'm

glad she is not. Because I cannot think of a more perfect person to stand at your side.

"With all the love and conciliation your grandmother and I can wish for all of you,

— PAPA FRENCH

Adella's knees buckled, vaulting her against a metal filing cabinet.

"Oh, Del," Maddy murmured, her tearful eyes reflecting Del's grief as they stared at each other in the dim light. "This is your blessing, for everything you had to go through…"

"How will I do all this by myself?"

Her childhood friend stared back. "You won't have to. I'll help you. But apparently, your grandfather knew someone you didn't."

"Papa… knew Desmond?"

ADELLA PLANNED to set up a sharing schedule within the family so everyone could have access to the house and vacation there without overcrowding or conflict. She hired a social coordinator to work with the family schedules and organize the family functions of the household.

"Excellent. I'll come back in a few days to see where we are and invite some of my aunts and uncles. We will start with them." She would sit everyone down so they could begin forming an understanding. She would not treat them as they treated her, or keep them out.

By the next morning, her family had figured out she was no longer in The Hamptons, but it did not matter. She and Maddy had stolen a few precious hours to review some key documents in the vault and some of her grandfather's journals and recordings. He'd written concerns and doubts about his children that he would never share publicly.

Solomon had set up a handful of ventures in Manuel Real Estate that had failed. At a costly price tag.

Two of her cousins had faced harassment accusations that her grandfather had to settle in legal agreements outside of court, with hefty payments for the accusers to stay quiet. Their indiscretions he'd never made public, but they had privately agitated him.

Lack of innovation.

Skimming off the top, here and there.

Failed ideas and enterprises that drained the budget.

Primarily, Adella's aunts and uncles had pursued mostly their own selfish motivations. Some of it Adella recalled, but she'd had no idea about the breadth of it all, particularly because she'd been a child whenever the issues had come up.

Her sister, Constance's, failed digital media company.

Her cousin, Afi's, failed wearable tech timer.

Her uncle's failed black-owned cruise ship line.

Her aunt's failed nail spa chain.

Failed restaurants.

They had been an enterprising family but with very little real-world experience. And they were mightily disconnected from what people on the street wanted.

Her grandfather had held discussions with his offspring about this, in private, never humiliating them publicly or crushing their entrepreneurial spirits.

But in their failures, they had wasted resources. And within the company, their excess and unrealistic goals had caused the company to sputter.

"I want an audit of the company's finances and oversight. I want to know everything. Before I play ball with Desmond's mother, I need a full picture of exactly what we're confronting."

Maddy nodded. "Jerrell's father, and his elder brother, Roland, all of them are on Wall Street and they can arrange it. An audit will take a few weeks, maybe even months, but they'll get it done."

Adella's chest rocked at the thought of challenging so many forces at once—particularly in her own household—but she agreed.

Now that her lawyers had access, they could get a clearer picture of Manuel Real Estate's shape. She would be splitting her time between her family's company offices and the hospital, at least for the next few months.

"It's crazy how my grandfather knew Desmond's mother. Why did he trust her more than his own children? And even made deals for the company with her that the family clearly didn't have a clue of?"

Though a lot of questions remained unanswered, she had finally gotten some insight into her inheritance, and Adella itched to see Wes.

She needed to explain. In her haste to inspect her grandfather's things, she'd had to hustle for three days to review documents, make phone calls, and set appointments with lawyers and financial professionals.

But by mid-week, she longed to face her love.

Before heading out of town, Maddy dropped her off at Healing Hands Hospital, where her girlfriend had learned Wes now worked his shifts. Throwing her arms around her Adella, Maddy whispered into her neck, the way she once had as a girl who did not want anyone overhearing her thoughts about the kids she didn't like.

"Good luck, girl. Once he hears what you needed to do, he'll understand. Call me and let me know how it goes."

Jittery legs took Adella to the doctors' locker room, just as Wes was leaving.

"Adella?" he said, staring at her.

"Wes." After not seeing him since Thanksgiving, the sight of his face unleashed her heart chambers so they were free to float again. Butterflies skipped through her vessels, tapping lightly along her veins.

His gaze roamed over her face, grazing her hair. "Wow. You sure are stunning."

"So are you. I've missed you."

The harsh locker room light could not cancel out the flecks in his gorgeous emerald eyes.

"I saw you'd gotten married. Front of the Society page." His dry, rose-red lips tightened, as if he'd drank dirt. "I had no idea you would actually go through with it." His body weight seemed to sway like a toppled building. "Congratulations?" He slammed the locker.

Why did its slam reverberate through the thin sheet metal that was her? "I came to explain. It was pretense, and nothing like it seemed."

"Really?" Those green emeralds flared. "Because in the full-page spread of the newspaper, it looked pretty genuine to me."

"It's not. I don't love him. But I could not give details, due to the sensitive nature of my grandfather's holdings and his requirements."

Wes's head forced a nod the way a child forced down unwanted beets. "I see. Well, whatever your reason, I hope it makes you happy."

"It doesn't. It hasn't." Her heart slipped through her like peas, pea by pea, drop by drop, until they were pebbles filling up her stomach. She moved toward him, to squeeze his arm, hoping he would squeeze *her* again, that she would feel him around her. Her heart valve opened and closed, the mouth of a fish panting to return to water, longing for oxygen, Adella's life forces panting for the oxygen of him inside her again.

"Wes?" a female voice called behind them.

Wes's attention shot over Adella's shoulder, past her heart.

Adella pivoted.

Dr. Renee Lovejoy stood at the entrance.

"Renee?"

"Adella?" Renee asked.

The three of them stared at one another, heads spinning like seagulls perched atop boardwalk brick walls underneath a granite-gray sky, the color of tombstones. Or maybe it was just Adella's head that spun.

"Are you working a shift here? I didn't see your name on the schedule," Renee said.

Adella's eye sockets worked to hold in her eyeballs. "I was dropping by to visit Wes."

"You two know each other?" Renee asked, but instead of addressing Adella, she gazed questioningly at Wes.

"Yes, actually—"

"Oh! That's right! You two were at Boston General together." Renee's eyes popped wider with the realization.

"Yes. We were," Wes replied, and that was all he said.

Adella longed—no, thirsted—for him to say more.

They loved each other, had planned to get married, and he was hers.

Five excruciatingly long seconds dragged her heart through a meat shredder, and Wes's further explanation did not come. Instead, he brushed by her, and greeted Renee with a kiss.

"Well, that was kind of you, and thoughtful, to come over and say hello. I'm sure you guys are missing Wes over there. But we are extremely happy," Renee said, pausing to suck his lips and put another emphasis on the point he'd just made, "to have him here." Her eyes fluttered. "Oh yes! You got married this weekend. Didn't you perform an open-heart surgery on your wedding boat or something? I saw it on the news!"

"Really?" Wes asked, his face a tossed salad of surprise and bewilderment.

"Yes. Wasn't that just, like, a few days ago? What are you doing here? Why are you not on your honeymoon?" Renee asked.

Despair wrapped its fingers around Adella's dry tongue, its hand forming a fist in her throat.

Wes picked up the conversation to fill the awkwardness. "She was just telling me that she needed to sort out some of her grandfather's business. He passed a few months ago. Right?" He swallowed, his eyes prodding her, maybe even praying she wouldn't disclose that they'd dated. "Since Adella was in the area, she decided to stop by. I'm glad she did." His good-natured smile and country-boy gentle laugh broke the fall of her heart that tumbled down the oakwood tree branches under which they'd sat.

"Sorry about your loss. But happy for your newfound love!" Renee replied. "We'd love to meet him. We'll all have to go out on a double date sometime. But right now, if we don't get out of here, we'll be late for the show."

Wes's final smile communicated that it was indeed final. "It was good seeing you again. Thanks for stopping by. Good luck."

On her exit from the locker room, Adella's heart valve slowed and the blood carrying her oxygen fled her. She was a fish flopping in the open air, struggling to breathe.

Moments later, she staggered toward the hospital front exit, since she didn't work here and had no pass for the more secluded doctors' exit.

Out on the street now in more ways than one, stupidly, she had no ride. Adella had anticipated she and Wes would leave together. Or at least sneak off to some place where she could explain and ask him to wait until this sham with Des was over.

She still searched for strength to raise her arm and hail a cab when an SUV instantly pulled in front of her.

Wes's slam of his locker, moments before, still vibrated through her brain, and down her nerves, making her too preoccupied to fear the unknown vehicle that stopped a few feet away.

Its door opened. A familiar face approached her. Adella fell into his opening arms as her legs collapsed.

LOVE HER

DESMOND

Desmond had expected her to be angelic. All women looked angelic and pure on their wedding day.

What he hadn't expected was the fierceness on Adella's face the night before the wedding, when she'd saved his cousin's life with practically nothing but her own bare hands.

Her boss-level command of the entire procedure, her hands whipping and eyes laser-focused, as if she could have done it in her sleep, all exerted a magnetic grip on him that was beyond sexual. And yet he wanted it underneath him. And on top of him.

She most certainly was no child. No matter how her family wanted her to be.

Hell-bent on hating her when they arrived in The Hamptons, Desmond could not.

In that procedure, Adella had established that she was more than a spoiled "other" now.

So the morning after the wedding, once he'd seen off some of his family and friends, Desmond had headed back to Boston. Even though Adella had given him her blessing to go fuck himself in Baltimore, an irritating tingle in his chest had redirected him north.

The way she'd jetted off, like she had fire ants in her panties and couldn't escape him fast enough, bothered him. Sure, she might have been way out of his league, but women didn't just dismiss him. So while her absence, in theory, should have brought him all the elation of a man with one-point-five million extra dollars sitting in his bank account, he was perturbed at her audacity to think he was some mosquito to be swatted. Ergo, the good doctor had both irritated and titillated him.

A lot of questions peppered his mind. First and foremost, was she scurrying off to see this white dude when she and Maddy were still riding Desmond's ass about Lana?

Although this wasn't a real marriage, Adella *was*—technically —*his* wife now. And it wouldn't kill anybody if he simply…

…ran a little reconnaissance.

As Desmond had touched down back in Boston, he'd had no name or info for this guy. So he'd paid a private investigator to follow her from her grandparents' home in Cape Cod, where she and Maddy had posted up for two full days after spending a day at the Manuel Real Estate offices in Boston.

But on the third day, the PI had called and said her friend had dropped her off at Healing Hands Hospital, which was not the hospital where she normally worked.

And damn.

His heart hurt to see his good doctor's legs buckle while she'd exited the front of the hospital.

As she'd walked out, Desmond saw a Mercedes roll by his Escalade, and inside it was the guy who'd showed up at Adella's front porch months before. Sitting next to him was a new black woman, and she wore doctor's scrubs. The license plate had Greek letters on it, representing a black sorority, so this guy was already driving another black woman's Mercedes.

Desmond had waited for Maddy to swing back and pick up Adella, but she hadn't. He did not know why he cared, but nevertheless, he'd needed to see with his own eyes what he was dealing with. And truthfully, who else did she have to comfort her besides Maddy? And Maddy could not stay forever.

Desmond had stepped out of his truck and around the front grill, rushing to catch Adella as she seemed about to faint under the weight of whatever she'd just witnessed. Her faded eyes met his, flaring wider with surprise. Yet she said nothing. He expected her to rebuff him. In his arms, he could feel quakes from the avalanche that must've been bursting inside her.

Guiding her toward his truck, he threw open the door. "Come on. I'll take you home."

They rode back to her home in silence, pulled into the garage without a word. She still sat dazed for for a while after he shut off the truck, until he finally got out. Once he opened her door, he waited a while longer for to realize she needed to get out.

Carrying her purse for her, he followed as she dragged herself up the stairs. In her purse, her cell phone buzzed. Unsure whether he should look at it or not, he decided to peer at the screen and see if it was something important that she should answer. It was Maddy. The call was followed by a text.

Maddy: *So how did it go?*

And then the icons of a thumbs-up and a thumbs-down. Out of respect for Adella's privacy, he shut the phone off and set down her things.

"You hungry?" He had already arrived at the house two days before and, while she still handled business at her grandfather's house, he had stocked up food in the refrigerator and ordered some meal prep for the week.

Her eyes drifted into space, so he went to remove her shoes. Then he started for her sweater.

"Don't."

"It was drizzling outside, freezing rain. You need to get out of these clothes before you get sick. You know that."

"Leave."

He would accept her talking to him like he was her houseboy, for tonight. But in the meantime, felt like an ass. Why was he here and not on the first plane back to his spot in Baltimore? Why was he posting himself here with her? He ticked off possible reasons in his head.

Desmond may have owed Adella, after humiliating her in front of her friends with Lana. No, that could not have been it. Because if any other woman had ignored and dismissed him—regardless of whether he deserved it—he would've been too happy to exact vengeance on her ass. But not this time. For some reason, he actually gave a damn.

Maybe he was here because she's a good person. Nope. That wasn't it either. He knew lots of good women.

Three days later, she had not come out of her room. So Desmond picked up her phone and called the last person in the world he wanted to talk to—Maddy.

He wouldn't go through Jerrell. This was a Maddy situation. And a tiny part of him wanted to gain Maddy's respect. Even though trying to deal with her was like negotiating with a cyclone, he respected how hard she rode for the people she loved. Maybe one day, hell, in some crazy alternate universe or the next lifetime, he might be one of those people.

"Adella!" Maddy said when she answered on the other end of the phone.

"No. It's Desmond," he replied, staring up the stairs toward his wife's bedroom. "Houston, we have a problem."

Maddy flew in from D.C. and landed in Boston International that night.

"She hasn't eaten in days. I've tried," he explained, and he also relayed what he had seen. "Dude is dating another black chick. And she's got money too. Loaded. Some doctor at another hospital where he's working now. Comes from a family just like yours."

"Who?" Maddy asked.

"Some Renee Lovejoy?"

"Renee Lovejoy," Maddy repeated. "Oh yes, I know her. Very smart. Not as accomplished as Adella. But she's proven her chops." Maddy let out a rough sigh. "I have nothing against her. But, damn, this guy's clearly got a type."

"My thoughts exactly," Desmond added, and grabbed his small suitcase he'd packed before she arrived. "Look, I'm going to hit the street for a couple of days. Handle some business of my own. Give you two a little time together. Call me if you need anything. Not that I think you will. Just offering."

"Desmond," Maddy called out before he made his exit.

"Yeah?"

"Thanks for calling me, and not one of her…"

She didn't need to finish the sentence. He knew Adella's family could not be trusted with this.

"Stays in this house."

An hour later, he was on a plane and seated in business class, on his way back to Baltimore. There was someone he needed to see.

THE NEXT MORNING, Desmond entered a Baltimore barbershop. Just as the door opened, he was the first customer. Snazzy, nice, it didn't look half bad. The place had been renovated recently, since he'd last visited four years ago.

He'd brought an extra coffee. Black, no cream, no sugar, if he remembered correctly. Several young barbers came out, offering to cut his hair for him.

"No, sir, is the owner still around?"

"Yes, but he doesn't give cuts anymore. He mostly overseas things. Is there something one of us can do for you?" one of the barbers asked.

"Nah. I'll just wait for him here then, if he's going to be in today," Desmond said. And wait he did, for the next two hours, until the owner arrived.

The man mostly appeared the same as the last time Desmond had seen him. Maybe his gut was a little farther out, chest slightly thinner, but still stout. A few more grays sprinkled in his whiskers. Now completely bald.

The owner turned to him. "Congratulations."

Desmond's heart squeezed at hearing the first word they'd spoken in years. "Thanks. Would've been nice if you had come."

"Oh, no. I don't belong in your new white-golf-pants-wearing, jet-set circle of people you're kicking it with these days. A street hustler like me? What would I look like being there with all them fools?" he asked.

Desmond tried not to get emotional. He lifted his shoulders before letting them crash down again. "I don't know. Maybe like my father?"

The moment he'd said it, the other barbers exchanged money, because earlier, they'd taken one glance at Desmond and began placing bets that he was the owner's son. Those who'd won happily received their twenty-dollar bills.

"So, I take it you didn't come here for a haircut. With all that money you sleep in these days, you can go anywhere you want for a cut."

"Actually, I did. That and," Desmond paused, fishing up the words from the well in his chest, "some advice."

Without another word, his father tapped an empty chair with a rattail comb. Minutes later, he was shaving Desmond up, and they stared at one another in the mirror.

"You must've been pretty goddamn desperate to bring your ass way the hell over here to the hood, from Mount Olympus where they've got you hangin' out," his father started. "So what happened? You gave this new wife of yours the clap? She's ready to divorce you already?"

Desmond rolled his eyes. "In another lifetime, with somebody else, maybe. But not with her."

"Oh, wow, you had a little attitude when you said that. So you love her."

"I didn't say all that."

Mr. McLain popped him over the ear with the comb. "You didn't have to, nigga. You might not bring your ass around here much, but I know my own goddamn son."

Even though it stung, Desmond couldn't help laughing at his dad's trademark way of disciplining him, just as when he was a kid squirming in his seat and his father popped him to stay still for a haircut.

"It's just… this whole marriage thing, man…"

"Well then, what did you ask her for, if you knew you weren't ready?" his father asked him straight out.

"Trust me. It wasn't my choice," Desmond said, not wanting to relay too much information about his mother. Even if she did irritate the hell out of him, he would try his hardest not to give his father ammunition to go in on her with the insults.

"So your mama forced you."

"I didn't say that."

"You didn't have to. I was married to her for seventeen years. There ain' nothin' you can hide from me that I don't already know. Especially when it comes to her ultimatums. And her control issues."

A razor blade shaved Desmond's windpipe at the painful reminder of his parents' long marriage. How well his father knew her. And though the man spoke about her with a bladed tongue, Desmond could still hear the love.

He worked up the nerve to ask, "About that, why didn't you come with us? Why are you still in the hood cutting hair when you could have, I don't know, done so much more? Moms could've set you up. You—"

"Set me up?" His father stepped back, aghast. "You mean her taking care of me?"

Desmond straightened his chest because he had anticipated his dad's blowback. "Not take care of you, but helped you out. You could've owned a bazillion barbershops all over Maryland." Desmond stretched his arms out wide around him. "Why don't you come with us?" He asked the question that had been burning through his mind for the last fourteen years.

His father's eyebrow lifted. "And be her little dog? I don't think so. I'm a man. And a man needs to be a man. But also..." His father stopped talking.

Between them, the only sound now was of the razor shaving off hair that tumbled to the floor. A quiet, low humming in a timeless ritual between a father and his son.

"That construction gig, her making all that money, was a hard pill to swallow," his dad said.

Desmond was shocked to hear the words. They fell on him like unexpected snow in the middle of a sunny afternoon.

Mr. McClain continued, "That's probably childish thinking and shit, I know, and if I could go back and do anything, I would tell her that and be real about it. And see how we could work through it. Instead of me getting all puffed up and vindictive, the way I was." His father's hands slowed, and his eyes drifted. "Me being a jealous asshole... may have driven her into another man's arms..."

Desmond's chest fell alongside his father's scissors. This was the first he'd ever heard of it.

"You can still go get her, Pop."

"I don't know. Sometimes I think about it," his father said, blinking back tears as he resumed snipping. "But what do I have to offer her?"

The man had asked out loud the same question Desmond had asked himself at least a thousand times over the past four months. His father spoke to his own internal nagging.

"Well, you see Mom hasn't married anybody else yet."

"She's still irritating as hell, huh?"

They shared a knowing laugh.

"That and then some," Desmond answered.

Mr. McLain paused the trim to stare at his son. "But if she forced you to get married, that shit wasn't right. And if you would have come to me before you did it, I would've told you."

This time, his father's stare wasn't chastising, it was one of sympathy. Maybe even regret that he hadn't been around to counsel his son.

"This girl… she ain't so bad. But I…" Desmond's words got tangled in the hairball of emotions now bunching up in his chest. "I wanna know how I might actually make this work. I mean, she is so much. And I'm so…"

"Not much." His dad smiled. And they both cracked up again. "I'm just playing, young man. My sons are awesome. And I couldn't be more proud."

His father's words, the amused gleamed in his eye, lodged deeper into Desmond's trachea. "But I fucked up these last few years."

"No, you haven't. You've been having a damn good time and living your life while you're young. As you have every right to do. Many young brothers like yourself ain been so privileged to have that experience. You're still figuring it all out. You're only thirty-three, with plenty of time to turn the ship around. I, on the other hand, am not so fortunate."

"Man, please. You're what, in your mid-fifties? No time is ever too late."

"To succeed in life, or with women? Which one are we talking about now?" Mr. McLain asked.

"Both." Desmond could see in his father's eyes he still loved his mother. No matter how tough he tried to act or how he tried to wall off his emotions.

The scissors started moving again, but slower now, as if Mr. McLain did not want this particular haircut to end.

"Love on her." That's all he said.

Desmond shifted.

"What do you mean?"

"I mean, no matter what, don't get distracted with how much money she's got or what she's buying or the job title she gets next. Just… love her. As a human." His father swallowed, his eyes flickering like a light about to go out but struggling to stay on. "It don't matter where she goes or what she's doing or who she's doing it with, just love her."

Desmond processed what he was saying.

The older man continued, "When the two of you lie down together at night, when you touch her or stand before her, you are human and so is she. You're not loving her title or accomplishments. Those are nice, and you can be proud. But focus on the human. Don't ever let your marriage stray away from that."

"Love her as a human," Desmond repeated, more to himself.

His father gazed at him. "I'm proud of you. You're a good man. And just because you got off track or got caught up while figuring out your path, does not make you any less of one."

The words Desmond had needed to hear, but his mother was too busy and preoccupied to say, were rain falling on his desert heart.

NOT KIDS ANYMORE

ADELLA

della finished her steak and potatoes Maddy had ordered from the local steakhouse before her friend took her plate.

"Good to see your appetite is back."

"I need to report to work and then head over to the real estate offices after I've done a couple of shifts," Adella grumbled.

"I know you're a grown woman, girl, and I'm not your mom, but you just got married on Saturday. You are fully entitled to take off two or three weeks after all you've done for that hospital. Take advantage of it. Rest. All this other stuff will be waiting for you."

"I need to do something with myself so I'm not sitting here wallowing in it and thinking about how she kissed him in front of me. And he didn't even say anything," Adella whimpered. She didn't mean to sound like a pouty child. Or for her voice to shake like a leaf rattling in the wind.

"I understand that. I was the same way a couple of months ago when Jerrell and I had a falling out. I was a mess. But don't forget all the opportunity you have right in front of you. For heaven's sake, you saved somebody's life at your *engagement* party, on a cruise ship! The top TV shows in America are competing to interview you!" Maddy said, shaking Adella's arm as if pumping her back to life.

Indeed, Adella still reeled from the phone call that had come in the day before, from one of the top television journalists in the country.

They wanted an interview of Adella's experience on the boat, of her being rejected as a doctor, and then performing an impromptu heart surgery to save someone's life.

And not only that, but she had been astonished to receive several offers for book deals from major publishing companies. The incident had received national press coverage, and Maddy had connected her with a publicist and an agent.

Then there were the phone calls that had come in from the cruise line, offering apologies and to make amends. Of course, she guessed they were buttering her up so she didn't file a legal suit.

Throughout Adella's career, she had received numerous awards and professional accolades, but this recognition was different. Strangers on the street, and all around the world, gave Dr. Adella English the respect that her family still had not.

"Yes," she replied, with a tiny crack of joy, "it is just a bit cool."

Right then the door opened, and in walked Desmond toting his luggage. He also sported a fresh haircut, crisp jeans, Timberland boots, and a beautifully knitted sweater underneath a classy wool coat and scarf.

Maddy put on her friendly face. "Hey! I was wondering when you'd make it back."

Adella did not speak her thoughts out loud, but she questioned where Maddy's upbeat tone toward him had come from suddenly.

"Hey," he said while his gaze examined Adella. Or rather, assessed.

"Hey." Adella attempted cheerfulness. After all, he did live there now. She could not simply be rude.

Maddy's eyes darted between the two of them. "Well, you're not alone anymore, and you should be in good hands now, so I'm going to head out."

Adella's chest cratered.

"Um," she stammered. She hoped Maddy would stay and continue being her shield so she wouldn't be left alone with Desmond. "You're not imposing. I thought you weren't leaving until morning."

She watched her friend take a deep breath. The pressure of Maddy's hand warmed hers. "You know I'm always here for you if you need anything, girl. But," Maddy lowered her voice, "I don't think I'm what you need."

Her head motioned toward the stairs where Desmond had made his way up with his things.

"Don't leave me here," Adella pled.

"I know you overheard what Jerrell said to me a few days ago, on the boat. That you are no longer mine to protect. And Adella," Maddy said, clasping Adella's arm, "he's right. And so are you. We're not kids anymore. You are not your mother's little sick girl, and I am not the standard-bearer for all Hamptons women. Time for us to be brave, sail our own ships. Right?"

Adella's heart chambers crumbled like sandcastles sliding into her veins. But she knew her friend was right.

The two embraced over the dining room table. Grateful for her childhood friend who had nursed her back to life, too many times to count, she whispered into her neck, "I love you, Maddy."

Her friend murmured back, "Love you too, Del. Jerrell says he might not be as bad as we think."

Finally, after kissing Adella on her forehead, Maddy let go.

～

ADELLA STARTED the long trek to Desmond's bedroom after Maddy left. Shoving down her self-consciousness that squeezed her lungs, she knocked on his door.

Total awkwardness fell between them when he opened it. She'd never seen him stripped down beyond his long-sleeved dress shirts and sweaters. Now he stood in his pajama bottoms and a tank top, displaying sculpted muscles underneath chunks of extra flesh, a stocky and healthy size standing at five feet and ten inches, four inches above her.

"Hey."

"Hey," she said back. "I wanted to know if you've eaten yet. I have some steak and potatoes left over from the steakhouse."

"Yeah, I ate on the plane ride back."

She didn't know what else to offer him. She had no clue of what they had in common. "Right."

She didn't want to go back to her room and be alone, because she would only cry over Wes and replay the kiss between him and Renee over in her head as it had for the past five days.

Defeated, she pivoted with the tray in her hand back toward the stairway.

"Did you guys order dessert?"

She stopped. "Yes. Strawberry cheesecake."

"I like cheesecake," he said.

He followed her down to the dining room and poured a glass of Moscato to drink alongside the cheesecake. While Adella grabbed saucers and forks.

Raising his glass, they toasted.

"We haven't killed each other yet," he said with a tired smile.

"I'll toast to that." A smile managed to find its way across her lips.

They ate in silence for a moment before she lifted her heavy head.

"Why did you come and get me?" she asked.

He shrugged. "I'm asking myself the same thing. It was probably stupid. Actually, the more I think about it, it was stupid. But I guess I didn't want you to be alone when you found out."

"How did *you* find out?"

Like a puppy waiting for food, she awaited his response as to why he had been keeping track of her.

"You and your people have your way of finding out about my sexual history. I have resources of my own. Since you would not answer the question I wanted to know, I went and found out for myself. I had a feeling that once you did whatever your grandfather wanted you to do, and you took ownership of his company, that you might go running back to that dude. If it were me, and my nose was wide open for some chick, I'd probably do the same. I wanted to see what the likelihood was that you and him would get back together. So I checked things out for myself."

That seemed like a logical response. Who wouldn't want to know what their future was going to be?

"You must be happy."

Desmond's head swung from side to side. "On the contrary, I'm not. You had a lot of hope and determination on your face when you were leaving The Hamptons. I kind of admired it. It didn't feel good that you blew me off for somebody else, but at the same time, you had my respect for wanting something so bad and going after it. I'm sorry you didn't get it."

"You're joking."

Desmond recalled the regret on his father's face from the day before. "Nope. And I guess that's why I've never been in love. Or never allowed myself to fall. Because I never wanted to have all that hope and anticipation, only to feel it burn. My parents went through separation. I decided way back then I wasn't doing it."

It was Adella's turn to raise her glass. "Wise on your part."

Wise indeed. Had she stuck to the promise she had made to herself, that she would keep her head focused on medicine and not give her heart to anyone, she would not be in this predicament now.

"I'm not so sure. How does the old saying go? Better to have loved and lost than to never have loved at all?" he asked.

"That is how it goes. But I can confirm your way is better." She finished the last of her cheesecake and wine. "I should get to bed."

He nodded. "Of course. Don't worry about the dishes. I'll get them. It's my thanks for dessert."

"Oh no, the mess is mine and Maddy's. I'll help."

She got up, still wearing jeans, a soft mohair sweater, her hair in the old updo style from the wedding. Desmond's gaze raked over her body, and again, the attention put her on edge. Behind his wondering eyes, what was he thinking of her?

Feeling like a fly under observation, Adella walked ahead of Desmond, sensing his eyes drill through her from behind. Evaluating her. Was he judging her because she didn't work out enough or diet the right way?

Since there were not too many dishes, they handwashed instead of loading up the dishwasher. For each one she washed, she passed it to him, and his hand always brushed hers in the system they picked up.

"Nice haircut. You found a spot here in Boston?" she asked.

"Nah. I went to see my dad at his shop in Baltimore. Decided that while you and Maddy were doing y'alls thing, I would go hang with him."

His father? "Was he at the wedding?"

"No. He and my moms don't get down like that."

"He does a nice job." She handed him a dish.

"That he does. He's one of the best in the city. And he needs to start acting like he is."

Adella switched toward him with more silverware for him to rinse and place in the drying rack, but no sooner had she turned than Desmond's mouth smashed into hers.

Her knee-jerk reaction was to pull back, but he had anticipated her. The pressure of his warm mouth pushed against her own, sucking until it was difficult to disengage from him.

A determined Desmond kissed Adella deeper. She shoved her hands against his chest. But even as his arms were dripping wet, he strapped on to her waist.

Fierce and far stronger than her, he held on, maneuvering and dominating her mouth, and refusing to let go until he'd had his fill. Finally, he relaxed his arms and let her go.

Parts of Adella began talking back to her head that screamed bloody murder.

What should she say? He was her husband. It wasn't like he had done something illegal. Wait. He had violated her space!

But did she... *like* it?

"You had no right." She backed away from him, grabbing the dish drying cloth from the countertop like it was a weapon.

"That's debatable, but let's say you're right. I wanted to anyway. And I'd do that shit again." Desmond licked his lips and let his gaze fall over her like his appetite was nowhere near satisfied.

Del's emotions wrapped around her like a spindle spinning wool. Gagging on what to say, she simply spun away. "Goodnight."

She couldn't rush up the stairs fast enough, almost tripping and falling with her sweater clenched over her breasts. Once she'd scurried back to her room and closed the door, she stared in the mirror, and realized that every time she bent over that night, her cleavage showed! Her palm smacked her forehead. He had probably been staring at her rack since he got home! She was so embarrassed. Her bra was loose and easily flopped open to reveal everything. And then that stare he gave her when she'd got up from dessert! How rude of him, and disrespectful! What did he think she was, a slab of ribs at the meat market? How dare he objectify her like she was cheap!

Her thighs were Jello, jiggly and moist.

What was happening to her? He had looked at her like…*nasty.*

Once Adella got ready for bed and lay down to close her eyes, eerily, it wasn't Wes she was thinking about.

For the first time in her life, her panties were soaking wet, her nipples hard as lug nuts poking through her silk gown.

FALLING FOR HER

DESMOND

With a swift yank, Desmond threw open Adella's curtains. Fully expecting her motor mouth to fuss until her gas tank sat on empty, he braced himself.

She jumped up, throwing her covers off her, panicked as if she needed to flee a catastrophe.

"What time is it?" she asked.

"Twelve-thirty."

"No, I didn't!"

"Yes." Humored at her moment of terror, he chuckled. "You did. Morning, Doctor Sleep Forever." He reentered her bedroom with a tray of coffee, cream, and sugar that he set down on the bed.

In a groggy state, she moved off the mattress. "The house. Cape Cod. I need to head back over there. Handle some things before the others start searching. Make sure no one is—"

"I already told Franny not to expect you today." He braced himself once again.

"That's not your call to make!"

"I know it's not, but I thought I'd try it out anyway. Franny won't be letting anybody into the house until you return. At your request. Your lawyers delivered cease and desist letters to your family members, so they'll comply—all of them—an hour ago. At your request." For a third time, Desmond steeled himself.

Silence.

When he shifted his focus from stirring her coffee, the way he'd seen her stir it at lunch with Jerrell and Maddy, she was frozen.

"You did what?" she asked.

His muscles stiffened as they once had when he'd been an offensive lineman ramming defense on the football field. "You heard me. I called your lawyer. And he was too happy to oblige. Says he's been chomping at the bit to get your people under control."

"That's a conflict of interest. Your company's interests and mine are not the same. He's *my* lawyer! Not yours. And that house is mine. Not yours."

Good thing he had prepared for this. "Actually, your grandfather put it up as collateral two years ago to keep things afloat when he took out a loan from…our company. So technically, because we do have a financial interest in that property that could be jeopardized by your family's actions, I do… kind of… have a right." He hadn't wanted to play that card. "Adella, I just want you to relax is all."

"Get out."

Unperturbed by the steam rising from more than her coffee, her new husband remained where he stood. "I'm just trying to have a time with you, since you told me I can't mess around with anybody else."

"Out!" she bellowed. "Or I will throw this hot coffee on you!"

The angrier she got, thinking she could scare him, the cuter she became. Lowering his head to hide his smile, Desmond tried to control the amusement shaking in his gut.

"You would't be the first person to scald me. Once, a girl threw hot oatmeal on me when she found me with her sorority sister. Though, I was hoping you would try this coffee and tell me how it tastes. I'm not much of a coffee drinker, so I'm not sure if it'll wake you up or kill you. Curious to see how this works out."

"What part of *I don't want you in here* do you not understand?" she asked, rising to her knees on the mattress.

A silk scarf covered her head, but his eyes followed the silk nightgown cascading over her ample breasts, thick biscuits of her hips, and full, squeezable waist he could grab for hours. Trying to reel in his erection, he licked his lips.

"Stop staring at me like I'm some animal!"

Adella's hands groped at her body for a robe to clutch over her figure, and when she realized she hadn't yet put it on, Desmond grabbed it from the chaise.

He tossed it away from her to the other side of the room. "I'm definitely not checking you out like you're an animal. But I will ride you like one, if you want."

Her disgust made clear that she couldn't decide how to interpret the offer—as bad or good. So he added, "That's a good thing, by the way."

"Give that back to me." She wrapped her arms around herself, seeming to shrink.

He found himself wondering if she'd ever been fucked right. Truly, lovingly, incredibly just had the shit fucked right out of her.

"Show me around Boston," he said.

"No. Would you please give me my robe?"

"No," he responded, mimicking her.

But her "lost lamb" helplessness struck him. His heart twisted at the sight of a rabbit who seemed to cringe while facing a wolf. He just might have given up his inheritance, anything, to remove her bewilderment. He went to retrieve the robe and handed it to her so she would be at ease.

Covering herself with it again, she chewed her lip while

worrying. "I appreciate what you're trying to do, but my family's going to be so…"

"So what? So much more disrespectful to you than they already are? Fuck that. Come spend the day with me. Just one, and I won't bother you anymore." This was a huge gamble.

"You're lying."

"I'm not." And he wasn't. "We can do whatever you want. Show me what you rich folks do when you're not busy taking everybody's money."

"I don't have to do anything else with you ever?" she confirmed.

Damn. He hadn't expected her to take him literally or to jump on the offer like a kid onto a seesaw. Now he started to seriously second-guess himself. He began to doubt the tiny softening of her body in his arms when he'd kissed her the night before…. Maybe he'd been wrong and just imagined it. If he was wrong, and this didn't work, he was screwed. For a very, *very* long time.

"Never. Whatever you want to do."

Half an hour later, when she descended the stairs with an abysmal scowl, he decided to accept that and threw open the front door that led to the circular drive, where a horse-drawn carriage awaited.

Her eyelids batted a few times; she clearly had not expected that. The surprise on her face pleased her husband, sending tiny shocks through him. He noted how, even when his bride tried to play tough, Adella's vibe was still sweet and vulnerable.

"After you," Desmond murmured.

"You like horses?" she asked.

"Hate 'em. Except at the race track when they're winning me money. Other than that, haven't been around them very often. So, where to?" he asked.

In a rare show of delight, she replied with a grin that might have bordered on sinister. "The horseback riding stables."

He pursed his lips as if he'd just bitten into a red jalapeño pepper. "Of course, you would choose that."

"You said whatever I want." She actually seemed happy, so he went with it.

The stables weren't far, two miles away, and within the hour, she was introducing him to her mare, Philippa, and her stallion, Curious.

She talked to them like they were old friends. "How's my boy doing, huh? I've missed you so much. Mama's been busy, but she's here now." Her voice had lowered to that of a gentle breeze. Leaning her head forward, Adella nuzzled the horse's ear with her nose, and the horse responded, almost as if hugging her back.

The two shared a connection Desmond hadn't seen her exchange with any other human but Maddy. He couldn't decide if he was impressed or disgusted.

She coaxed him into petting Curious. When Desmond stalled, returning the same spooked-out stare the horse was giving him, Adella shocked him by taking his hand. Placing hers firmly over his, she guided her husband's palm down the horse's forelock.

"That's it," she murmured in a gentle voice that…did things to more than Desmond's hand. She pushed his fingers over the horse's ear toward its crest and down its girth. Their intertwined hands ran through its hair that gleamed like threads of silk. She patted his other side. "Wow. He doesn't hate you."

He chuckled. "You were hoping he would."

"Kind of," she replied laughingly, and the two of them cracked up. "Let's take him out for a ride."

"Oh, no, that's all right. I'm good. You go ahead."

Five minutes later, the stable keeper had brought them Adella's grandfather's riding boots. As Desmond put them on, he felt somewhat like an imposter, stepping into the shoes of a man so many people apparently respected. Adella must've been kicked by a hoof of pain, because she looked away from him for a small moment before mounting the horse.

The stable keeper led out the mare, Philippa.

"You've never rode a horse?" Adella asked with a smirk. She stared down at an unwilling Desmond. "We'll go slow. I promise I won't be too hard on you."

Now that was a goddamn first. A woman promising that *she* wouldn't be too hard on *him*. Until now, he hadn't thought it possible, no matter how badass a chick was in bed.

For right now, there was no way in hell he was humiliating himself to impress anybody.

His new wife's eyes dropped to his, and for the first time, they actually seemed inviting. She didn't look like she wanted to throw up.

The stable keeper helped Desmond mount Philippa.

As she'd promised, the two of them took off slow while he struggled to adjust to a living thing underneath him besides a woman. Adella led his horse's reins, her voice a steady stream of calm as she soothed all three of her subjects.

Around them, the earth was sprouting lush green grass a few weeks early, and the Cleveland Pear trees had begun to blossom green buds. The horses trotted around a bend that offered a spectacular view of homes facing the waterfront, trees clustered in patches on the hills, and the glistening horizon of the Atlantic Ocean in the distance.

Once they arrived at a clearing, Adella left Desmond to gallop faster on her own for a bit and get exercise.

At ease, she seemed to slip into another mental space, riding with confidence across the Massachusetts rolling hills, her plump turkey legs in surprisingly good shape. The animal's muscles rippled, responding underneath her, and Desmond was just a smidge jealous of the horse.

Somewhat mesmerized, he watched her slow up at the top of a hill. Her erect posture, mastery of the reins, and the connection with the large creature beneath her, all whispered to Desmond. Determined, she stared straight on, her mouth set, gaze surveying the land as if she were about to conquer it.

When she brought Curious back, she and Desmond dismounted, and he joined her while she rubbed her horse.

"You're wearing your wedding ring." Desmond observed their rings next to each other. He had not really paid attention before.

"Of course, I am. Why wouldn't I be?" she asked.

He shrugged. "Maybe because you don't want to be married to me?" He tried to laugh off the truth.

"I took vows. I'm going to honor them."

"Is that what you were doing when you went to see your white guy?" It was an uncomfortable question to ask. He probably should not have gone there, but he could not pretend she didn't feel the way she did. Judging by the way her back muscles straightened like wood, he might have been right. But the two of them needed to air some truths that day, and to learn what they would be to each other.

"I was going to explain and ask him to wait. I could not do that a few months ago, when all my family was in the house and with lawyers advising me to keep quiet, to not take any chances. Besides, he was shocked. He rushed out of the house and never answered any of my calls."

Desmond let out a low whistle. "For him not to answer your calls like that," he paused, treading lightly, "makes me wonder if he really loved you."

Adella's eyes cut away from his, and she started to slip away from him. "If you want today to go smoothly, I suggest you stop talking."

Desmond rolled his tongue around his mouth as his hand made its way across the luxurious coat of the horse. "Why didn't you two marry? And then you wouldn't be here."

For the next few moments of stiff silence, she must've been asking herself the same question. "I wasn't brave enough. Scared of my family. What everybody would say."

A tide of skepticism rolled through Desmond. He didn't totally buy her answer. "You sure that's all it is?"

"Yes," she replied quickly, maybe even defensively, as if she'd picked up on his disbelief. "I had finally worked up the nerve to tell them over Christmas. I had already met his family, and they were wonderful. Kind. Warm."

"Everything your family is not to you?" Desmond finished.

He could see there was more bringing her eyes to water than the chilly winds.

"Everything my family is not to me." She repeated the words like her subconscious was digesting their truth. "My family is loving, but complicated, just like everyone else's."

"But not loving enough to you. Why aren't they?" He dared to satisfy his curiosity.

She still brushed the horse, but her thoughts had galloped elsewhere. "I was sickly. And not all that cute. Not very fast or nimble at playing games. Always easy for them to sideline or forget me. They still do, out of habit. Now that Papa has left me everything, they are forced to deal with me. And they lash out from resentment."

"How did you learn to ride these things if you were so sickly?"

"I learned later, after my surgery, in my teenage years. Had to play catch-up. My grandfather took some time with me. So did Maddy. And during college, I would come alone, to take breaks and get away."

"And your white dude's family did not take you through that stress." It made perfect sense to Desmond now. The attraction of someone who offered her the kindness she'd never had. "What was so great about him?" Yes. Desmond would go there, and get her to open up, let her vent her feelings for another man, so maybe they could finally at least live with one another in peace.

A different expression crossed her face.

"He was like lying down in the grass during summertime, like walking on soft sand in Hawaii in your bare feet, or swimming in the warm waters of a lagoon that are turquoise and crystal clear. Everything pure and natural and unassuming, that's Wes." Her chest rose and fell, with her apparently wishing she could inhale him now.

The shit sounded poetic to Desmond. Simply listening to her, he might've even shed a tear. "Do you always describe your feelings so beautifully?"

"That's not anything beautiful. It's just true."

"Damn. It was beautiful to me. You could have been painting a picture with your words and shit. A Monet."

"What do *you* know about Monet?" Adella asked, surprised.

He drew back. "Why'd you say that like I can't know Monet?"

Her bashful grin was only interrupted with a jaw-drop, and she likely realized she was stereotyping him. "I don't know. You just don't cross me as the type."

They walked the horse around a bend of trees, their boots splashing over sticks and soggy ground.

"Well," her husband began, "this area here looks like Monet's *Luncheon on the Grass*, and that over there, with all the trees, looks like his *Women in the Garden*." Desmond watched her mouth part with astonishment at his artistic knowledge, and he mocked her, letting his mouth fall open also.

Apparently humored and impressed, she stared at him with expectation. "So are you going to tell me how you know that, or should I believe you're an art thief?"

"I had to take art class in college as a requirement for graduation. It was either that or classical history, and I'd be damned if I was going to spend my time reading all the white-washed conquests of Caesar and the others. So, art it was. Monet and Van Gogh were two who stuck with me. All the nature scenes reminded me of places outside Baltimore that I wanted to see one day."

From Adella's expression, she processed what he'd said. "What else do you like?" Hit with an afterthought, she shot a finger at him. "And don't say football." Her face broke out in a knowing grin. "You don't get off that easy."

"But I do like football. Why can't I say that?" Hell, he was stunned she even troubled herself with what interested him.

"That would be like me saying I like medicine. It's a given. So, what else?" she shot back.

Thinking, he rolled his eyes.

"Come on," she prodded. "Surely, there are other activities you participated in when you were growing up besides drinking, girls, and barbarianism."

Her humor sent a laugh bubbling out of him. She was a little more relaxed around her horses, unveiling slivers of the real Adella.

"Glad you think so highly of me." On the outside, he smirked, but in his stomach, he was tickled. She wasn't too far from the truth, but he wouldn't tell her too much truth during this probation period. "Actually, it was video games, swimming with my friends at the Boys and Girls Club when my mom and dad worked, sometimes comic books. Amusement parks. Oh, and—" He stopped himself.

"*And?*" she pressed. "You were going to say something else."

He smiled. "No, I wasn't."

Her eyes flew wider. "Yes, you were! Oh, so I see how this works." Her face turned suspicious. "You hound me for information you can throw in my face later but you won't let me do the same."

"I'm not going to throw anything in your face later. I'm just trying to understand the person I live with. Whether you are a crazy lady who might murder that other dude, or worse, take your frustration out on me."

At that, she cracked up.

Enjoying her laughter, he continued, "Like some *Fatal Attraction* type shit."

Adella laughed even harder, and underneath her cable-knit

sweater, her sizable breasts were shaking too. Desmond could stand there and tell a few more jokes just to watch them jiggle.

"You're laughing, but that happens for real," he replied. Her cackling strummed his arteries, turning him into her percussion instrument. "I'm just trying to figure out which side of crazy you're on." He paused for effect, listening to the clacking sound in her throat. "I see you're not answering, though."

"I think I'll let you keep lying in bed at night and wondering," she joked with a mischievous smile.

It was Desmond's turn to shake at her humor. "Uh-huh, yeah, okay. If you're trying to get me to leave, you're making good progress," Desmond joked back.

Finally, all her teeth gleamed in the morning sun. "So you liked amusement parks. I've never been to one."

"You're lying!" He jumped back.

"Nope. Couldn't do it while I was sick. And later, my mother was too afraid I would break."

"One of the EMT guys on the boat mentioned you having a surgery, too?" It was the flirty guy Desmond almost thumped. "What sickness did you have?"

"Scoliosis." At the mention of it, her eyes darkened in the middle of day. "There was a lot I missed out on."

Her wishful voice blew through his insides, touching him. This sense of caring that rose in him was weird, seeing a woman as a human, something more than a target to be pounded. In the past, he was only wining and dining, clubbing, showering them with grocery store flowers, putting in the minimal amount of time with the clear objective of sex.

This was new territory—spending time simply to... spend time.

"Let me take you," he said.

A dismissive chuckle flew out of her. "We're supposed to be doing whatever *I* want to do."

"It sounded to me kind of like you *did* want to, and never got the chance." He took a risk and eased his arm around her waist. His chest at her back, he leaned closer to her ear. "Let's do it tomorrow."

Adella's floral, oceanic scent hardened his manhood. His erection was welcomed by the softness of her fleshy ass against him. She didn't push him away, and instead, her mouth fell open at feeling his desire pressed on her. And Desmond enjoyed how her eyes fluttered in dismay.

"I can't." It was almost like she had her answer on autopilot, as if an unconscious part of her was still trained to avoid any new risks.

"I think you can." With his hands still stroked her waist. "And you're just scared of what you really want."

No smart-aleck comeback to that.

Before they left the stables, Desmond actually said goodbye to Curious, letting his fingers run through the stallion's hair one last time. He could see why a person would come here, to get away from all the noise and annoying humans and embrace the calm of animals who wanted nothing but affection.

"Wow, did you almost just kiss him?" Adella joked.

Her surprising humor tickled his heart. In more ways than one.

"Come on here, woman." Now it was Desmond's turn to pull on her.

THE NEXT DAY, after Desmond called around for which amusement parks were open in early spring, they hopped in his truck and headed for the Wild Wild East theme park.

The giddiness and childish excitement spread over her face infected him. And Desmond's blood rate pitter-pattered at the prospect of showing her some of the ridiculousness he'd loved as a kid.

He purchased them day passes, and because it was still early spring, they didn't have to worry about long lines of kids and teenagers. He checked out her wig perched atop her head.

"You might want to get your scarf and tie it down real tight, so that up there doesn't fly off." He smiled, and she gave him a playful shove. For the first time, she didn't seem defensive about it. "I honestly don't see why you need that."

But in a way, now that they'd talked more, he did see. Someone had made her believe she needed it.

In the scary house, each time she jumped, cringed, or fell backwards, her hands flew to her mouth or her body leaped against Desmond's. Her animated shrieks were loud enough to scrape his ears, and still, when she whipped around, burying her face in his chest, he took her in his arms. The moments of her softness wrapped up in him, the waves of her ocean-scented fragrance wafting into his nostrils, all sent his mind to carnal places. After they left the scary clowns and knife-wielding axe murderers from all the famous spook films, they moved on to the rides, specifically his favorite twisters.

With a devious grin, Desmond guided her toward the high-speed thrill rides.

"You're already taking pleasure in this," she complained.

"I am." He grabbed her hand and led her through the turn-stile, until they found seats at the very front of the roller coaster.

Cringing, Adella stared at all the rows. "We're sitting right up here?"

"Where else would we sit? We've got practically this whole thing to ourselves." Genuine happiness filled him for all the screaming he was about to hear. "No more controlled environ-ment for you, Doctor Good Liar."

Desmond was not disappointed. Adella bellowed at the jerks, swift turns, and long drops so steep it felt they would keep plum-meting through the earth. The adventure reminded him of his family when his parents were still together, how his father had laughed hard as his mother lost her mind.

His hands waving in the air, Desmond relished the heart-racing thrills. It had been too long. Out of the corner of his eye, he checked on Adella, who had shut up and stopped screaming. Now her fingers gripped the bars in front of her for dear life, and her eyelids did not close a single time. Swinging from side to side, her flesh pressed backward from the tough wind velocity, he wasn't sure if she'd died or not. Maybe he'd made a mistake bringing her on here. He managed to throw his arm around her, but she was so stiff she did not move, and the ride yanked them around so fast it was hard to comfort her.

"It's almost over," he managed to say.

What seemed like a million years later, the ride finally ended. During the slow return to the platform, he leaned over to ensure she hadn't shaken out her soul somewhere back there.

"Talk to me, Doc. You all right? A little too much for you? This kind of thing isn't for everybody, you know?"

Oh shit. Something else he would have to explain to their mothers.

As if coming out of a trance, Adella stared at him with eager anticipation. "Let's go again."

Desmond sat in shock. "For real?"

Her chest rising and falling, she seemed to be finding her breaths.

Adella rode the twister three more times before she finally moved on to the others. Spinning and looping, she laughed, her mouth wide to take in all the adventure filling her up.

At the bumper cars, she sucked, but she amused Desmond while trying her best to beat him up with one.

"I'm going to have so much heartburn tonight," she said at the sight of chili cheese fries and a chili dog he handed her. "If this is what you grew up on, I can see why your family members are having heart attacks on boats."

Desmond actually guffawed at that. "But we were happy though. Bad health and all. I can't believe you didn't ever have you one of these."

"Nope. My grandfather was not into junk food. We had chili, but not chili *and* hotdogs *and* cheese, all lumped together at the same time."

He stopped her before she began to eat. "We can't do any more roller coasters after we eat this. I don't want you throwing up everywhere. And I actually like this coat."

"Understood." She took a bite, and he watched her eyes roll back. "Mm, junk food." She moaned, sinking into it as if she were going to Heaven.

Desmond shoved some of the fries in her mouth so she gagged and laughed, and the whole botched effort sent them both into fits.

Sliding the rest of the food inside, his fingers met her lips. For a moment, their eyes connected in more than a passing glance. Suddenly self-conscious as the center of his attention, she seemed not to know what to do with herself.

But Adella felt the connection, and Desmond saw her feeling it, before her eyes darted away.

He did not want to scare her. So, for what must've been the fiftieth time that day, he tried thinking of any subject other than how her mouth was absorbing that long stick.

THIS WHOLE NOTION of marriage was growing on Desmond. He kind of felt guilty with her riding next to him, her ring finger dangling near the center console in the truck. The rock his mother's company had selected was nice, beautiful, big, but he had not picked it.

"Where did you get this ring I'm wearing now?" While at a stoplight, he studied the platinum-and-gold band he wore.

Seeming to be caught off guard, she shrugged. "I don't know. I presume either my mother or one of my brothers bought it."

"Hmph." The wheels of his mind turned, or maybe it was the gears of his heart, or a little of both.

"Why?"

"I was just wondering. Will everything we do for the rest of the time we're together be choreographed by everybody else in our lives. *All* the time. The way they apparently have been for a long ass time."

For that, she did not have an answer. When they arrived home, she twisted her head toward him with a question mark in her eyes. "Thanks. For… whatever this was."

"Date night for two married people? Who are still, technically, on their honeymoon?" He shut off the truck and came around to open her door for her. Then, he unloaded the stuffed animals he had won for her at the games and challenges. They were so huge she needed help carrying them.

Her gaze was unsure once they got in the house. "So will I be getting my nightly set of cocktails?"

"How about a nightly cup of tea? Or some nightly ice cream?" he asked. "I refuse to be responsible for making you an alcoholic. And if you are one already, I don't want to perpetuate it."

He could not have that on his hands.

"I'll take the ice cream then."

On her way up the stairs, her husband hoped—maybe even *prayed*—she'd come back down in nothing but her birthday suit. Then, he could properly make dessert out of her ice cream. A man could dream.

He whipped up vanilla bean banana split with lots of hot fudge, and instead of making separate bowls, he prepared one. By the time he was done, she came down in cozy cotton pajamas. Again, it surprised him when he was more intrigued than disappointed. She could've been wearing a trash bag, and he still would have been excited as hell for what was underneath it.

Taking out one of the gifts that they'd received from the wedding, he set a candle bouquet on the center of the table and lit all sixteen candles. Then he took out some of the other candle gifts they received and set them around the dining room and living room.

"Where did all this come from?"

"You never went through the gifts. But I like getting surprises. So I did while you were at your granddad's."

She eyed him with a skeptical raised brow when he set the one bowl between them.

"Don't worry, Doc, I didn't lace the ice cream with rat poison." He scooped up some hot fudge and banana and ice cream, and held it out to her with chocolate dripping over the edge.

Hesitant initially, she scoped him out. But Desmond remained steadfast, and would sit here all night with that damn ice cream if he needed to. After a few seconds, his bride leaned forward and parted her mouth.

Down, boy. He struggled to calm his rising erection.

"I enjoyed the rides today." She sucked up the ice cream, her tongue sliding across her bottom lip to lick up the fudge. "Thanks for taking me."

Watching her lips and tongue lap up chocolate sauce was thanks enough.

"Don't worry about it. It was a good time just hearing you scream."

He longed to hear more of it, on a different kind of rollercoaster ride.

This demureness in her—with eyes that questioned, and feared, and examined—he was not used to it. He was not used to seeing more behind a woman's eyes than temporary lust. Or actually, he'd never paid attention. Desmond normally entertained bold, brazen women who came at him for the quick and dirty purpose of tossing him around in bed or jumping on him in the car.

And yet, Adella's Penelope Pussycat fright turned him on. Her sensuality was a candlelight rather than a blowtorch, quietly lighting different parts of his body at the same time instead of just one part. And with his parts roasting over a low flame, he was Pepé Le Pew wanting to give chase.

But he would take his time, kind of the way one observed a flower garden in bloom. The flowers didn't all bloom in a day, but rather, petal by petal, a little more blossom every day, with care, water, and sunlight.

As he fed her more bites, he cupped her elbow. The smooth, superior-quality Supima cotton fibers of her pajamas cooled his fingertips.

Subtly, he massaged the soft fabric over her skin, but did nothing more. He didn't make any sudden moves to overwhelm her. Scaring her away from him was the last mistake he wanted to make. For now, he'd have to be satisfied to watch her open up petal by petal.

Instead, with only his thumb, and his eyes, and his ice cream, did Desmond communicate to Adella, and to himself, that he was falling for her.

A MONET LOVE

ADELLA

*B*efore the sun had begun to announce its presence on the Eastern seaboard, Adella yanked open Desmond's curtains. Gleefully, deviously, she moved to his closet, cut the light on, and picked out his clothes. For a while he was in such deep sleep, he didn't realize she was there. Finally, she made enough noise that he stirred.

"Adella?" he grumbled into the pillow. "What's up? Everything okay?"

"Of course everything is okay. Why wouldn't it be?"

Still groggy, he hid his face from the light. "Because you're in here. Little Red Riding Hood in the woods. Where wolves can attack you. Seriously. Especially first thing in the morning."

She chuckled and kept putting together the clothes he'd need. "Too bad the wolf won't have time for that. Get up."

"What time is it?"

"Five forty-five a.m."

"And I would do that because?"

"I can't tell you. It's a surprise. Just get up."

After more jerking and tossing, he obliged her, with an attitude. "Girl, if there's not a damn good reason behind this..."

"You'll do what?" she cracked.

"I'll figure it out when I wake up some more." He swung himself from bed and stomped toward his shower, not bothering to close the bathroom door. In a sleepy daze, he started getting out of his clothes.

Since his door happened to be open, Adella allowed her eyes to drift a bit. His five feet and ten inches of thick flesh coated his bulky muscles, as if he worked out but also didn't turn away a plate. He caught her watching him through his mirror.

"Excuse me? Privacy?" he fussed with a sleepy grin. "You staring?"

"No!" she snapped, her eyeballs rolling away as she bit back a rising smile. "I was just… checking these clothes I found, making sure they're appropriate for the weather." She smacked her forehead and stumbled out of his room. Her MIT-trained mind couldn't come up with a better lie than that?

And why were humming birds flapping their wings against her rib cage?

Why was she acting this way? She'd lived with a man for months when Wes was around. This was different though.

It was almost as if she and Wes were more brother and sister than a couple. And though she had not wanted to admit it with Desmond the day before, she was disappointed to see that Wes had gone and literally replaced her with another professional black woman so quickly. He'd said he'd never dated a black woman before her.

Now she questioned the truth of that. She understood that she'd hurt Wes, but it nevertheless stunned her that he'd rejected every one of her calls the past few months. Now she wondered if she had truly been in love with him. Or as Desmond pointed out, had she loved that Wes was nice to her?

Wes's eyes did not scour her figure or make her feel so seen, so *uncomfortable,* as when Desmond visually undressed her.

In The Hamptons, her friends had always gotten those looks

from guys. Maddy, Chrissy, but never her—Adella, the sickly, awkward third wheel.

Initially, Adella had not known how to receive Desmond's attention, whether to be offended or flattered.

But yesterday, his beefy arms circling her waist, his breath blowing along her neck, had shot tingles across her body. Then, his arousal was a brick against her back. She'd never felt anything that hard on Wes when they'd kissed and messed around. In fact, since none of the dates in medical school or college had panned into anything serious, she'd never reached that point of sexual vulnerability with any man but Wes. Now, Desmond had stroked the hidden corners of her.

"What are you in here smiling about?" Desmond asked, cutting into her thoughts.

"Nothing." Adella threw on her coat, turning her back to him so she could compose herself. "Just excited about the drive. It's been a long time since I've done it, but if it's as pretty as I remember, it'll be fun. We should probably head out."

She had already packed her car with lunch and blankets. So about 6:30 a.m. they took to the New England coastline.

The sun pierced through the clouds, spraying pinks, lavender, and apricot across the sky. He had reclined his seat, so Adella expected him to be asleep when she peered over. But instead of closed eyes or light snoring, she found him gazing out at the landscape and sky.

"Those are some pretty colors," he observed.

"Yes, they are." She had almost taken him to an art museum today but decided the location where they now headed was even better.

The entire two-hour drive, he absorbed the scenery, cranking his neck to see better, turning his head, whipping out his phone to capture shots. Three times, she pulled to the side of the road for him to take pictures of the ocean, harbors, farms, and boats sitting against the skyline.

Finally, they arrived at their destination, and she parked alongside a dirt path on an upward-sloping hill. Very few people were out on the chilly spring morning. Through her peripheral vision, Adella took in what may have been Desmond's wonderment.

His eyes did not blink, and he almost seemed too afraid he'd lose this vision if he did. Clusters of blooming magnolia trees wished them good morning, as well as masses of crocus flowers, daffodils, tulips, and azaleas, in numerous colors—apricot, peach, rose, cobalt, cream, canary—spreading for as vast as their eyes could see.

Realization blossomed on his face. "You brought me to the Monet painting."

Leaving the food in coolers back in the truck, they took a walk through the path.

"I left the bikes behind. I wasn't sure you'd be able to hang," she cracked.

"This is the shit. I mean, it's gorgeous. I've never seen anything like this before. In all my life. Not in person," he said with a bewildered laugh.

He shoved his hands in his pockets, and she could see he was maintaining his discipline, respecting her space. His deference was attractive.

"To be here at sunrise, we would've had to leave at four-thirty in the morning. The flowers would've looked like they were dipped in paint. All the colors across the sky meeting with the colors in the fields... it's pretty sick."

"We should do it."

Taken aback that he was willing to get up that early, she stared at him. "*Really?* You would have to get up at three forty-five a.m."

His face didn't flinch. "Why don't we spend the day and stay around here overnight? We can get up in the morning to see it.

I've done all kinds of overnight craziness—yacht parties, clubs, strippers. Why not see a sunrise with my wife?"

His gaze was a wind blowing on the piston inside her petals. When he licked his lips, Adella escaped and shifted her focus. The morning air dried her throat and pricked her skin as if she stood in the middle of a flower field with no clothes on.

As they proceeded, she hooked her hand in the crook of his arm. A bit farther ahead, past blooming dogwood trees and tiny blades of grass, they were welcomed with fresh scents, dew, and birds singing. He took his hand from his pocket, so hers slid into his that was warm and smooth like good leather.

She told him about the times she had come here with her grandmother, who loved nature, who brought the grandchildren to ride bikes and play. Though her parents were busy working when Adella was a child, and they spent most of the summer between Alabama and The Hamptons, occasionally, they still traveled once or twice a year to upper Massachusetts.

Laughing, she recounted funny stories of her brothers breaking arms and legs, falling off bikes, jumping from barns, losing kites in trees.

"They're not always cold. Our family is just highly competitive. People have been so busy working hard for profit and success, the family ties sometimes fall to the wayside."

"That shouldn't be the case. Not in any family. Ya'll sound like the Jacksons, or like Queen Elizabeth's family—claiming to love each other while stabbing one another in the back at the same time," Desmond replied.

As his indignation landed between Adella's ears, she recalled her grandfather's letter. His reasoning for his decision to leave the entire family estate to her was becoming more clear. He had also dropped another bomb in the letter—that he felt Desmond was an excellent choice. The dandelion seeds of her thoughts scattered in her mind.

How did her grandfather know Desmond?

"Earth to Adella," Desmond called, snapping his fingers in front of her. "Where do you want to set up?"

"Have you ever met my grandfather?"

His eyes indicated a quick scattering in his own head before his playful gaze returned to her. "No. Why? Did he leave me some money too?"

After they took some of their things to the driest clearing they could find, they put down plastic bags underneath their blankets and set out food baskets in the warm morning sun.

Desmond paused after picking up his croissant and egg sandwich. Instead of taking a bite, he handed it to her.

Butterfly wings fluttered in her heart cavity. "What do you want me to do with this?"

He opened his mouth.

She longed to run and hide in the flowers.

His eyes did not leave hers.

"That whole sandwich could take forever." Her voice sounded wispier than she'd intended, and her saliva would not leave her mouth no matter how many times she gulped.

Desmond's voice rose no higher than the breeze. "I've got time."

Again, the lenses of his eyes could have been microscopes the way they examined her. God, why did he have to ogle her?

Her fingers quaked harder than the grass blades blown by gentle wind. She cut up some of the sandwich, but when she picked up a piece to hold it out, her fingers shook too hard. Too many terrible memories flooded her mind, Kevin Middleton's taunting voice most prominent among them. She dropped the sandwich.

Tears welled around her eyes. How could she be a world-class surgeon operating on people's hearts but couldn't feed a man a sandwich?

Through the blur of her emotions, Desmond took another piece and handed it to her.

"I can't," she muttered.

She started to hyperventilate, and sounds of Kevin Middleton's ruthlessness reverberated through her. Then Lana Gilley cackled between Adella's ears. *You want me to show you what he did to me with his tongue?*

Desmond must have sensed her torment, because he gently shook her chin. "Hey."

He stuck her croissant sandwich against her mouth for her to eat. Adella dipped her head to bite off a piece and strugged so no scraps would fall out. Playfully, Desmond tugged the food back, watching her stretch her neck to break it all off before he cracked up. His antics put her at ease again. She shot him a side-eye, while he kept using food to torture her.

Finally, he held his sandwich to her again.

She took it. He opened his mouth. His bride slid the piece inside. Not removing his eyes from hers, Desmond sucked her fingers. He slid his wet, messy tongue around her fingertips, and licked her whole world silent. She could not bring herself to pull her fingers away. Then, he absorbed the food and swallowed, his gaze still arresting his wife. The only birds chirping now were the songbirds in her head.

Then came the fruit and cream tarts she'd packed that they fed each other. With the last piece she placed in his mouth, he closed the space between them.

Sweetness was still on his tongue. Delectable kiwi, strawberry, and orange exploded on her taste buds when his mouth fused with hers. The aftershocks ricocheted down her nerves, titillating the tips of her breasts, shooting past her navel, and setting off an entire fireworks show between her thighs. Sensual, moist and deep, Desmond's tongue dipped and sucked, and his hand was warm along her neck and collarbone, stroking her exposed skin. In a trail down her throat, he smacked on her until she couldn't take it anymore. Adella's shoulders bunched up, and a whimper escaped without her permission.

"You see?" Desmond murmured, his face in the crook of Adella's neck. "You can do more than you think you can."

BLOCKED

DESMOND

He might have climaxed in his pants, just from the turn-on of her helpless little moans.

That damsel-in-a-forest vibe tugged at his heartstrings and kept him as hard as a brick. He knew it wasn't an act. Adella was terribly, sweetly, deliciously *innocent*.

And also a little damaged.

While she'd clearly done a decent job of healing herself, or rather of surviving, she still clammed up when it came to a man's attention. When it came to her attractiveness.

Her wide eyes blinking as if she was terrified of ecstasy, fat lips opening and showing off her moist tongue, chest heaving up and down like a platter ready to be served, Adella was far more sensual than she might have been comfortable acknowledging. He'd known a few church girls—*"good"* girls—who weren't comfortable with sex. They'd been raised to believe it was bad and felt guilty just thinking about it.

So Desmond didn't push once they arrived at a seaside bed-and-breakfast for the night.

"I'll go first in the shower." Avoiding eye contact, she swept by him.

"You sure you couldn't use some help in there?" One hand on his hip, the other rubbing his manhood, he shrugged. "I could scrub some parts you haven't been able to reach. You know?"

Adella turned and shot him a bashful side-eye. "You sure about that?" But he heard the laughter in her voice.

"Ha! Oh! Is that a challenge?" Dr. Good Liar had a smart mouth on her. "I knew you had a little freak in you. You don't have to say nothing but a word, girl. I will come right in there and show you—"

Adella slammed the door between them.

"I'll be out here. In a g-strap. Waiting patiently."

For his turn under the shower, he handled his man needs to avoid jumping into her queen bed in the night. Still, a few minutes later, he stared at the double beds with real hope in his heart that she'd ask him to enter hers. She was already in her bed watching the news, and Desmond moved in slow motion.

The wait was a torture chamber. He'd played hard positions on the football field, but none of them compared to climbing into a different bed than his wife. Sex he was legally entitled to, he couldn't have.

Adella switched off the lamp. "Good night."

The stadium lights all over him shut off. Should he walk over to her bed and take her by surprise? The past two days had been so cool, and she was finally letting down her guard. He didn't want to ruin the good vibes. If she wasn't ready, he couldn't force it. But despite him knowing this, an urge overtook him, and he started toward her bed. Feeling for her in the dark, he scooped her into his arms.

"Desmond."

"Come on, Doc. You know I wouldn't do anything to hurt you." He fumbled for her forehead and kissed it, and then moved to her mouth. "And I know you won't let me touch you tonight, but I'll be damned if we're going to bed like Papa and Mrs. Smurf. Let me sleep next to you. That's all I'll do."

Strong and sturdy, Adella's arms were shields between them. He hated that she felt she always had to protect herself. Who did she keep expecting to hurt her?

At this point, he wasn't courting her for sex. He was courting the bewilderment in her eyes at his every touch. The skies must have opened and the Lord heard his prayers, because her fortress softened. For an astonished Desmond, she slid aside. She even curled up and lay in the crook of his arm, and just as he'd promised, he behaved himself.

The next morning, sunrise over hills of flowers wasn't as breathtaking as Adella. The absence of sex only intensified his desire to be inside her.

Once they were back in the city, and out of the countryside where phone signals didn't exist, they turned on their phones.

Desmond read several texts.

Jerrell: *You two kill each other yet?*

Smiling, he shot off a quick reply.

Me: *Still ticking. ;)*

He kicked off his shoes, changed into loungewear, and straightened up his room since they had left so suddenly the previous day. Adella put away picnic items downstairs.

When he went to join her, he asked, "So what'll it be? Tea or ice cream?"

"Popcorn," she replied with deviousness on that innocent face. "We should have some around here. I was thinking I'd go change and we could watch a movie. How about... *Fatal Attraction?*"

"Hahaaa. How about *no*. Let's see something safe like *Avengers Endgame*, or *Friday*, or *The Notebook*. Doesn't every chick like *The Notebook?*" To be honest, he wasn't sure what women liked, since he could count on one hand the number of times he'd watched movies with any besides his mother and sister. And the times he'd tried, they usually lasted ten minutes before they were between the sheets.

She laughed. "You make the popcorn. I'll go get the mail and change."

"Deal." He headed toward the kitchen.

Five minutes later, popcorn in hand, he emerged to find her entire vibe crestfallen.

"What's wrong?" he asked.

In her hand, she held up a note. A heavy feeling already weighing him down, he trudged over to read it.

Where are you? We need to talk. You have no right to shut us out of the house. Please unblock our calls and texts so we can speak!

— SOLOMON

The note was signed by her brother Solomon, who had dropped it off while they were gone.

Desmond bit down on his bottom lip, and guilt filled his lungs until it nearly suffocated him.

Adella blinked. "I just turned on my phone and went through it. I don't see any texts or voicemails from my family members. And I never blocked them."

He'd seen her angry, and her expression at this moment wasn't that, but it was one of distrust.

Manning up, squaring his shoulders, he prepared himself.

"I did. A couple of days ago, before I came to wake you up, I spoke with your lawyer. And then I went through your phone and blocked them."

"You should have talked to me first."

No yelling, no throwing, no punching, or finger-pointing. Adella's calm may have scared the shit out of him more than if she'd just thrown a lick. That kind of anger, he was familiar with. Instead, her eyes flared like a city before a power outage, and inside them, Desmond was once again her enemy from the opposition forces, trying to take down her family's company.

"If I had asked, would you have agreed?"

She shook her head. "No. Still, that's my call. I know they're not the best, but they're still my family."

"It's not only that they're not the best. They are nowhere near the ceiling and should actually be under the floor. Lower than the worst," he insisted. "And have you not been happy these last forty-eight hours? The happiest you've probably been since your grandfather died?"

The last two days had changed Adella's energy. Her swaying hips, the smile that glowed brighter than sunrays beaming through trees, had also shined into him. Her change was changing Desmond, so he knew he wasn't mistaken.

The answer to his question glimmered in the deepening of her pupils and the softening of her mouth. But she stiffened, as if conflicted on how to feel about this, before coming down on the side of being firm.

"Don't make decisions without me again. Especially when it comes to *my* lawyers, and *my* things, and *my* family."

Her family didn't deserve for her to defend them after how they treated her, but he had crossed the line. And fucked up.

"Of course not. I'm sorry. I wasn't trying to… I only wanted you to have some space. And peace."

Desmond had never cared when he disappointed his mother. He hadn't cared when he'd slept with Lana, and Adella found her hair on his hotel bed. At that point she'd been no more to him than a spoiled Cape Cod and Hamptons brat who needed to be checked.

But right then, his new wife's upset was a meteor catapulting into Desmond's chest cavity, screwing up his respiratory system.

To see her turn away and head toward the stairway dismantled him.

Yet she didn't make a single phone call. Not even to Maddy. Instead, she powered off her phone and set it on the table.

Desmond's gaze trailed her up the stairs, expectation and

hope thumping in his chest that she would turn around and forgive him.

His bride trudged into her bedroom and closed the door, shutting off the possibility that he might follow her inside tonight.

I'M NOT PLAYING WITH YOU

ADELLA

Blaring smoke alarms snatched Adella from sleep. The stench of burnt meat curled into her nose, and as her groggy eyes opened, she could've sworn a gray haze marched through her room. She sprang into the hallway and swung around the banister, flying down her stairs.

In the kitchen, Desmond was shoving open the windows and running amok. Black bacon still fried in the skillet, raw eggs spilled across the counter, and biscuits were blackening beyond recognition in the very bottom of the stove. Adella shut off the fire and turned on ceiling fans to vent the smoke. When they finally fanned some of it out, she glared at him, hand on her hip.

A shamed Desmond could barely hold up his head. "I was trying to fix you an apology breakfast."

"Or you're trying to destroy my house, as well as take over my grandfather's house, take our company…" she observed.

Her insides shuddered as she spoke the worries that had kept her up half the night. Sleep-deprived, she had finally managed to close her eyes until moments before.

"No, that is definitely not it. I'm not trying to—"

Not wanting to hear him lie to her, Adella scooped out charred food, prying it from the cookie sheets and pans.

"Would you please stop?" he asked in a low, humble voice. "And listen to me?"

His humility disarmed her.

But she hardened, reminding herself, as she had all night, not to be naive.

"So you can shoot me some bullshit about how you're only concerned about my happiness. Save it. You're only playing nice because your mother wants my grandfather's company. You're only concerned for the seven figures that just dropped into your account. There's no need to cook for me. You'll still collect your next seven figures after I have a live birth," she grumbled while nursing the pain shooting through her chest.

A visibly upset Desmond wiped down the counters like he was fighting them.

"Do you think I care about some house in a white neighbor-hood, in Cape Cod, where you and your people are the only black specks out there? Or moving to a city where I don't know any-damn-body, and I'm stuck in your house all day? You think this is some big party for me? It's been hell. Because I *do* have friends. I *do* have a social life. I *do* like to have fun. But you asked me not to embarrass you, or sleep around, or get drunk. So I haven't. And what's my reward? I'm lonely as shit, and I stay horny as fuck. I'm not getting any from my pretend-wife and I'm not getting it from anywhere else. You could at least jack me off or something."

"You'll feel better as soon as we do IVF and have a kid, and you get more cash, plus shares of my stock. It'll buy you some extra blow jobs when you go back to your old life."

"Would it surprise you to know I haven't spent a dime of that money?"

"Yet," she popped back.

"I've been too busy here trying to make you happy, be your friend, take care of you, support you, let you reject me. Even while you pout and cry over some dude who was only nice to you for your money. I wonder which is worse—my mom forcing me here and I get paid, or that white boy scheming you of his own free will because that's just who he is."

The words sliced into Adella as would a scalpel. And she couldn't defend Wes, because after all, the speed with which he'd replaced her had spoken volumes. In silence, she scraped a scouring pad over the cookie sheet with all the power of Rosie the Riveter going to war.

"Adella."

"You've said your piece. Please, just be quiet now," she said, her back to him, head down so he couldn't see the hot tears forming.

Desmond's hands eased onto her back and then around her waist. She hated how her nerves snapped to attention now when they felt his touch.

Desmond didn't speak above a whisper. "I don't care about any of this shit."

"I'm not your fool."

"When we started back in November, yes, all you meant to me was dough. I thought you were a spoiled-ass brat. But then I saw you turn into a warrior, a completely different person when you did that surgery, on the spot, with my cousin. I wanted to know more about that person. How did she become so incredible while dealing with all the mess from her fam? Me being married to you became about more than the money. And when I heard you describing that other guy, all poetic—someone who couldn't even hear you out—I was thinking, *damn*. Before you, I didn't care about love. After I heard you say those things, I wanted somebody to love me enough to describe me like that one day. I know this might sound crazy, but... I'm starting to like this. I like you."

She stared at his reflection in the window, staring back at her.

"You're trying to cut me off from my family, so your family

can move on us. No. Let's just stick with the plan we agreed to. The marriage and two babies, and then we're done."

That way, she could protect herself from getting hurt again.

But her husband remained at her back, intertwining his hands with hers in the dishwater. "If that's your concern, I won't talk to any of my relatives or anyone from our company. I'll give you my phone, my computer, and the passwords. As well as to my bank account."

Was her breath trapped in her chest because she'd slid to the bottom of the dishwater? "What?"

"You heard me. You can monitor me. And see for yourself. I don't have some game I'm running. And whatever plans my mother has, I don't know them because we haven't talked much. Her company is thriving, she's traveling, and she's been busy." He pulled Adella closer to him, nibbling her ear, and dipping his soaked hands under her pajama shirt. "You and I have been busy too. The only family that's truly tripping is yours, Del."

How could she reject his offer? Hell, the throb between her legs demanded that she accept.

She needed to keep her focus. "Your mother is thriving because she has my company cornered while you're here distracting me."

"What you and her do is between you and her. I've been here with you." Drying off his hands, he moved to get his phone and brought it back to her. He powered it up and handed it to her. Immediately, text messages rolled through his screen.

Where are you?

What happened? You trapped with them bougie Cape Cod Negroes?

You do remember you were born in Baltimore and not Boston, right?

Adella laughed.

"Keep it." He squeezed her waist.

"I'll see everything?" She still questioned if there wasn't some catch she couldn't see yet.

His eyes reflected the morning sunlight, so they glistened at her. "Everything."

Even as the sun warmed her insides, she still wondered if she should trust this. "And what do you want from me?"

"You." Desmond's serious expression studied her the way she'd studied her books. "I'm not playing with you, Adella. Stop fighting it."

He pulled her to him, and his mouth brought the sunrise to hers.

Adella relaxed and kissed him back. His hands under her butt, he lifted her onto the kitchen counter.

"And I don't need to buy a blow job," he said, his lips sucking her neck before meeting her face to face. "I'd rather wait and get one from a woman who describes me like a Monet."

Buckets of paint splashed through her veins, painting Monets with every word he poured into her. Her marble-hard nipples skipped against his chest.

With both her hands, Adella touched his face, shutting off her doubts and kissing him deeper. She allowed her fingers to play at the nape of his neck and rub the short, smooth waves of his low-cut hair. Their tongues met in her mouth, where he snaked his over her teeth and around her taste buds.

Her breasts danced in his hands that sent her head into a tail-spin with him squeezing them into his mouth and sucking as much of them as he could. Adella was his breakfast.

"Mm," she moaned.

Shocking her, Desmond's fingers grabbed her pajama bottoms.

"Raise up," he whispered, and she obeyed so he could pull them down. His impatient hands pushed open her legs, where he lowered his face.

Adella's jaw fell slack. "What are you doing?"

He flung her legs over his shoulders, and her ass cheeks

jumped when the moist softness of his tongue slid across her oozing, pink core.

Oh, goodness. Adella sizzled up to her navel, through her trachea, in a spontaneous reflex that escaped out of her throat. Her delirium forced Adella's head back. "Ahhh."

"Stay with me, Doc. Let me teach you some CPR real quick. I'm about to revive you," he whispered, his breath tickling her wet folds.

She stared down at his eyes. Peering up at her from between her legs, Desmond winked.

He gripped her thighs tight. He laid his tongue at her opening, and skated it up her folds. Adella gripped the edge of the counter, her legs wrapped around his shoulders.

"Del, you taste so damn good I might be having you for breakfast every day," he whispered.

Between the thickness of her thighs, he shoved his face and slurped. His every tongue stroke deeper, wetter than the last, Adella now gasped hard enough that she was learning a new CPR technique.

Hot in the center of her belly, an orgasmic flood started to swirl, better than any climax Wes had ever given her, or she'd given herself. The ecstasy washed over her, almost catapulting her body into a seizure. Adella rocked and jerked, and Desmond held her tight, sucking up her gushing cream as her orgasm continued.

Adella felt faint, but he kept going, his head wagging violently while he feasted.

Her husband's eyes locked on hers, he ate her like he'd starved for months.

Adella shuddered at the pleasure she wasn't sure she could handle. His tongue pressed, each devastating lick sending more shock waves into her abdomen.

"Des…" she gasped. "Haaah…"

The sound barely escaped her throat. Her moans mingled

with his slurping sounds and filled her kitchen. Feasting and dipping inside her core, he pulled her toward him until her butt hung off the edge and he had full access.

"Don't worry, I've got you, baby."

He pushed her legs open wider and dipped his two fingers inside her opening. Her eyes closed, mind blown, she dropped the rest of her defenses and succumbed to the pleasure. Her legs that clung to his back while his fingers moved in and out of her. Slippery and wet, Desmond's mouth softly attacked her pink nub.

His fingers twerking on her G-spot conjured another scream from her chest. A thunderstorm of tremors cracked through her insides, lighting up her female walls and center until Adella came again.

"Mm," she moaned, grabbing his head.

Desmond held on to her waist, his mouth still slurping up all of her juices.

Adella's fist came down on the counter. "Aaagh!"

Her legs were getting weak, but he clamped her ass to his face.

"That's right, baby, come for me. You're going to be coming all day. I promise," Desmond said before his tongue dived into her opening again.

DOOR OPEN

DESMOND

A gasp here. An eye flutter there. The delicate skin flapping at her throat, little breaths tripping from her mouth, all did more than arouse him sexually. They endeared him to her. He might have shaken harder than she when he slid his fingers in her panties, stuck his tongue inside her oozing wetness, savored her moans and yelps.

And though Adella's limbs were quivering, begging him, and her muscles relaxed in his arms, she still hesitated at times. She was still nervous.

So Desmond stopped himself. For the first time in his life, he wanted to be a gentleman. He cared about her. Not her money or her status and position. But her. The woman who had already been through so much. And Desmond also cared what she thought of him.

Besides, this romance stuff wasn't so bad. He kind of relished the mystery and intrigue, this painstakingly slow way of catching feelings for somebody. Watching her as she caught feelings for him, and the way they were both changing toward each other.

For the next several days, Adella took Desmond all over Boston—the art museum, Arboretum, even roller skating, the movies—followed with long walks through her Toney neighborhood. More horse-drawn carriage rides, holding hands, and pulling her into his jacket when she shivered in the spring cold. Her body was starting to fit against his just right. It even stunned him the first time he turned his head toward hers, and instinctively, she tilted her face up so their lips met.

Spring days warmed up from more than the weather. Each time she stared at him she thawed another piece of his player mentality. Desmond may as well have been on the operating table while she performed emotional surgery on him.

After she returned to operating at the hospital, he went back to work on his studies for his MBA. Being Adella English's husband compelled him to be a better man, one who was worthy of her. Not only that, but he remembered all too well how his mother exceeding his father led to their breakup.

Now Desmond understood what his mother meant with her words, "*She just might be the catalyst that gets you off your ass.*" He also wanted to show his mother he was good for something besides waiting for her money.

Sometimes, he video-called Jerrell, who talked him through some of the lessons and principles.

A big grin spread over Jerrell's face one afternoon while the two of them worked via video, and Adella was still at the hospital.

"Maddy mentioned she hasn't heard from Adella in a while. So I'm guessing you and her, um, aren't racing toward divorce yet."

Desmond's eyes dipped down and bashfulness crept over him.

"Don't worry, man," Jerrell continued, laughing. "You don't have to tell me your business. That whole vibe is answer enough. I'll tell Maddy she doesn't have to call the hounds on your ass."

Desmond attempted making dinner for Adella a couple of times, both of which were disastrous. His feelings were somewhat crushed that Adella laughed until her stomach hurt while trying to doctor it up with spices. But he didn't care about embarrassing himself because her tired face came to life, making his efforts worth it and lighting him up inside.

They had been living in a closed universe for about three weeks, and he was okay with that too. Coworkers asked if he was returning to Boston with his bride, and Adella showed him text messages from his siblings who had reached out.

But he was in no rush to get back to the real world and leave this little piece of paradise they'd found. Desmond feared that returning to their families, and wrestling with all their competing interests, the prodding and prying from both sides, would place them at odds with each other again. He and Adella were finding their rhythm, and he refused it to die.

However, the moment she entered the house after work one night, her mood flat, it became clear their honeymoon truly had ended.

"I spoke with my mother today," she reported.

His wine traveled over his tongue and down his throat as if her words had turned it to vinegar. "Really? How is she?"

Adella smiled at how the fake politeness of the question contradicted the disdain in his voice that he hadn't attempted to hide.

"She wants a family sit-down between her, my siblings, and me." She took a sip of her own wine. "I can't put it off forever."

"I know. We're not on our honeymoon anymore. So we can't use that as an excuse, huh?" He wished he could shield his good doctor from them for eternity.

Adella's head fell back against the chair. She stared into the candle flame dancing in front of them, the kind that had a wooden wick and made popping noises like it was a fireplace. She must've sensed his trepidation, because her finger moved over to caress his. Her touch caressing more than just his skin, the candle fire may as well have danced in the center of his rib cage.

"They don't own us," she murmured.

He laced his fingers with hers.

"I don't want them hurting you. And I can't promise I'll be respectful if they're not respecting you." He spoke his worry straight across the candle fire and into her eyes.

"As far as they're concerned, our marriage is property that they negotiated and that they own. That's exactly how they will treat it."

After finishing their dinner with the shrunken appetites they now had, they cleared the table and washed up the dishes, as they did every night now. He moved behind her, his hands over hers in the dishwater, Desmond pressed himself against his wife's voluptuous physique. She tilted her head as if he held a string that pulled it aside and exposed her neck. Velvet and sweet, her skin almost melted on his tongue.

Then, he could not believe the words that spilled from him before he had actually thought them.

"I love you, Adella."

Her closed eyes snapped open. She turned toward him, her jaw hanging between them.

"Damn," he said, standing close enough to hear her breathe. "You're making a man feel self-conscious. You don't have to be so quiet. If you don't love me back, it's cool. I get it." He'd gotten too caught up in the moment and had said it too soon.

"You love *me*? Or the money you get from being with me?" Her instinctive distrust wielded knives through her glare. He had learned it was her default protective mechanism.

Checking himself real quick, having asked himself the same question over the past few days, he second-guessed himself again.

But his delay must have raised the hairs on her back. Suspicion darkened her face and she jumped like a deer leaping from the road. Desmond grabbed her arm before she could flee, bringing a terrified woman into his arms.

"Adella, not everybody is out to hurt you. I don't care what your family said. Or how much money is involved. I would not let those words come out of my mouth if they weren't real. You've got my heart, Doc. Don't rip it up."

The lasers of her eyes scanned him for just how real he could be, if underneath all his organs and blood, he spoke from real emotions. Real ability to love. To love *her*.

The weight of her hand pushed against his chest, and she turned away.

Damn.

He had not fully thought this out—how fragile she might still be, the devastation that had kept her in bed, without food, for three days only a month ago. She clearly still wasn't over that other guy, and here Desmond was complicating things by declaring love she couldn't return. He finished up the dishes and put the last of them in the drying rack. She still had not come back downstairs a half hour later, so he shut off the lights on the first floor and made his way up the stairway.

But this time, at the balcony, a thin sliver of gold light extended toward him. It peeked from her bedroom door that stood open.

HEAVEN

ADELLA

Should she stand?

Sit?

Lie to her side?

A million questions about how to do this flew through Adella's mind.

Desmond really did just say what she thought she'd heard.

No matter how many times she'd wondered what he was feeling, if he truly was interested in her, to actually hear him say it was like dropping straight down on that roller coaster. The disbelief and questions all had her mind and body in freefall.

Was she being naïve if she believed him?

But for weeks now, Desmond had kept his distance and given her space. He would climax her on the couch with his fingers and then pull away. He'd defended her with his family, and in a way with hers, and his deference had to mean something. The lust on his face tonight, the desperate way he'd asked her not to go... *had* to mean his feelings were real. That he'd taken their marriage vows so seriously, from the first moment—when she had dismissed them—could not be fake.

Heart racing everywhere except inside her, she fretted over

how she looked. Of what he would think. She was finally wearing one of the wedding nighties that Maddy and Chrissy had helped her. That day, Adella had made it very clear she would never wear it. Now the new wife ran her hands over its champagne-colored silk and chiffon bodice that was see-through in some places yet still elegant. She was too preoccupied with questioning her appearance.

"You look like heaven."

Desmond had approached her as quietly as the sunset, his eyes drinking her up. By the time she realized his presence, his hands already claimed her waist, and clawed down her hips.

With longing in his eyes, his tongue slid out with desire and he sucked her cheek. Gently savoring her, he nibbled her jaw and licked his way down her neck.

Her body relaxed, with each of Desmond's kisses unlocking her mental doorways. Letting him have his way, Adella trusted him, sweeping her arms around his shoulders.

Like she was dough, he kneaded the flesh over her stomach. Playing with her breasts, he he munched like he wanted to pull each one off her.

The muscles under her navel pulsed and throbbed at the way he groped her.

"Haah…" she gasped, not quite knowing what to do with his appetite.

But he did all the work, his teeth yanking down her bodice. Then his football-strengthened arms scooped her up, fulfilling a fantasy Adella had been too scared to ever imagine for herself.

Staring at his treasure, he carried her to her bed, laying her down, where Adella fell back.

His hulking frame, twenty-seven inches wide, towered over her, and she trembled at the sight of him. His flesh glowed from the candle she'd brought up and placed on her nightstand. Seeing a far different man than the haughty one she'd first met, she reached for him. Lifting his shirt, she rolled it over her head. The only time her fingers moved so surely was in surgery, but now she didn't fumble with the strings on his sweats. Rising from the bed, she stared at him.

"Desmond McLain." Her heart pumped so hard it may have dulled her senses, and she wasn't sure if she'd said it.

"Mrs. McLain," he murmured, pausing to wait for what she had to say, maybe even expecting her to tell him to stop.

"Thank you for being the sun rising in my heart, the sun setting on my pain, morning dew on my thighs, evening tea that keeps me sober, my Midori Sour that helps me relax, a long seaside drive on the road to joy, hazardous cooking that might kill me..."

His big body shook with laughter.

"... my living, breathing Monet, I love you."

Desmond's gaze on her deepened like she was—as if she'd never be anything other than—precious to him.

Within moments, nothing remained between them, and he was at her doorway. Her *other* doorway.

"Your first time?" he whispered. His heavy hand on her cheek warmed her face.

"Yes," she murmured back, finding concern and love in his eyes.

He moved his hand between them. "Squeeze it."

She did as he'd instructed. He kissed her hand.

Then, her husband pushed inside her, inching forward as the sharp sting forced her to shriek and her lungs to grasp for air. He sucked her lips, lovingly sliding his tongue against hers while he slowly filled her with all of his steel. She might have squeezed the blood from his hand while Earth's plates were grinding inside her.

To ease her discomfort, he rubbed Adella's breast, lifting it for his tongue to tease. Biting and pulling her hard nipple, he softly tugged its edge. The sensations helped Adella relax a bit in her hips. Desmond sped up his strokes as her walls adjusted to him.

"Shit, Del, I'm never coming out of your tight pussy."

Underneath him, she held on through the initial bolts of stinging in her womanhood, until his motions weren't so jarring.

Moving tenderly, his fingers rubbed her face while he stared into her. Feeling his warm breath on her cheeks, his lips kissing her eyes, and the loving hand he laid on her chest, Del opened up.

And Desmond drove deeper into her, which hurt for a moment. But suddenly, sexual sparks began to match the pain.

"Oh!"

Shit. Hot tremors tingled deep in her abdomen and grew more demanding. He'd found her G-spot. The sensations intensified with every stroke of his shaft drilling into her.

"Damn," he half moaned, half whined, pushing faster, deeper.

It was him squeezing her hand now while his steel mined for the diamonds in Adella.

Sparks popped in the center of her. Desmond's hunger stirred her craving for more, and she slipped her hands around his back. With her legs strapped to his waist, the gates of her body opened wider.

Locked into one another, their kisses were deeper than carnality. Had she known sex was this freeing, she might not have waited so long. Then again, she would have been utterly disappointed if her first time with someone else had been a fraction less than the love Desmond was now putting on her.

Wanting to feel his passion deeper inside her, Adella thrust her hips to match his rhythm. In the heart of her womanhood, Desmond took her to the edge of ecstasy where she met the repressed side of herself.

Lost in her wetness, Desmond pounded on her G-spot, his moans increasing her delirious state, making her wetter, hotter. Their newfound love exploded in the center of Adella, her back arched, legs tensed, feet balled to handle the heat flowing between them.

Their earthquake cracked through her, elevating her screams to new octaves that filled the house.

Still buried inside her wetness, panting harder, speeding up, he followed her into ecstasy. Like he couldn't have enough of her, and it had indeed been months since he'd been inside a woman, his exhilarated breaths now filled her ears and he erupted between Adella's thighs.

They lay for a moment, catching their breath. His heart thudded on top of hers.

Desmond planted soft pecks along her cheek, jaw, and then her neck. "How do you feel?"

Adella would never grow tired of the way Desmond's eyes shined at her.

"Can we stay like this forever?" she asked, still holding him inside her.

He laughed, kissing her eyelids. "We can't hide from your folks that long," he replied, to which they both chuckled.

"But we can try," she cracked as he started up again.

"So what are we doing about kids?" Desmond asked a few nights later after making love again. "Are we trying for a baby or what?"

Adella's gut shook from humor at his question. "Don't you mean, when can I bring you another inheritance distribution?"

"No!" He tickled her and they rolled all over her mattress. "That is not what I'm asking, Mrs. McLain!"

Her lungs grabbed oxygen after he'd tickled it all out of her, and Adella caught her breath. "Why would I want to get bogged down with a baby so soon? I just discovered sex."

"And I love sexing you." He placed his lips on her temple. "Watching your eyes pop like confetti, hearing the little kitten hum in your throat, and feeling you squirt all over me is dope."

Guffaws erupted from inside her at how he'd described it.

"I'm not ready to give this up either, girl. It's up to you. Whatever you want. But you know damn well that's what all of our people will ask. I'm not the only person with something to gain. You get more voting power over your board after a live birth. Don't pretend it's all on me."

"We only just started. We haven't been married for years. I want this for all my nights and mornings for a while." She covered half of her face with the sheet in a genie pose. With a sneaky smirk, she slinked underneath the covers. "To go to bed horny."

"Wake up horny." He dipped under the sheet with her and bit her cheek.

"Take a shower horny," she whispered with a smile.

"Horny in the jacuzzi…"

"In your truck…"

Their tongues found one another again.

"So it's settled then. No babies for now?" he asked.

"Just fun," she said.

He chuckled. "Because you don't trust me…"

"Because I need time." Adella sucked her bottom lip. "And more sex."

His lips against her ear, Desmond's sensual laughter filled Adella's eardrums and marched down to her heart. "As long as you don't break it, girl."

"Good thing I got that IUD as a backup in December," she admitted laughingly.

Desmond drew back. "Oh, really? So, Mrs. McLain, you were being slick and dishonest in the negotiations." He tickled her under the covers.

She squirmed from his fingers. "Are you mad?"

"No." He yanked the covers down and kissed her again. "I don't blame you. We'll be doing it a lot. I need plenty of time to tame this." His hand slid up her leg, and his tongue foll.

"Mm," she moaned at the trail of moist heat he licked along her skin.

He lifted it over his shoulder and pushed inside her. Adella's eyelids snapped back to her brow bone, and a pleased Desmond came toward her.

"There's my confetti."

After he put her to sleep that night, and every night after, she practically hopped from bed each morning and raced to avoid starting her work shift late.

"Ow!" She tripped over his long shoes.

He had started sleeping in her room, and she stumbled over their clothes on the floor before facing gobs of toothpaste he'd left in her sink. It was a far cry from the neat bathroom she usually kept, but she didn't have time to fool with cleaning.

As soon as they returned to normal life, and full schedules, her days were filled with Board of Directors meetings for various non-profit projects, her alumnae society, professional organizations, and women's groups around the city.

For the increased workload around the house, she had to arrange for the cleaning service to visit more. As well as a professional chef to prepare and send meals a couple of nights a week. Though she adored the cute hopefulness in Desmond's eyes when she came home to the smell of burnt meatloaf stuck to the pan. It tasted more like packed sand with tomato paste smeared over it, but Adella didn't have the heart to ask him to stop trying. Instead, her heart oozed a warm, gooey adulation for the efforts of a man whose only knowledge of domestic life was placing batteries in a TV remote.

Then, there was prying herself from him to leave the house.

"Why don't you call in today?" Desmond was good at catching her on the way out the door.

But she was sharpening her exit game, packing her things in the car the night before so he had less time to taunt her.

Sometimes, when she returned home, she overheard his video

calls with Jerrell talking him through his business classes. She tried not to listen in while going through her mail and business documents, but their adorable joint laughter couldn't be ignored, especially when Jerrell teased him.

"How come you didn't know the answer to that, man? It's super easy. How late were you and Del up last night?" Jerrell's voice would call out louder. "Del! Why aren't you helping this boy with his homework?"

"Because he gets an A-plus on *my* homework assignments!" she called back.

But all the business talk reminded her of their family's outstanding commitments.

Adella would soon have to decide who in McLain Construction she would approve to work in her grandfather's offices.

She'd been able to delay the choice this long because Jerrell's eldest brother, Roland, was still conducting his audit of Manuel Realty. Her body was a ball of hitch knots, twisting and tightening inside her as she awaited what it would reveal. Which of her family members bore the most responsibility for its decline? Whom would have to be ousted to right the ship? How did she keep the family together so they could at least put up a pretense of peace?

These questions she'd put off for months under the guise of planning her wedding and then the audit. Her new married life had also bought her time to delay family drama, but now the clock ticked.

In the meantime, she and Desmond savored one another's favorite spots. From him throwing his leg over hers in the middle of the night, to the pressure of his hand on her waist or her butt in his sleep, to his erection poking her first thing in the morning. They made love at sunrise, her windows thrown open, the chilly breeze sweeping in, her curtains fluttering as Adella's joy seemed to float right through them.

For her next trip down the stairs, a mail courier was awaiting her.

"Dr. English?" he asked when she opened the door.

"Yes."

"For you. Could you sign here, please?"

She opened the envelope marked "Confidential." It had arrived from the audits unit at the bank where Roland Rouse worked.

SUPERTANKER

ADELLA

*A*della had to force herself away from Desmond. His taunting laughter, the loving way he held her, rubbed her, massaged her, took his time… gave her new life. And the way he received love from her, stared at her, made the insides of her panties skip with new life. She couldn't stop smiling, giggling, or rolling her eyes.

But still, he was right. She could not put off family obligations forever. It had already been weeks, and she was hoping that with space between her and her family, the situation would've calmed down. Without their lawyers, maybe they could talk reasonably, and see one another as family, rather than an empty house that shut off when Francis Manuel did.

Desmond serving them with cease-and-desist papers had bought her more time to comb through her grandfather's things. She'd read his letter and journals again.

She could also ponder how he could have known a man was good for her, whom he'd never even met. His journals and notes didn't contain a word about Desmond's mother.

A month after her wedding, she prepared to go meet her

family again. Desmond refused to join her, despite Adella offering.

"You're a member of the family now, just as much as my siblings' spouses. You have every right to be there."

"Not if they want to see light of the next day, no, I probably shouldn't. But I think everything you shared with me sounds like far more than they deserve from you." He spoke while finishing a paper for a class.

On her way out, he walked her to the door and gave her the forehead kiss. "Once things settle down, and you all work it out, if they're showing you your respect, then I'll come. But I don't want to say something out of line that will have you and me here arguing about them."

He had a good point which, admittedly, he often did.

A few minutes later, she was on Route 28 for the two-hour Sunday drive to Cape Cod. Maddy was flying up to meet her for moral support, and after the gathering, they could debrief to exchange notes over lunch. Since Desmond wasn't coming, Adella welcomed it. He would go hang out with some of his classmates, while she spent the night in Cape Cod.

Maddy was already waiting in the foyer after Franny had let her in. They'd arranged to meet early, before the rest of the family arrived.

"Oh my God. Look at that face." Her childhood friend threw her arms around Adella's neck. Maddy pulled back, her gaze dancing all over Adella. "Girl, tell me it isn't so."

Adella smiled from her toes up her spine and out of her vocal cords. "It is so. So very, very much so," Adella reported as her eyes rolled up. "In every imaginable way."

"I can't wait for this to be over with, so we can head to lunch and mani-pedis. But for now, how did you two possibly...? I mean... you and him hated each other!"

"I know. But he is," Adella sighed, "so not the way he comes off initially. I think we were both coming from a place of being forced into this and not knowing each other. But when we got rid of our families, we were left with only each other."

Maddy squealed again, linking her arm with Adella's.

"So, speaking of being madly in love, what is happening here?" Adella touched Maddy's growing belly. "What are you? Four? Five months?"

"Girl, I'm four months. And guess what else?" Maddy held up her hand, a huge yellow diamond glistening atop it.

Adella screamed. "Get! Out! Jerrell is not playing around! He is tying you up. *You.* Miss Independent Woman, Miss I-Will-Never-Marry-Anybody."

Maddy hosted a sunrise of her own all over her face. "We're having a boy. He is ecstatic. I am so glad this is all coming together. Just six months ago, we were all sitting in my backyard…"

"Don't remind me. And this had been thrown on my lap like hot burning coals. I was dreading my life." Adella's head fell back until she stared straight at the ceiling.

Maddy then turned to her. "No matter what's said in here today, remember this feeling that's all over you right now. And you'll get to feel it again soon enough. Forever. You ready?"

"Thanks, girl. Yeah."

They walked out of the sitting room. And into the hallway to face her mother and siblings who were gathering.

"Well, if it isn't Miss Married Lady," her eldest sister, Constance, noted. "Seems he's locking you down. We were wondering what he had done to you. If you were buried in the woods somewhere, you've been so quiet and invisible."

"Constance, that's enough," her mother chastised. "Glad to see you are well, Del. You do look happy. Should I be expecting a grandbaby?"

Adella was certain of what her mother really wanted to know. How much more power would Adella have now if she were expecting a child? And how soon?

"Mom, we should all catch up on what's been happening in Manuel."

"The rest of us are caught up already. You're the one who's been slacking," Solomon snapped. "We've attended the court proceedings, where your lawyers have served papers on us, preventing us from entering our family home, preventing us from making deals in the company without your final approval, the board can't vote, the executive teams can't act. Meanwhile, you've been lying up over there with a sleaze who's good for nothing. Now you're probably carrying his child as his family prepares to ruin us."

Her big brother's upset shot straight at her. But she let it roll off, intent on keeping the conversation calm and reasonable.

"Here's what I'm offering."

"What you're offering?" Solomon asked, leaning over the library conference table. "You are offering me a piece of the company that *I* run?"

Summoning the encouragement in her grandfather's words, she faced her elder brother head-on. "That is what Papa intended." Adella's voice lowered; she was grateful she had Maddy at her side. "Since you can't successfully run one. Correct?"

"What do you mean?" he asked.

Maddy reached under her chair and pulled out the chestnut wooden box that Franny said they had all been searching for. The reason Adella's mother, aunts, and uncles had delayed calling the rest of the family when Papa had been dying. Using the key, Maddy opened it up. Their eyes widened, every one of them.

"Those are my father's things! I was looking for that!" her mother cried, rushing to grab it.

Maddy snapped the box shut.

"He left it to me." Adella reminded them, and turned to the maid, Franny.

"Yes, he did," Franny confirmed. "He wrote a letter to Adella that I witnessed him write, along with his lawyer and accountant, and we all signed it."

"I've already sent it for filing with probate." Adella stared at each of her siblings. "Here's what I'm willing to do. We will all share the house. But I will have final say on what's done with it. Papa used as it collateral, so it has a few outstanding liens. And we have debts to pay."

"Papa's company was sound. I handled the books. Went over it with his accountant," Solomon defended.

"As did your uncles," her mother added.

"From the looks of things, your accountants are slippery, and they've been fixing the books to cover you. You all had some pricey dreams and expectations. Papa took out a number of loans to fund them for you, and he did it against the value of the company. To push your dreams and make you happy. Fortunately, we have enough holdings that we should be able to cover much of the debt. But the sad part is none of you created anything that helps Papa's legacy. You only sought to use his company for yourselves and your own projects."

"And who are you to judge, heart surgeon? Who paid for your fancy education at MIT?" Constance shot back.

Adella didn't bat an eye. "You are absolutely right. And that's why I will start with my contribution of all my shares to the reduction of that debt. Are you willing to do the same?"

Squirming in their seats, none of them spoke a word.

She continued, "As a heart surgeon, I am not hurting. I can even sell my house. I can downsize."

Constance twitched, exchanging looks with Solomon. "Of course you can. You're married now, to a man who is inheriting a heap of dough just for being with you. And if by some chance you go broke, you can happily run off to Baltimore and live with him and his family. So don't stand there and act like you're making some grand sacrifice."

"I'm trying my best here. If we sell off some of our holdings, we can use the remaining proceeds to restructure Manuel Realty, downsize it, and work with the McLain family to innovate. We could bring Papa's properties into the twenty-first century, into the future."

"You need to go back to practicing medicine and let me do my job," Solomon retorted. "Do you even know who Margaret McLain is?"

That question leveled Adella like a dilapidated building. But the gigantic eruptions of debris sat inside her, under the detonation of their stares.

"What?"

"She was Pa's whore," Adella's mother said, sucking her teeth.

Adella plummeted to a seat.

Mrs. English continued, her voice cratering, "That's right. They had an affair. She left her husband. We never knew until a few weeks ago when we sent lawyers to Baltimore to poke around. Part of the reason she rose in the construction industry was because of Papa's help starting out. He introduced her around, got her into the right doors, mentored her."

"At the end, he left her a part of his company," Solomon finished. "And the rest of it to you. With conditions."

Batting her eyes the way one batted at a gnat, Adella huffed. "Is Desmond…"

"No. She already had the children. But Papa and Desmond have crossed paths."

Desmond had said he'd never met her grandfather when she'd asked. The new information was vexing. Why wouldn't he have told her when she asked?

"Del, there's a lot you don't know." Solomon rubbed his chin. "And whatever you have in that box probably isn't the whole story. But our company is holding up just fine, and we will figure it out. You are not the person to give me directions after I've run the company for twelve years."

The news had jarred her, and she took a moment to inhale.

"I know this is hard for you to accept, but I understand now, why Papa made the decision he did. I am the only one who did not want his company." She stared at each one of them. "But now that I have it, the responsibility rests with me to protect our legacy. I'm asking you to help me."

"We don't trust you. What have you been over in that house scheming up with him? What did the two of you cook up?"

"Nothing," Adella answered.

"Oh, really?" Constance asked, her eyes narrowing. "Well in that case, maybe there are a few other things you should know, Miss I-Want-To-Help-Everybody. You can't even help yourself."

At that moment, they brought in someone else. Adella's cousin, Afi.

Afi's strut into the room was confident and eager, and she pulled out her phone as if it were a bomb she couldn't wait to throw.

"Afi?" Adella asked

"What is this?" Maddy asked.

"Just listen," Solomon insisted.

Afi pressed play on the phone.

Suddenly, an audio recording of laughter filled the room, and in the background, the swishing sounds of water.

"Yeah, man," an all-too familiar voice said, "I'm going to have this damn girl eating out of the palm of my hand. Once I put this thing on her, gas her up a little, take her for a couple rounds in the rain. Beat up on the cat real good, all her shit will be mine. Then I'll have her money on top of mine too."

Another voice spoke in the recording. "But she's, like, a heart surgeon. That's pretty badass. Aren't you curious on whether it could actually work? She might make an honest man out of you." This voice seemed familiar, as if Adella had met the person before but did not know him well.

"Hell, I never wanted to get married. That's some bullshit. She ought to be glad to pay me to marry her. She can't pay me enough. My mom is paying their bills and keeping their lights on. And what do I get? A supertanker. But don't you worry, I'm getting mine on the backend. Literally."

The two men's ricocheted between Adella's ears.

"Dude, you are a trip. What the hell is a supertanker?"

"It's those big-ass vessels that Aristotle Onassis built for carrying lots of oil. It's what he called Jackie Onassis behind her back because she cost so much money for him to buy. She cost more than one of his supertankers."

Maddy's eyes nearly popped from her head. "That's enough!"

Afi let the recording continue.

"And that's exactly what this chick is. My family is buying a supertanker and I'm stuck with it."

"Shut it off!" Maddy demanded.

"So you see," Solomon said, leaning toward Adella once more, "all is not so perfect in paradise. He is waiting for the best moment to play you and turn you against your family, so you'll walk in here and declare us your opponents. You are in no position to school us on Manuel's interests. And you need to stand down and let me run Manuel Realty."

Adella sat back, not allowing one tear to fall. She would not give them the satisfaction.

"Del, we love you," her mother said. "You are a very smart girl, but you've never been able to fully see after yourself when it comes to dealing in the real world. Let Solomon handle the family affairs, and you just focus on your career. You need to keep an eye out on Desmond's family that you just married into, and report back to us what you learn. We'll all make the necessary decisions for Daddy's company. It shouldn't all rest on you."

Hot devastation rolled through Adella. "Woman."

Confusion crossed her mother's face. "Excuse me?"

"I'm a very smart *woman.*"

Her mother's fixed smile spread across her but didn't eliminate the disagreement in her eyes.

As always, Adella shifted her focus away from her mother's loaded face that said nothing and spoke volumes at the same time. Rather than be sucked into paralyzing questions of what her mother thought, Del would have to keep reminding herself that her mother's doubts of her capabilities no longer mattered. Adella had proven herself too many times to count at this point. So she cast a side-eye at Ilyana.

Ilyana's face flinched. "I'm sorry, Adella."

"You knew about this?"

Her little sister shifted in her seat. "They told me it was best if we waited to verify the information first. That's what you said, right?" She waited for an approving nod from Solomon.

"When was this recording?" Maddy asked.

A self-satisfied Afi answered, "March twenty-fourth."

Constance added, "The night before your wedding. A few minutes after you saved his mother's cousin's life."

Her mother rose and shooed them all out. "Maddy is correct. That is enough now. Everyone, give Adella some time." Once the others filtered out of the room, her mother then turned to her. "I told you not to let your guard down. The world is a terrible place, filled with users. That's why I always taught you to keep your nose in your books. You did not listen."

An ambushed Adella struggled to breathe and keep her composure.

Her mother closed the distance between them, at least physically anyway, and placed her hands on Adella's shoulders, a paltry attempt at a connection. "I always told you to stay ahead of the game. And instead, you allow yourself to get played." Mrs. English grabbed her purse and headed toward the door. "Call me so we can discuss your turning my father's personal items over to his children. And quickly."

THE BEST OF MY LIFE

DESMOND

*D*esmond wasn't screwing it up tonight. Dinner was going to be perfect, because he'd ordered it. Steak, lobster, and the entire spread. More wedding candles from their gifts completed an elaborate layout along with the dining room table. Marvin Gaye played over the intercom. He'd ordered every color of rose in the flower shop so the house resembled the fields of flowers where she'd taken him on their first day out. Last but not least, *The Notebook* was cued up for a movie if she wanted. Or if they made it that far.

He knew she'd spend an afternoon with Maddy having a girls' day, so most likely, she would come home smelling and looking good. He had done his part and freshened up himself.

Finally, a car pulled into the front yard, which was strange because she normally parked in the garage. But he didn't hear the car door slam. Instead, the headlights remained on as they flooded the dining room and washed him in extreme brightness.

Had she shut off her car? What was wrong? He went to meet her at the door. On the other side of it, her sandals clacked over the porch in a rush up the steps.

"Out!"

He'd barely opened the door.

"What?" Stunned, Desmond instinctively reached out to calm her, but she slapped his arm off.

"You heard me! Get out of my house!" Not only did Adella's voice tremble, but it seemed her entire existence shook out those words.

Maddy marched right behind her.

"Adella, talk to me."

"No need," Maddy responded as Adella hurried up the stairs. She pulled out a phone. Her finger hit "play."

"A goddamn supertanker. That's what I'm stuck with. She ought to be paying me for marrying her. Not the other way around."

Desmond's fist flew in his mouth. Scott Gooden. He had only had that conversation with one person, the night before his wedding.

"Adella!" he called, racing up the stairs, taking three at a time. "That was before I knew you. That's not fair!"

"What's not fair is having somebody in my house, in my *home*… in *me*…pretending he loves me when I'm only a mark to him!"

"It was two months ago."

"When you were making all these offers for us to be friends, get to know each other, go on walks, try and endure this together. But this whole time, you were running a game where you would make me the fool." She tossed his things in a trash bag. "I'll have someone come and get the rest. Or you can do it while I'm at work. As long as you are out of here, completely, by the end of the week."

Desmond stood in front of her because he wasn't above begging now. "Don't do this. I love you."

"Do not ever say that to me again."

"Baby—"

"Do not call me that."

"Adella, these last few weeks I've had with you have been the best of my life. I was dumb and said some things that night I should not have. You were a stranger to me."

The sadness that she tried to mask with anger ignited fireworks in his heart chamber.

"And what about your mother sleeping with my grandfather?"

All the bottle rockets, Roman candles, and comets could not start a larger fire in his brain than those words.

"What?"

"You're going to tell me you didn't know? I asked you straight up if you'd met my grandfather, and you said no, but you have."

"N-no, I did not!" His mind raced to think of something, anything. But it was kind of hard when hit with the failure of his parents' marriage, one of the biggest catastrophes of his life. When had he met Adella's grandfather? How?

"So now you're going to play dumb," she huffed, dragging his things down the stairs. "And tell me. What was I to you on Friday night? When your lawyers moved on my company after business hours? They filed papers in court demanding to see all our books. And waited until late in the evening so we couldn't do anything until Monday. Or when your lawyers moved against my stock, to freeze my holdings so I cannot control them? You said you wouldn't touch it."

This new information she spouted off was news to him.

"I-I don't know. I have no idea."

When he tried to touch her shoulder, she jerked away as if he were leprous.

"Of course you don't. Because you think I'm dumb enough to believe you. Because all I am is a piece of dull-brained metal, a *supertanker*. And nothing more."

The heart attack on her face shut down the flow of blood inside him.

She continued, "But I'm impressed. You knew what a supertanker was. And you knew who Aristotle Onassis was. So you're not the dumb jock you pretend to be."

Struggling to see through the sandstorm of Del's wrath, he fought not to choke, and tried to find his voice. "Baby, you don't mean that."

Inches away from him, her furious sand winds kept blinding him. "*Baby*," Adella repeated mockingly. "Believe me when I say I mean every word. Especially the part where I tell you to get the fuck out."

Maddy opened the door.

The headlights from Adella's car still washed out their faces from streaming so bright.

All her surgical tools could not have sliced him into nearly as many pieces as the despair on her face.

He knew another word from him would do nothing. In his bare feet, Desmond grabbed his keys and walked to his truck. It was stunning how he'd played against some of the toughest defensive linemen in the NFL, and none of those plays had pummeled him like pulling away from her, away from the house he had finally come to view as home.

THE NEXT MORNING, he sat in his mother's company, where he had not visited in two and a half months. He would start with Scott Gooden.

"D! My man!" Scott called as he entered his office. He leaned his head out the door into the main office of cubicles. "Look, everybody, you see who's here? It's D! He's back from the land of milk and honey!" Scott whipped around, his arms open wide. "You finally sick of slumming it in The Hamptons and Cape Cod, decided to come back and schlep around with us commoners?"

Desmond's family and friends did not know he had arrived. He hadn't bothered going to a hotel the night before. Instead, he had driven straight to the airport and caught a flight to his hometown.

"Sit down, man."

Scott took one look at Desmond. And backed away. He remained standing.

"What's up, dude. Y-you okay? Do I need to call Keenan to come and help you out with something?"

While assessing the situation, Desmond rolled his hands over one another. "Who came to you?"

"What?" Scott's face wrinkled up as if he'd been struck by a termination notice.

"I asked who came to you, and offered you money to set me up?"

Before Scott could open his mouth to lie, Desmond found the realization in his eyes.

"No, no, man. That never happened."

"I already inspected the payroll books from March and April. And I see that you received a special bonus of double your regular check. Two months in a row—once in March and again in April. No one else got that, man. So I'll ask you again." He stared at Scott hard, one of the few people on Earth he had actually considered a friend. "Which one of my siblings came to you?"

Scott's jaw muscles rippled, his Adam's apple traveling up and down his throat. Desmond waited, watching the internal debate his co-worker was having with himself.

"Chaitra."

Desmond stood.

"D, look, man—"

"Don't gas me, dude. I expected better from you."

Within two minutes he was sitting inside Chaitra's office.

"Why did you do that? How trifling are you? I haven't been here. Nowhere around. You have this place all to yourself. So why?"

"You need to be reminded of what you're doing there in the first place—making good on our deal. Mom hasn't been paying attention, but I have. You and that chick have spent too much time over there being quiet, you're not talking to anybody, and she's been avoiding us. None of our officers or auditors have been inside Manuel, and we haven't been able to inspect their properties. You're not holding her accountable, and that hurts McLain."

"Adella didn't deserve that. She's never done anything to you. She saved Furonda's life."

His sister's arms folded across her chest. "And we are saving her grandfather's company. Quid pro quo. You seem to be confused, though. So I sent you a little reminder."

Desmond clenched his jaw. "Buy me out. Buy all my shares, and you can have them, and then I'll be done with this."

Chaitra scoffed. "*Or,* you could just give them to me. You don't care about this company."

He leaned forward in his seat, confronting her from the opposite side of the desk. "But since I'm so money-hungry, like you say I am, *pay* me."

Chaitra snickered. "Oh, isn't this cute? Chick's got your nose wide open and you can't even see straight."

"And that bothers you, doesn't it? That I'm not down in the mailroom, drinking and smoking, so you know exactly where I am and what I'm doing at all times. That way, I'm not a threat to you." Desmond sucked his teeth. "Yeah. Don't think for a moment that I never knew. You love me especially when I'm in your shadow." He stood. "And you wanted to fuck with Adella, because you know with her at my side, I'm not some dried up jock anymore. You're actually worried now."

Next up was his mother's office.

"I heard you were in the building. They told me you had a glow about you, but I didn't believe it." His mother smiled. "Well, I'll be damned. I wonder if somebody sitting in this office was right."

He couldn't fake the chitchat. That's not where his head was. "You served Adella's lawyers with papers freezing her stock options. Those are my rights to her stock, and you didn't talk to me about it."

"Damn right I didn't. Adella isn't dumb. She knows what time it is, that eventually, she will have to deal with me. Manuel can't keep delaying forever."

"You should've discussed it with me first. She's your daughter-in-law now."

"Then maybe I could have tea with my daughter-in-law. Dinner with my daughter-in-law. Maybe go out for a brunch or something with my daughter-in-law. But you've had her hemmed up since she left that night and you went chasing after her. So I don't know, you tell me."

A pissed-off Desmond scoffed before mimicking her. "Well, I don't know, *maybe* if we hadn't been pressured to marry, we wouldn't be using all this time to learn each other's names."

"I'm glad you're back. I've heard you're taking classes, starting to move the needle with your life."

He prepared himself for his next words. "I want out. I'm going to start my own life somewhere else."

A snicker escaped through her ruby lipstick,and she stared out of the high-rise overlooking the city in which she'd come up. "Doing what?"

"I don't know, but not this. Chaitra and Keenan can have this."

Her attention shifted from the city streets she'd survived to one of her children she'd survived. "Boy, shut your fool mouth."

"I've made up my mind."

"You don't have a mind to make up." Margaret McLain's long eyelashes tightened together. "For the last five years you've been getting drunk downstairs. You're only now beginning to understand who you are or what you want. I will not let you walk away from a secure thing to go and screw off in the world with no plan."

"It's not your choice to make. I'm hiring my own lawyers, and they will be in touch to work things out."

His mother threw all her attitude into a wave of her hand between them. "This is *my* company. You need new lawyers to help you work out what…concerning my company?"

"This whole inheritance situation."

"Do you even know why you're married to her right now?"

Desmond shot a bullet of his own at her.

"You were fucking Adella's grandfather or something like that? Yeah. I know about it."

His mother's arm struck faster than lightning. Margaret McLain slapped her son so hard he had to blink several times to get his vision straight again.

"Not that it is any of your goddamn business," she muttered through curled lips, "but we never fooled around. French Manuel was a kind, good man. He treated me with respect when other men in this industry talked to me the way *you* just did."

His mother's body shook until she appeared to be having a standing seizure.

"French had *nothing* to do with mine and your daddy's problems. Your daddy and I were scraping to get by. I wanted to leave the hood, but with three young kids, I thought my life was over."

Her voice began breaking as if it stumbled and bled on broken glass.

"I was working my ass off from one temp job to the next. I spent a month temping at one of French's holding companies. While he was in town, he saw my work ethic and took me under his wing. He made some phone calls, helped me find a permanent position at a construction company, with a decent salary and benefits. For the next few years, I worked my way up, and when I had questions or issues, French took my calls. Back then, practically the only women in the construction game were secretaries and cleaning ladies. The two or three female executives I met were catty."

He'd never heard about her career climb, but had only felt her absence in the many nights of canned ravioli that he, Chaitra and

Keenan grew accustomed to living on in the evenings. She'd never shared why days would pass that Desmond and his siblings saw her laundry list of after-school chores more than they saw her. Now, his mother's story trickled through the rocky cliffs of her eyes.

"So French made time to meet me when he flew through town to check on his properties. He'd help me figure things out. How to deal with assholes at the office and such. But of course, jealous-ass people saw me on the come-up. That's how rumors started, and your daddy believed them."

Desmond's insides shrank at the sight of yet another woman he loved hurting in front of him.

"When you were a little boy playing football in the park, French would watch you play while he waited for me to get off work." As she spoke, her eyes watered. "He would buy candy for all you kids and order pizza for the entire block."

"Whoa. That nice old guy we all saw sometimes?"

She nodded. "Yes. That nice old guy. And then later on, you met him again when you were in college. You'd had a bad game and you were in a mood. French was with me, because he'd been wanting to see you in action. After the game, you said out loud, 'I don't think I belong here.'"

The memory played in Desmond's mind. "I kind of recall that."

"Do you remember what he said to you?"

Desmond rubbed his chin, thinking back to that game where he'd performed well but suspected his coach was only putting his favorite boys on the field. He'd started out strong in the first half, with three offensive tackles, but his plays slid when the coach didn't reward him with more time. Instead, the stingy old man positioned another lineman for the better plays, and it was a hit to Desmond's focus. He knew that day he should not have chosen Norfolk State, but University of Maryland.

His heart still hurt just thinking about it. "Yeah. I'll never forget that day. But what he said confused me. I had to take a minute and think on what he meant. It was something like, 'Well, if you don't belong out there, then none of those sorry suckers do.'"

"That was Adella's grandfather. He appreciated that you had heart. You never got cocky or considered yourself bigger than the game. He saw how well you got along with your teammates and how you protected other people on the field. French said, 'I hope my Del winds up with somebody like your boy.' But, Dezzy, your heart was also your weakness."

Crossing her arms, Mrs. McLain sat back on her desk.

"You were always bending over backward for your friends. You did all the work, they got all the glory. Desmond, it's no accident that French reached out to me when his company was in trouble. French helped me in my time of need, and he knew I would help him in his. He spoiled his kids rotten, and in his later years, as he got older, they bled him dry. Now they're mad because they don't get to sell off his company and pocket the change. They're taking it out on me, and on that poor girl."

"Well, Ma, if you're helping, why all the sneak moves with your lawyers?"

"If I don't move, there won't be a company to save. And as your mother, I still must protect my child's interests. I have no clue what her family is planning for us. I realize they don't like what's happening here. They never agreed to it. But I'm only doing my due diligence. That's why my lawyers served hers. Out of respect for French, I still plan to help his company. I am not going to take it down. If anything, I'm hoping we can make it stronger. So yours and Adella's children will have both my wealth and French's. And as for you, I'm happy she's motivating you to finally get your life back on track. But you are not making any stupid decisions here today."

She handed him a sealed envelope.

Desmond took it and read the sender's name on the front: Francis Manuel.

"Why am I just now getting this?"

"He told me to wait until you were ready to quit," his mother replied, going through the mail on her desk.

Desmond opened up the letter that was short.

So, young man, you're my grandson-in-law now.

I know my family can be rough.

Survival of the fittest is how I raised them.

But if you don't belong in the Manuel bunch, none of those sorry suckers do.

Take care of my sweet girl.

— FRENCH

Desmond sat astounded. Adella's grandfather had chosen him to be her husband.

"Now that you have reentered civil society, you've got a week to bring that damn girl in my office, because I'm tired of playin' with y'alls little young asses. Now get out."

Desmond scratched his head, a scheming smile rising on his face.

His mother's suspicious eyebrows lifted. "Uh-uh. No. Whatever just popped into your head, no."

"Come on, Ma. I just have one thing I need. If you want me to get her here, then please, help me out."

SEPARATION

ADELLA

*A*della couldn't believe how much she missed him. Every time she dragged from one patient appointment to the next, she hauled the Boston Harbor with her.

Forcing herself out of bed. Ignoring his phone calls. Rejecting the flowers he had sent to her home and to her job. She had donated them to cancer patients, the children's ward, the pregnant mothers experiencing childbirth alone, and then sent other bouquets out to domestic violence shelters around the city.

Maddy found her a publicist to arrange interviews with national television media, requests she had ignored during hers and Desmond's time together and after her breakup with Wes, after her wedding. Since the boating incident on her wedding weekend, so many opportunities had poured in that she had ignored, including requests that she join various boards of directors around the country and receive an award from her alma mater of MIT.

But when she came home from the meetings, media, and fixing people's hearts, she carried the one broken thing she could not heal—her own.

He had seemed so sincere, so genuine.

Maddy called her with news by the end of the week. "You can have the marriage annulled. And you won't have to worry about giving up your inheritance."

"What?" Adella asked.

"Yes. You can keep your grandfather's holdings, still be in compliance with the stipulations of his will, and annul your marriage to Desmond. There is an old, little known court case that says it's illegal to set a condition so narrow that you are confining the person's freedom, and on that ground, you can seek to have that condition of the distribution nullified."

Her childhood friend had come through for her and provided her with an escape valve.

That was Maddy, always on top of everything, always sniffing out a workaround.

But how would it affect Adella's family? They would feel like she'd cheated, that she maneuvered her way out of doing as her grandfather asked, and still escaped with the family money. They would never forgive her.

"But you know it won't be that easy with everyone else in my household. They'll take me to court and use that as a basis for why I should give back the inheritance." Adella fretted.

"But it is an option."

"Or I can just stay married to him so I can keep looking after Papa's holdings."

Maddy shook her head as if she hurt for Adella. "Don't torture yourself. Not for some guy who talked about you that way."

Adella was torn, her heart feeling like it was divided and thrown in opposite places. "Maybe Solomon is right. He can take over and I wouldn't be stuck with the family burden."

"But that is clearly not what Mr. Manuel thought was best." Maddy tried to think up a solution alongside her friend. "He felt like the company was falling short, and you were the only person who could be trusted to know what to do. He said as much. In writing."

In that case, Adella knew her options were limited as far as what she did with Desmond, because if she sought divorce, her family would weaponize it against her.

She would agree to a separation contract. Technically, they would not divorce. They could still use IVF to have children, and that way, he could receive more of his inheritance, and she could receive more voting power in her grandfather's real estate company. It seemed a perfect solution, and they would not have to live together. He would have no right to the use of her home, to share accounts, or to breathe the same air.

But God, how she missed breathing the same air.

When she turned over on her mattress, the nerves criss-crossing her whole being expected the warmth radiating off his body heat, the tiny snores escaping his mouth, and the puffs of his breath tingling her flesh.

Walking in the door, out of habit now, she waited for, "Is that you, Mrs. McLain?" She craved the little blip in her blood flow when his voice dipped to say their last name.

Now, at 3:00 a.m., she lay on her back, unable to sleep, very much alone and yet every part of her filled with her husband.

A CHILDISH, FOOLISH ME

DESMOND

esmond swayed as the legal process server walked away.

After opening the separation papers Adella had just served on him, he almost dropped them once his hands fell limp, followed by his body that slumped against the doorframe.

An hour later, he was a robot operating on battery power as he spoke with his own lawyer, who then spoke with Adella's lawyer. They would meet in the next few days in Boston to work out details of a legal separation. Desmond had requested that they meet in person, and though Adella asked that it happen via phone call, he objected and concocted excuses for why it should be face to face.

Every moment throughout those eight days was torture. Every breath that dragged through his trachea and into his air sacs was an act of labor.

She had refused every one of his gifts, phone calls, and text messages, and finally, his wife blocked his number. Crickets were her response to his emails begging her to just give him thirty seconds.

Now every time Desmond passed a hospital, any hospital, he

thought of her—what her schedule for the day was like, how many lives she had saved, if she was eating healthy, drinking too much. Or if she was eating at all.

From his brother, Keenan's, couch, he watched her news interviews that she gave after the videos of her saving a life on the boat had gone viral.

The world was incensed at the reports of how she'd been treated on their wedding cruise by the boat crew. Many people were asking the question, "Would they have demanded to see her medical license if she were white?"

His baby looked beautiful on television, poised with her natural hair blown out into swinging curls. A lovely peach, springtime dress draped her gentle, curving shoulders in a scooped boat neck that showed her graceful collarbone. Lush, soft and ample, Adella was luxurious. He couldn't think of her underneath hm without his mouth watering. Then, there was the joy he got from watching her startled innocence leap through her eyes.

"Why are you moping around here with us? You're getting on my nerves with that pathetic vibe you're giving," Keenan complained on their way to work that morning.

"I've tried calling her. She's not having it," Desmond reported.

"She's not having what? You? Or the lazy-ass way you've handled this so far?" his brother challenged him.

Desmond thought about that question. "What do you mean lazy?"

"I mean, what is this really about? Have you asked yourself that?"

"Stop playing. I know what's up. She didn't like my attitude and how I talked shit about her the night before we got married."

"You remember when Mom and Dad separated?" Keenan recalled. "And Dad was so wrapped up in his damn pride that he could not go to her and say what was really bothering him? Instead of admitting he was jealous of her success, he got caught up with a bunch of other shit, about her cheating and hanging out with her boss too much, not paying enough attention to the house and all that. When really, he could have just said he was tripping on his woman bringing home more money than him."

Desmond's shoulders slouched further. He ached to hear it retold.

Their parents' breakup had hit him hard at age thirteen. His dad may have only been a barber, but back then, his dad was his world, a god-like figure in his eyes.

Keenan continued, "He was lazy. Pop let Mom go, instead of manning up and copping to his own immaturity. Now is that you? That's what I'm asking. Is this really about you talking shit on the boat? Or is this about you approaching the whole marriage situation like a boy instead of a man? You thought of her as a cash cow, referred to her like an inanimate object, instead of the woman who was to be your wife. You had a bias toward her, and people like her, who grew up with money that we didn't have. You objectified her. And you projected your own stereotypes and shortcomings on her in that conversation. Now she doesn't trust you."

"Well, damn," Desmond muttered to his little brother. The young buck was maturing and growing up.

Later that day, Desmond called Jerrell.

"I heard what happened."

Desmond's head practically lived in the palm of his hand these days. "The only way I can reach Adella is through Maddy."

"You are correct. But you do know that your credit card with her is about to be maxed out, right? You can't keep calling us every time you blow it with Adella."

"It'll never happen again. This is the last time. J, nothing new has happened since our vows. It's been perfect. Just this one thing came up, some old shit. And I need Del to know that. It's old shit. Completely."

Jerrell agreed for Desmond to come to The Hamptons where

everyone could meet for breakfast that Saturday morning. But Desmond flew in early that Friday night, so Jerrell could do him a favor at *Sharon's*.

The moment Jerrell brought Maddy into the restaurant, and she laid eyes on Desmond, she immediately pivoted, storming back out. Her stomach was noticeably big. The last time he'd seen her, she was kicking him out of his home and he'd been so distracted he clearly hadn't noticed she was pregnant. Adella hadn't breathed a word. Christ, these rich folks sure were good at protecting each other.

"Maddy!" Desmond called. "Just hear me out. I'm sorry!"

She strutted right out the door and down the sidewalk.

Desperate as if he were fighting for his life, he took off after her. "I screwed up when I messed with your co-worker, Lana. And I deeply, *deeply* regret that now. I didn't regret it at the time, but I sure as hell do now."

Maddy's legs slowed down. Desmond rushed to approach her, and when he looked to Jerrell for an assist, Jerrell backed up.

"I brought her here. Now you're on your own."

Maddy glared at her man. "Why didn't you tell me about this? You should not have kept this from me."

"Bae," Jerrell said, throwing up his hands, "because I knew you wouldn't come. Hear what the man has to say. If you're not satisfied, I won't say a word. But we're talking about a marriage here, and your girl's happiness. You said yourself that Del was happy."

Maddy rolled her eyes, eviscerating Desmond with them. "You're just now feeling bad about screwing my co-worker while you were engaged to my childhood friend?"

"No, I'm not *just now* feeling bad." Desmond placed a hand on his chest, where these new emotions of tenderness and loyalty were truly changing him. "But I did not feel bad at the time. No. I hated you all. I hated the situation. I tried to sabotage it, and I was honest with you about that a few months ago. I'm honest about it now. But I have learned things. Adella has shown me a lot about humanity between then and now. I need her." He swallowed and took a moment to check in with himself, before he spoke words he could never take back. "I cannot live without her. She's everything to me."

He paused, letting the ocean's breeze cool his forehead and underarms that perspired under the weight of Maddy's stare.

"I was being stupid that night on the boat, acting like the football player who talks real big and sometimes gets caught up in bro talk. Locker room shit-talk. Saying things when we don't really mean them. But the truth is, I would not have married Adella for any amount of money if I wasn't feeling her already. I saw her sweetness the moment we met, her class, how phenomenal she was, how much bigger than me she was. It terrified me and intrigued me. I did not know what to do with that. Especially when I saw she loved somebody else already and that there may not be space for me in her world. What you heard was a childish, foolish me. It was not the man you see standing in front of you...." His voice trembled. "Who loves Adella more than I can put into words."

Maddy's eyes cut from Desmond to Jerrell, who threw up his hands in a mea culpa. They slid back to Desmond.

"I don't know if she'll take you back. She's hurting right now. And besides, Adella has her own mind. She doesn't just listen to me and repeat everything I do or say like she's some kind of bird."

"I know. But she and all the other women do look up to you like you're the Statue of Liberty and shit," Desmond replied before he and Jerrell broke into chuckles.

"True," Jerrell muttered, using the moment to silently chastise Steely Maddy.

Maddy squinted. "What's that supposed to mean?"

"It's a good thing. You empower people," Desmond responded to reassure her. "You're like Angela Davis for the rich Black folks. Fighting for your right to be rich and Black without judgment. I can dig it. I should not have been flirting with your co-worker in your own backyard while engaged to your good friend, your sister, my wife. And if you help me, I swear I will spend the rest of my life making it up to both of you."

Maddy leaned toward him, jabbing his chest with her finger. "If I stick my neck out for you, when I should be supporting my girl, it means that if you screw up again, I will jack you up in every way I possibly can. Legally, socially, financially, anally…"

Desmond laughed, relieved and happy that she was willing to help, even though he had no clue if it would work. He threw his arms out to hug her, and she accepted it.

"I apologize, Maddy. You are one of the few people on the planet whose respect I actually want to work hard for."

"I'd better be. Adella had better be."

With this new energy, he could hardly stand still. "She is."

PRICELESS

ADELLA

Adella arrived at the amusement park, and confused, she turned to Maddy. "I thought we were going to get our nails done?"

Her friend remained silent behind the steering wheel, and only stared ahead, where Adella found her answer.

Several yards away, near the entrance, out walked a figure.

It was Desmond.

"No."

"Adella…"

"I'm done, Maddy. I wish you would have asked me before you brought me here. You were the last person I expected to sneak behind my back."

"Adella, I'm the first person who wants your happiness." Maddy gazed at Adella with warmth in her eyes.

"He's not it." All of their mornings together, many of their nights, his voice in her ear, hands all over her, memories with which she'd tossed and turned for the past two weeks, rolled through her. The nuclear reactors of her emotions clashed until she could not see past her anger.

"I don't think you're being honest with yourself, Del. I've

always had your back and kept it real with you, always in your interests. Always lifting you up. You know I would never recommend you take a step that I think would hurt you. It's why I was so devastated that I was starting to trust Desmond and then we heard the audio."

Del's anger might have been hot enough to produce fire. "Exactly. So why are we here again? Why are we not learning from our mistakes?" Adella fought the urge to turn on Maddy's ignition and switch the gears for her so they could go. Even if it meant Adella's heart would be trailing the back bumper while they drove.

"Because this is a growth process, Del. It's not a mistake. You never told us about Wes. And I'm not here to second-guess if what you felt for him was love. I know you and I haven't talked too much in years before December. But still, if you were getting ready to *marry* Wes, you would have called me about that. And I'm wondering if you didn't call about Wes because you weren't quite sure about him yourself."

At that, Adella shuddered.

Her husband must have felt her quaking from forty yards away, because he lifted his head from staring at the ground to peer at her.

Maddy continued, "Before that meeting with your family, before Afi played that recording, I know what I saw in you. I have *never* seen you look like that. I've never seen you glow the way you've glowed these last two months."

Silence filled the car, but the noise of confusion filled Adella. It clanged from her pumping heart, through her pulsating blood vessels, and into her eardrums.

Ahead, an anxious Desmond shifted from foot to foot.

Her friend didn't let up. "You're a grown woman. You make your own choices. We chart our own paths. But that man right there is not the man I met five months ago. Far from him. And you, Adella English McLain, are not the woman you were six months ago. You have found your voice, and stepped into your-self. Some of your growth might be due to him, but a lot of it is you. Once you finally pulled away from your family that treats you like you are permanently ill and weak. And these changes could be wonderfully good for both of you. But don't take it from me. Check in with your own evolution."

In the heavyweight boxing ring of her rib cage, Adella's fear clashed with her hope.

She opened the door and got out, placing one shaky foot in front of the other. She arrived to stand before a husband who looked as terrified as she.

His gaze met her as one would meet the rainbow.

"Five minutes," she said.

"I don't even need that. I was wrong. You are right not to trust me. When we first got together, I had every intention of scheming on you."

"Talk about how you said seeing me operate on the boat changed you. But those statements you made in that recording were *minutes* after I saved your cousin's life. You said all those awful things right after the moment that supposedly changed you. So you weren't really changed. You lied."

He nodded.

"I was putting on a front for a guy I worked with. What you did was the most impressive thing I've ever seen. But I couldn't be man enough to say it to Scott after I'd been complaining about marrying you for so long. I couldn't tell him that I was already starting to fall in love with you. Not after I had spent years being the life of the party, Mr. I'm-Rebelling-Against-My-Mother. I was the guy they all wanted to be. But I was a man still acting like a child. Adella, you married a boy that day. Who wanted to be a man and was trying to figure out, very quickly, how I could get on your level. *That's* what was recorded—a terri-fied boy trying to adjust to somebody who is definitely a woman."

His chest heaved up and down, and nervous breaths floated from his lips at a fast clip that brushed her face and skin.

"Adella, baby, I wanted you, but you were so much more than me. You started growing me from the moment I laid eyes on you. When my mother's company lawyer moved on your lawyer, I had no idea that that happened. I have now spoken to her about that. I'm getting my own lawyer and my own accountants."

Adella's mind slashed his thicket of charming words and promises. "And your team will simply work with her. It'll always be your people against mine."

He wrangled something out of his pocket and handed her envelopes. "No, it won't."

"What is this?" she asked.

"Open them." His eyes pleaded with hers.

First, she pulled out a check. For $1.5 million.

"That's my inheritance I got for marrying you. You can have it."

Her hands shook as she stared at the zeroes in her fingers, made out to her.

The next envelope included a renouncement of his rights to her stock options and shares that his mother's lawyers had negotiated with her grandfather's lawyers. "I don't want it. You keep all your stock options, shares, voting rights, everything," he said.

Then, from the final envelope, she removed another document voiding out the part of his mother's will that bequeathed to him one million dollars for each child they had.

"I'm not saying you'll take me back, but if you do, and we have children, I receive nothing. I don't want anything, Adella, I don't need anything. Just you. In my life, in my arms, in my heart."

Her disbelief rocked her. He had transferred to her everything he had wanted. "You would give all this up for me?"

His gaze penetrated hers, and they didn't waver. "Yes."

"You called me a supertanker."

"I like supertankers." He smiled. "Have you ever ridden on

one? They're powerful, pretty badass actually, unsinkable. Just like you."

She chuckled.

"Adella, my mom reminded me that I have met your grandfather. I had no idea that French… It was your grandfather. I didn't know the nice guy who did stuff for all the kids in our neighborhood was your grandfather, or that he had come to see me play in school. We had a conversation, and he encouraged me."

Adella had almost forgotten that part. "He and your mother did a lot more than that, Desmond."

"No, they didn't. I talked to her, and the rumors were blown way up. It was only gossip, which your family's lawyers heard on the streets of Baltimore. My mother was very emphatic, they're not true." He touched his cheek she'd smacked. "Trust me, my head is still spinning from her knocking the hell out of me when I brought it up."

Adella's jaw fell, and her eyes widened as she covered his hand with hers over his cheek.

"He knew my mother, helped her as a young secretary starting out in construction. He had been following me since I was a boy."

Desmond handed Adella the short note.

She still couldn't believe what she was learning. Her grandfather had chosen her husband years—decades—before his death.

"Del, this is not what you think. Your granddad helped my mom to come up back in the day, and now my mother wants to repay the favor. She really does, Adella. But your family doesn't agree with his decision, and so naturally, she is using her attorneys to protect the agreement she and your grandfather made. That's where she's coming from. I think the two of you do need to talk."

He slid his arm around her waist, and Del's hips immediately welcomed his easy touch. Her gaze slipped onto the merry-go-round of his dancing irises while he squeezed her.

"Whatever you decide, I don't have to be involved. Not if it means I'll lose you. Your trust is more important to me. Your happiness… our marriage is most important to me."

But astonishment struck Adella as Desmond's body lowered.

Feeling him take her hand, gazing at an ocean of love in his eyes, she marveled. He had dropped down to one knee.

"Adella, baby," he said, trembling, "will you marry me? Again? Not for my family. Not for yours. But for us. For better or worse. 'Til death do us part. Companies or no companies. Whether we're rich or broke, I just want to feed you ice cream and make you bad dinners. But hopefully, they'll taste okay sometimes. So I'm asking just you… to marry just me, Desmond."

He opened a ring box, and when Adella saw its center, she almost had a heart attack—it was a red diamond.

"For real this time."

The most expensive and rarest of all colored diamonds, including pink and blue, the red rocks usually cost between one and two million dollars per carat. They were worth fifty times more than white diamonds.

All the oxygen swept right out of her collapsed lungs. She might have floated outside her body because she could no longer feel any of her own vital signs. "This is rare."

He smiled. "So is the woman who'll hopefully wear it. And everywhere you go, the world should know how priceless you are. You're worth every penny, and more. Adella, I'm so sorry for hurting you."

"How did you get this?"

"I pulled some things together. Sold a few investments." Light from the sky reflected in his eyes. Or it might have been his joy at putting the shock on her face. "Plus, my mom also likes super-tankers."

Through her tears, Adella burst into chuckles. "Does she now?"

Desmond sucked his bottom lip. "So what'll it be, Doc? Will

you have a man who's trying to be your man? Without cutting me up?"

The ocean overflowed from inside her. "Yes."

He stood and drew her to him, and Adella did not hesitate to receive all his passion she'd been missing the last two weeks.

Suddenly, clapping and applause surrounded them. Two of her siblings, Ilyana and Martin, as well as her mother and his family, joined them. And Maddy and Jerrell.

Adella handed Desmond his documents back. "Here. I'm not taking these."

"But you can. It's yours. You need to know how serious I am," he insisted.

She shoved them into his chest. "And I do. But I don't do broke men."

He laughed. "I'm not broke. I've still got a few assets, but I won't argue with you." He took the documents, kissing her.

Adella relished the warmth of his fluffy lips on hers again.

"And the way we build generational wealth is not by taking from each other," she added.

"Thank you, Adella," an annoyed Jerrell commented, his hands in his pockets as he rolled his eyes. "I tried to tell his ass when he was sitting in my brother's office talking crazy."

Maddy turned to him, her eyes needling him. "You wouldn't do that for me?"

All eyes in the group pinpointed Jerrell.

He took a deep breath. "Yes, babe, I absolutely would."

The group clapped.

"Good save, fam, good save," Adella giggled, feeling Desmond's arms around her.

Minutes later, she screamed as she rode every thrill ride in the amusement park. Twice.

But her loudest screams she saved for the best ride, which she straddled endlessly when she got home.

THE MRS. MCLAINS

ADELLA

Desmond comforted a nervous Adella in bed two weeks later.

They were spending a few days in her family's Hamptons home. She and Desmond had driven down a couple of days early to prepare the house.

"You don't have any reason to be nervous," he said, unable to stop tee-heeing. "She only bites when you insult her."

Nestling in his arms, Adella laughed. "It's not funny. She's your mother. That's reason enough."

"And you're the famous Ivy League doctor who saved her cousin's life, one of the brightest women we know. You're so smart that you're *rejecting* a job as a television show host," he said, biting her arm. He rattled off her new accomplishments while nibbling different parts of her. "Medical correspondent for a national news syndicate." He nipped at her back. "And soon-to-be author. Not to mention, you're my *wife*. The woman who tied me up. That would have been impossible six months ago. Trust me, she's nervous about meeting the point guard who scored that game-winning buzzer-beater."

Adella could not help the giddiness in the middle of her chest. She sat up, turning to him, her fingers searching his face. "But what will my husband do while his wife is making big-girl moves?"

He grinned at her. "Is that your way of hinting that I need to pick up a job?"

Del stroked his face. "It's my way of checking in on your happiness. And your peace of mind."

She'd read the statistics on injuries to football players and the emotional and mental trauma that came later as a result, as well as the listlessness and displacement once they put the ball down for good. Del wanted him to have the support system to ensure he thrived. She was especially concerned about them being stable in their infant relationship before they started a family.

He kissed her palm. "I get it. Yes, Jerrell and I have been talking. He's introducing me around. Honestly, baby, I respect how that dude broke away from his family's hustle and started his own thing. So I'm touring some breweries and looking into a black-owned beer operation."

Del held her jaw up. "Really?"

He nodded, blessing her with a joyous smile of his own. "It sounds fun, something I can throw myself into, and invest in. If I handle it well, it could add to our businesses. But first I need to learn these business ropes for myself. So I've been offered a summer job in the manufacturing department at the Boston Ale Company. I'll start at the bottom and working my way up. I can learn the beer business and get experience."

Stunned, Adella hugged him. "Baby, I'm so happy for you. And you didn't say anything?"

With a proud grin, he kissed her hand. "I wanted to lock down the position first and then surprise you."

A bursting joy sprouted from her chest and gathered in her throat. "I'm surprised. And so thrilled for you." Between kissing and squeezing in the small celebratory moment, they linked hands. Her vocal cords shook her words. "What about your mother?

"My mother's coattails were never what I wanted. I'll help out where you need me to, but for the most part, you and her will figure out the real estate thing. Right now, I want to figure out me. I hope that's all right with you." The hot caramel of his eyes poured into her. "Mrs. McLain."

A pang of loneliness shot through her when she thought of the upcoming obstacles she'd confront on her own. She didn't doubt her abilities, but Del had anticipated them tackling the family business hurdles together. "I was hoping you would help me turn down the drama between your company and mine. But you following a dream of your own is more important. That is perfectly all right with me. Mr. McLain."

Where their fingers played, the new red diamond gleamed with purple specks in the sunlight. The rock winked at her every time her gaze hit it.

"I still can't believe you did this."

Desmond was no longer paying attention to the ring. Her husband's eyes were already getting drunk on her nakedness.

"Believe it." His tongue slowly crawled from his mouth, and glided across her lips. "Why don't you show me how much you like it?"

Wearing a hooded gaze of lust, he grabbed one of her breasts, and licked her thick nipple. Soft, wet, his tongue sent shivers down to Adella's core. His mouth pulled on her hard tip before he gently bit it.

"Mm," she moaned, losing herself in rising heat.

He stared up at her while shoving more of her breast into his mouth. With his other hand, he inserted two fingers between her thighs, into her opening.

Adella's mouth dropped while he fingered her. She swept her

hands over his head, cradling it while he kept munching and sucking. Rocking and thrusting against his fingers, her core burned with desire.

"Why are you fucking with my appetite?" he whispered after wetting her breast.

"What do you mean? You just ate?"

"I mean, I don't care how much I eat, your man is gonna stay hungry for you?" Ready to handle his appetite, he tossed, her onto his rock-solid erection. The flesh over her belly danced under his fingers massaging it.

The Ivy League doctor decided to let her guard down. "And what if I'm hungry for you?"

Easing off of him, she took Desmond's shaft in her hands.

Shock froze him at the sight of his wife shifting down, between his legs. Adella kept her eyes locked on his and placed her tongue at the base of his stone-hard dick. Starting at his balls, she licked up with her whole tongue. Then she put him in her mouth.

Desmond's jaw dropped, eyes glued wide. The sight of his chest heaving in and out urged her to keep going, inserting as of him in her mouth as she could fit, until his head was plugging her throat.

She bobbed her head, up and down, until Desmond's innocent doctor disappeared and she morphed into somebody else.

Tasting and sucking, Adella let herself go. Her tongue and head motions wet him up, as if his wife's appetite just might exceed his. Her hands at his base while her tongue and mouth slurped on his tip, she jerked her head around, smacking on him. His size stretched bigger, and Del licked faster and nastier, pushing him back in her throat.

Desmond gasped under the pressure, his fingers cradling her face.

"I love you so much, Adella." He lifted his pelvis and pressed himself in and out of her throat. "Your mouth is so sexy. I've wanted this since the day I met you. Baby, get up here."

His low, guttural voice drove her heat that now clanged between her legs.

He yanked her up, but Adella remembered his mother would arrive soon. "I have to get ready. We don't have much time."

His starving eyes stared at hers. "Don't worry. We won't need much."

"Ah." She bit her lip as he lifted her and set her down on the length of his long shaft.

She was still getting used to him filling her to the hilt. Adella rocked on top of him, her walls pulsated with his wood cradled inside her. Husband and wife moved in unison, thrusting their pelvises together in a love song.

"Mm" he grunted, gripping her hips to submerge deep into her and disappear.

The exhilaration sent her head back. "Des…" she whined.

Hanging on, clawing and tugging, they disappeared in one another. Adella rode out the intense shocks overtaking her until her walls overheated and then erupted.

His face mirrored her ecstasy, and his trembling flowed through her. "Del!"

Their chaotic breaths intertwined, they no longer breathed or moved as two separate souls, but they exhaled together, reaching the heights of their love as one. Del rode her man even once the aged headboard unexpectedly cracked from hitting the wall so hard. Grinding out the ecstasy, they finally returned to Earth.

Damn. When Franny the housekeeper arrived from Boston in a few days, Del would have to explain that new repair.

By late morning, Adella was readying the lunch she'd prepared the night before. Desmond wouldn't stay for her meal with his mother, since he felt they needed to build their own rapport. He'd finalized plans with Jerrell and other Hamptons guys for the afternoon.

A lot weighed on her mind as she worked. Despite all the good news happening for her, Adella's thoughts clouded with big issues for her to undertake.

Aside from meeting with Desmond's mother to discuss upcoming corporate restructuring, Del still had to face the largest challenge—her family.

They were still nursing defeat and fighting in probate court. She had to find a way to right the ship with them. Papa had trusted her to.

On a mid-May day, the temperature still carried a brisk bite. Pulling open the wooden shutters, Desmond helped her crank open the old cast-iron vintage casement windows. As fresh spring air filled the house for the first time in months, the muslin whirled, as if welcoming new a new breeze, and new life, into the Manuel family compound.

They'd already switched out the heavy winter brocade drapes for light and summery silk charmeuse with airy muslin. She'd traded out the darker velvets for fluffier linens. No one stayed in the family home now except the two of them. She'd sent all the staff away.

Just as her grandfather once had, she consumed herself with the attention to detail. She worked to infuse freshness and modernity in the home—fuchsias placed by the window and on the table, lemon vanilla potpourri in the corners and shelves, paintings of Alabama sharecroppers and old schoolhouses moved to accompany paintings of Black revolutionaries and activists. Then also, there were wrapped candies in old vases.

Then, Desmond slid his arms around her for a hug and pressed his lips into her ear. "Baby, you are the fittest. In every way."

Their fingers gripped one another's faces while they shared a deep kiss that brought their foreheads together.

"I love you," Adella murmured. Her eyes closed while she processed the heavy lifting ahead of her.

"I love you too. Supertanker." He clasped his hands tightly at her back to reassure her. "You *are* a supertanker. Unsinkable. Or you wouldn't be the one standing here."

Hearing him recite the principle her grandfather had spoken to him was air blowing the doubts from Adella's nerves.

He then made his exit to go meet Jerrell and others for golf.

In her grandmother's oven mitts, she set out one dish after another, of salmon cakes with creamed garlic sauce, spinach salad, and fresh buttered vegetables. Sweet iced tea she placed alongside lemon meringue pie. All of it she had made herself.

Once Del had set the table, she put on a pale-yellow summer suit and unwound the twists in her natural hair, separating her crop into a shiny twist-out.

Mrs. McLain's car pulled into the front drive. Adella carried the frogs jumping in her airway out to the front terrace to meet her new mother-in-law. Gulping large breaths that begrudgingly moved down her throat, she waited.

The thick-boned woman stepped from behind the wheel of a Rolls-Royce, wearing a simple navy summer suit, gold buttons, and large hat that she clamped to her head to keep it from flying away. Adella smiled a genuine and nervous grin as she greeted her husband's mother for the first time in months.

"Well, well," Margaret McLain began, her eyes soaking up Adella as if she were a masterpiece. "Let me get a look at you, the woman who has turned my son inside out."

Shaking her head, surprised at the warm demeanor, Adella replied, "I haven't done anything, ma'am. I just managed not to kill him."

They exchanged a hug tighter than Adella was used to, and also longer, forcing her stiff body to release some anxious tension.

"That's probably the most important step."

Both women laughed, and Adella stepped back for the elder woman to enter the quiet Manuel home.

"Desmond told me you wanted to meet at your offices in Maryland," Adella said. "I don't know about you, but I could use this scenery. I hope that's all right."

"It is. Where's the rest of your brood?" Mrs. McLain peered around them and up the stairs as if she were half-expecting, half-dreading Adella's mother.

"They don't arrive until tomorrow. I wanted to meet you privately first. See where things lie between us before I climb my next mountain."

A knowing giggle was the older woman's reply. "Very wise." His mother's eyes danced around the Manuel's Hampton home overlooking the Atlantic Ocean. "It's been a long time since I've stood in this house."

"You've been here before?"

"Yes. Quite a while ago, when I got promoted to vice president, your grandfather allowed me to hold my industry party here. Sometimes he let his friends borrow this place to host their events."

Adella nodded while walking her to the dining room. "Mh-mm, I remember that."

Many famous celebrities, corporate types, and politicians had spent time at the Manuel property dating back before Del was born. Some of their portraits lined the halls and library.

"He allowed me to host some of my family and friends here for a nice party. I was impressed with it then, and it is no less impressive now. You all have kept it up well."

Adella fixed her plate while she wandered across to the pictures of family and famous cohorts.

"Where are your helpers, dear?" Desmond's mother asked.

"No helpers. Just us. More personal. My grandfather taught me—though I didn't know it at the time—that serving someone is one of the highest forms of showing honor and respect."

Tears welled up in her eyes, recalling all the times she'd carried her grandfather's briefcase, his tackle box, fishing pail, and pails of worms or crickets. When he'd opened it all up, she'd watched the painstaking selectiveness with which he would catch his fish, or shoot a duck or deer.

The weight of Mrs. McLain's stare settled on her daughter-in-law. "To hell with this long, fancy table. Let's get comfortable." Mrs. McLain kicked off her shoes, and then fixed Adella's plate.

Adella found a bottle of good gin, while Desmond's mother grabbed glasses. Removing their suit jackets, they moved to the living room and tucked their feet underneath them, with their plates and liquor.

"Now. How are you doing?" Desmond's mother's eyes furrowed. A crease of concern formed on her forehead.

Adella could have pounded a hole into the ceiling while she stared at it. "Hmph. A nightmare. Desmond has been the brightest part of all this. I totally thought he would be the worst."

They broke into laughter.

She tried to cage her elephant-sized tears, but they refused to hold their peace. Her chest heaved as she hyperventilated with thoughts of her family and her dread of seeing them the next day. She would need an armored tank to protect her emotions from their barrage of opinions.

The more seasoned woman reached across the sofa, clasping Adella's hand. For several seconds, Mrs. McLain shook it, wagging Adella's arm from side to side, and they both shed real tears.

For one of the only times in her life, the younger woman felt understood. Like their separate journeys might have been much the same.

"You are indeed French Manuel's granddaughter," Mrs. McLain whispered. "And wherever he is right now, I know he is so relieved that you accepted his offer."

The searchlights of Adella's gaze drifted up again, as if scanning for Papa somewhere in the room. How could she be having a conversation with a woman deeper than what she had with her own mother?

"How did my grandfather know Desmond?"

"From mentoring me." Mrs. McLain grabbed the tongs and placed another salmon cake on both their plates. "I wanted Desmond to see a positive male businessman, not just the ones on the street that he saw all the time, but a bigshot, an executive. Many men in my neighborhood were working behind counters, under cars, cutting hair. Nothing wrong with that, but I wanted my sons to see other kinds of men too, the white collar kind. Sometimes, I would arrange for Desmond and French to cross paths before my meetings with French. After seeing Desmond play ball as a kid—the way he looked out for his friends and protected his sister—your grandfather was adamant about Desmond and you."

Del ate slowly, thinking over it all, and how he'd never said anything. Del had never known until she'd read through his journals. She had spoken aloud the words of his letter so many times, she'd practically memorized them. Papa's forethought both warmed and chilled her.

She handed Del a shot of gin. "And your grandfather wanted me to mentor you."

Del was too blown away to toss it back. "Mentor me?"

"Yes. I accepted. A trade-off. He got Desmond, and I got you."

"How can you help me? You're from the opposing company."

The woman's eyes glistened. "I'm for the greatest wealth. Your grandfather knew that. If you do well, we do well." She tossed back her gin. "So. What do you need from me?"

The weight of Del's worries tripped out in a long sigh. "We should repurpose some of the commercial properties. Assess which buildings are too old and should be sold or destroyed. Which communities we could revive? And we have not been in front of technology readiness. Or revitalization. I believe

Solomon has just been keeping the company afloat barely, so it would be financially solvent for him to sell after Papa's death. But we could be so much more than that."

Desmond's mother nodded. "Agreed. Who do you plan to keep in charge of the company?"

"Solomon. He knows it best. But with a co-chair. I'm willing to accept a liaison from your company who will work alongside him, exercise your voting rights, and serve as a check against him."

Mrs. McLain nodded. "Good thinking. I'm amenable to that." Her focus on Adella deepened. "My son is very happy. I've never seen him this way. I'm honored that you're my daughter-in-law."

Adella smiled from the flashbacks of the past three months that played in her head, of how far they'd come. "Thank you. I'm honored he's my husband. Not sure how I feel about the whole arranged marriage thing, but I am grateful for Papa's foresight. That he didn't leave me alone in this."

Mrs. McLain poured more shots. "No. You are definitely not alone. Adella, I want you to know that, no matter what happens in the boardroom—whether we agree or disagree—you are what Desmond needs. You are part of my family now, Adella. My business and my family will always exist apart from one another. One will never affect the other. For the growth I see in him, I love you already. That is unconditional. Deal?"

Her mother-in-law became a blur through her tears. Del nodded. "Deal."

The woman's face shifted to a more analytical, business-oriented expression. "So which properties did you have in mind?"

Del thought a moment before pouring the next round. "Desmond tells me you're interested in breaking into The Hamptons."

"I am. Something in particular you're eying?"

A smile broke across the younger Mrs. McLain's face. She passed her mother-in-law the drink. "In fact, there is."

Curiosity animated the businesswoman now. "I'm all ears. Shoot."

CHAIRWOMAN

ADELLA

On the dreaded Sunday afternoon, Del waited for her family to arrive. Maddy had offered to come with her as a source of support, but Adella declined. It was time to do as Papa had expected and rise to the occasion. Survival of the fittest.

The fittest is you.

This time, she wore no suit. Instead of expensive dress clothes or a tennis outfit that matched the spring pastels and easy yachting attire, Adella threw on an apron over jeans and a button-down shirt. She heated the large meal she had been cooking on her own since she and Desmond had arrived three days prior—duck, chicken, steak, salads, and vegetables she'd been preparing for the past two days.

None of the food had been catered. Rather, from memory, she recalled her grandmother's recipes, on which her grandfather often tested her.

She now understood what Papa had wanted. Why he had always quizzed her. Why he always assigned her the mundane tasks. Why she had always been in charge of food and setup while the others ran off to play.

Ilyana entered first. "It smells good in here. Which caterer did you bring in this time?"

"Madame Del's catering service," Del said with a smile.

"Get out! You had time to do all this?"

Her sister came in and threw her coat over the foyer chair, not realizing that Adella had dismissed all the waitstaff.

Del paused. She set down the dipping sauce, walked to the chair, and picked up Ilyana's coat in front of her before taking it to the coat closet. While hanging it, Adella rolled her eyes at Ilyana.

"My bad. Where are all the service people? The help?"

"You're looking at it." Adella returned to the dining room table to arrange her dish settings.

Chastened after Adella had admonished her, Ilyana joined her to grab drinks.

Rachel arrived with Constance. And then Martin appeared. As did her Uncle Bryce and Aunt Lizelle. Once everyone was present, they wondered where were the waitstaff and help.

"This is an all-hands-on-deck family meeting," Adella announced. "No one else will serve or wait on us. I know it's what we've become used to. Papa's priority made sure we were accustomed to being served. But today, we will be serving ourselves an one another. No frills or trappings or underlings to make us feel big. Just us."

Solomon huffed.

Afi shoved her arms across her chest as her mouth tasted a quart of vinegar. "We are not poor. We don't have to work like poor people. Papa never tolerated that for us."

Adella handed Ilyana a stack of plates to begin passing around. "No, but he also didn't tolerate laziness and selfishness either," Del replied, staring straight at her elder brother. "I know you don't like what Papa decided, but he did it. It will not change. My first priority is our family, the homes, and personal accounts. My second priority is the company and making sure it is in sound financial health. We will not be selling it."

Grumbles rolled around the table, particularly between Solomon and Bryce. Adella had read Papa's suspicions about their scheme to divide it and sell.

Her Uncle Bryce's massive body swung one leg over the other. "So how will you keep a dying company afloat in a dying industry? When did you become an expert in the real estate business since you haven't been working in it? Why don't you just stick to fixing hearts?"

"I plan to. Starting with the heart of this family. If you want to walk out of here and not come back, that's your decision. But I am committing a portion of my earnings to the family estate."

Gasps erupted around the room.

"You're lying!" Afi snickered.

"I am not." Adella studied each of them. "Among all of us, we have the resources to get the liens removed from the Cape Cod home. We can share that debt. I invite you to join me and help pay off Papa's debts that he incurred to secure our futures."

"I have business of my own that I need to handle. My money and investments are tied up elsewhere." Bryce's shoulders clapped against the chair so hard, she feared it would collapse.

"And you had hoped, with your share of Papa's company, you could untie some of your other dealings," Adella concluded, her gaze narrowing on him.

"Don't talk to him like that," Afi threatened.

"Fine," Adella responded. "Very well then. But don't complain about the decisions I make if you are not willing to put skin in the game to save our properties."

"Since these are your houses now, why should we pay into them?" Bryce asked.

"In exchange for all of us paying on the liens, I would transfer title to all of us jointly. And we would all be owners with a sharing schedule. Hopefully, we could pull this family back together, with holidays, reunions, and celebrations. Of course, we would continue gathering in Alabama as we always have."

Her gaze fell over each person in the room.

"Solomon? Will you contribute to paying off the liens on the Cape Cod property?"

Solomon shifted in his chair, biting his lip, having a hard time lifting his eyes from his plate of steak. "I'm afraid I'm unable to, sis. You haven't left me with many options, so I'll be heading in a different direction than you."

His words punched her in the gut because she was really hoping he'd get over the hurt and the two of them could work together.

"Solly, I want you to stay and we do this together."

In his furrowed eyebrows, he seemed to carry some feelings he refused to share. "I love you, Adella, but you're doing what you believe is necessary, and I'll have to do the same. I'm starting my own venture, a restaurant. Maybe Papa leaving you the company is my blessing in disguise, a chance for me to go after a dream of my own."

Adella stared at her big brother, inclined to run down the laundry list of times he'd abandoned her, particularly all the conflicts where she endured Kevin Middleton without Solomon's protection. The resentment bubbled up in her chest. She almost felt as if Solomon owed her since he'd never been supportive in the past, and that helping her was the least he could do. But she bit her tongue. Having an angry Solomon in the fold would be more harmful than helpful. Nevertheless, the words her tongue held back she unloaded on him through her side-eye.

"Aunt Lizelle? Afi? Constance? Any takers? Anyone care to join me to save our properties and contribute to lifting the liens in the amount of four-point-seven million?"

She scanned all of her relatives, stopping at the eldest of her grandfather's children. Her mother.

They'd never needed to speak to communicate. And for

Adella to feel her mother's burning disdain, no words were needed now.

"What point are you trying to prove, girl?" her mother muttered.

"No point. It's just a question. Are we devoted to Papa, or are we devoted to ourselves? "There are more than enough of us to eliminate these liens together, and we should do this as a family, not just me alone. Please don't force me."

Three people raised their hands. Rachel, Ilyana, and Uncle Bryce's son.

"We will contribute to lifting the liens," Rachel said.

Adella nodded. "Then the matter is settled. Bryce Junior, Rachel, Ilyana, and I will be the new stewards of the Cape Cod property. This property in The Hamptons, I will transfer owner-ship to all of us—a life estate in each of us with it passing to a person of my choosing upon the death of every person in this room. Our lawyers can work out the specifics."

Astonishment silenced them, their gazes darting around the room at each other as if they had expected Adella to be greedy enough to take everything and not share.

"I'm curious to know." Solomon piped up. "What would my role be if I stayed on in House Adella?"

"It's still House Manuel, and you would be Chief Operating Officer. But, there will be a liaison from Margaret McLain's company who will work alongside you."

Grumbles across the room once again.

Solomon pounded the table. "A liaison? Tuh. You're in with those McLains now. That's what you and your frat boy have been over there doing the past two months? With none of us around. I could never find you so we could talk."

A sinkhole of isolation opened at the pit of Adella's stomach, churning and swirling to suck her into it. That hole always opened up whenever one of her older siblings undermined her.

And once again, she sank into it, suffocating and unable to breathe.

She shook her head. *No.* She was among the fittest. Adella had more than survived. She had thrived. Despite them. She crawled out of the sinkhole and forced her lungs to clamor for oxygen. And stared from Solomon to Constance to her mother.

"If you think I would hurt what Papa built, you don't know me at all. And maybe you have no clue of my character because you never bothered to *see* me as anything other than your sickly little sister you were stuck with. If you had, you would understand why Papa left this to me. Because I would never do such a thing. But *you* would."

Her brother flinched as she called him out for his selfish backroom dealings behind Papa's back. They all stared at one another, like slow ships passing in the daytime.

"Your meal tastes really good, Adella," Rachel complimented her, in an effort to cool the emotional temperature. "Who was the caterer? It tastes so similar to Grandma's."

"Me." Flat and lifeless was now Adella's response for a meal that was made with so much love.

A gentle wind seemed to blow emotions around the room, from one to the other, before they dropped somber spirits to their plates.

"This entire meal, all this food, *you* prepared it? No waiters, no chef?" her mother challenged.

"All me." Pangs of disappointment cracked across Adella. "But thanks so much for your faith in me."

"It's been years since one of us prepared the meal," Aunt Lizzie observed.

"We've all been too busy." Bryce sipped his lemonade, his eyes avoiding Adella's in what might have been his attempt to suppress guilt.

"We've all been so disconnected," Adella corrected him. "So busy chasing profit, and the next shiny thing." Her gaze landed on

Solomon. "I will host a crab boil here in three weeks. The first time we've had one in a while. I hope you'll join me for some of the things we used to do, that helped to keep us together, that Papa tried to keep alive after Grandma was gone."

Adella set pecan and sweet potato pies on the table. "I'm willing to share Papa's empire. Once I trust that you will handle his affairs responsibly." Del finally parked her gaze at Afi. "Without vindictive, backstabbing schemes."

Afi's face hardened.

Adella finally understood why Papa never confronted his children about their transgressions. It stirred too much animosity that risked tearing them apart. Rather, he'd gone into debt instead to accommodate them.

Adella would not say more to her cousin. Afi's stubborn sour-grapes face indicated she had gotten Del's message loud and clear.

"I love all of you. My offer stands to work together. Anytime you're ready. I don't want to do this alone." Del shot a final glance across all of them. "But I can."

～

ADELLA and her friends enjoyed the afternoon sun on the terrace of *Sharon's*.

Desmond and Adella were set to renew their vows privately that night on the beach, with just a handful of close friends and family.

But at the moment, they discussed the hottest topic in Sag Harbor—Kevin Middleton being so close to purchasing the *Ivory*, the historic black-owned restaurant that meant so much to the Sag Harbor community.

Chrissy, Maddy, Adella, Desmond, and Jerrell all sat at lunch with Chrissy's cousins, Neera and Cher.

"I'm not ready to give up on the *Ivory* just yet. Yes, it seems like Lana is in a strong position now that she's got Kevin on her team, but I think I found us a loophole. We can have the *Ivory* declared a historic landmark because it's been around for so long." Maddy sipped a Shirley Temple.

"That requires a ton of red tape and bureaucracy," Adella replied. "The city wants the tax dollars of a thriving Ivory that's fully operational, and not a museum, so they will fight you behind the scenes."

Next to Adella, Cher, squirmed with some apparent discomfort.

"What's the matter with you?" Chrissy asked her.

"Nothing," Cher said, with a strange look on her face, as if she'd been caught with her hand in a big jar of chocolate.

"Howdy, folks," an irritating, high-pitched voice scraped Adella's ears. It sounded like a fork crawling against a skillet.

Lana.

"Why are you here?" Maddy stared at her Capitol Hill co-worker, and Desmond's former lover.

For his part, Desmond rolled his eyes and parked them on his wife. They seemed to say: *Baby, I'm so sorry.*

Then, yet another stray person appeared with her. Kevin Middleton.

"Hamptons fam! What's good?" How could somebody be equal parts handsome *and* evil? His gaze landed on Maddy and Jerrell.

Lana and Kevin were now the two most scandalous people in The Hamptons.

Lana grabbed the back of an empty chair Adella had saved. "Ya'll can't speak? We're all black in The Hamptons. Would it not be rude if I walked right by you and did not say something?"

"It's rude that you came over here like a gnat," Jerrell replied.

Lana's attention shifted to Desmond. "I haven't seen you in a while. Not since the *Oasis Cove*." Devilish in the way she threw a hand on her hip, she cast a side-smile at Adella. "How are you two doing? Does your man need another tune-up?"

Adella shot up and knocked over the chair. That was it.

Desmond's attention remained on Del, asking her not to move.

"Don't you have dog food to eat somewhere?" Chrissy asked Lana.

"Lana," Desmond spoke, his attention steadfast on his wife, "I'm sure you've met my wife, Mrs. McLain, the woman who tunes me up so good she wears my three-million-dollar ring."

Adella waved with her left hand as the sunshine confirmed the rock's quality.

"Th-three *million?*" Kevin repeated, never one to deprive the world of his thoughts.

"Three million," the others at the table repeated smugly.

Lana's eye sockets seemed to cave in upon hearing the price tag.

"Congratulations." Kevin coughed. "Damn, Del, your cat must be the Garden of Eden and the rest of us never knew."

"Motherf—" Desmond lunged at him.

Jerrell's arm shot out to shove a livid Desmond back in his seat.

Kevin snickered at Maddy, and his eyes dropped to her four-month visible baby bump. "Madison, good to see you're being fed well. With plenty of cakes and pastries, jelly donuts and such."

Jerrell let go of Desmond to squabble with Kevin himself. But Maddy stood and shoved herself between them all.

"Don't tell me you're upset, are you, man?" Kevin taunted Jerrell. "I was just about to invite you all to my private gathering I'm holding at the *Ivory* in a few weeks. We can celebrate your new baby, and Del's wedding, and Chrissy's… well… Chrissy's impending divorce. Sorry? Congratulations? I'm not too sure which applies here. But anyway, you all should come. We start construction in late summer once the sale is finalized."

"But the sale's not finalized *yet*," Maddy reminded him.

"It will be, though," Lana replied.

"Don't be so sure," Chrissy intervened.

Throughout the entire conversation, Adella observed Cher, the way she stared at Kevin. The way Kevin's eyes seemed to connect with Cher's indicated more than a passing glance between the two. Del questioned what was going on, and she stored this exchange in her mental notes to raise with Chrissy later.

For now, Kevin snapped at Maddy, "It's a done deal, Mad Dog, and you may as well start accepting it. You *lost*." He scoffed. "Who else can stop us now?"

"Me."

All eyes at the table sailed to Adella.

"*You?*" Kevin asked, throwing back his head to laugh, its arrogant snarl reminding her of all the times he'd mocked her when they were kids.

Adella ignored the astonished faces of her friends, with whom she hadn't yet discussed this. As well as the mollified expression on her husband.

Del's book deal had snagged her $4.8 million. She had turned down a job offer to host a television show on health and medicine in the black community, because the $225,000 annual salary didn't match what she earned as a heart surgeon at $436,000.

She planned to keep part of her schedule available for Manuel Realty and shepherding its comeback. If she could turn it around successfully, that payoff would deliver far greater dividends and investments than a talk show.

Plus, she would appear as a regular medical correspondent on CMN, and that job would garner her $3 million per year. With the addition of her new stock shares, Adella would add over $20 million in wealth to her portfolio before the year was out.

"Yes. Me."

"Ahaaa." Kevin flicked his nose for effect. "Adella. Sweetheart.

I know you're a heart surgeon and all, and that's very commendable. But even to be some doctor, your money's not that long, Del. How exactly would you pull off a seventy-million-dollar project? You're going to need a big assist with that, don't you think?"

"She's got help." All heads swung to another figure entering the terrace. Margaret McLain. She joined the table, first kissing a stunned Desmond on his forehead, and then an expectant Adella. The elder businesswoman took the seat that Adella had saved for her.

Del had invited Mrs. McLain to brunch, to start the process of introducing Desmond's mother around in the New York circles.

And right behind Mrs. McLain was Mr. McLain, Desmond's father.

Desmond froze in his seat, his mouth falling and grinning at the same time, as the elder McLain pulled out the chair Adella had also saved for him. Adella's husband turned to her and squeezed her hand, his gratitude pouring from his eyes.

All of the others at the table could have been statues of black marble. Del's announcement had frozen their mouths in time. Especially the mouth of Kevin Middleton.

Del sucked her teeth as she faced her longtime tormentor. "Oh, Kevin, I'm not just *some doctor* anymore. I own a company now. And I'm the chairwoman. *Sweetheart.*"

The End?

BOOK 4 EXCERPT

OVERHEATED FOR SUMMER

CONTINUED FROM CHRISSY & SHELDON IN BOOK 2

"Alright, so you think you got it?" Sheldon Rouse asked, among the screaming children and anxious teachers on grass.

Little Blake's eyes danced with delight on his Field Day. Excited for the last day of third grade, the boy bounced his projectile in his hands. "I think so."

"No, you don't think so, young stunna. You *know* it. Keep your feet steady while you pull your hands into your chest. Ready up. Lock your eyes onto your target. Arms firm. And when you send it out, let it rip. Your arm is a rubber band. Stretch it nice and tight, let it go, and then snap back!" Sheldon instructed his girl-friend Chrissy's nine-year-old son. As he did so, he stood behind Blake, guiding the boy's small but stalwart arms through the motions.

Sheldon thought the kid had a good football physique, and only needed a steady arm. He was certain the issue was Blake's confidence.

"Okay," Blake said, taking his object, focusing and pulling it into his chest, tight as Sheldon had demonstrated.

"What do we say to being a scaredy cat?" Sheldon asked.

"Fear *no* one," Blake responded.

He ran back into the festivities.

"You've got this! You're a stallion!" Sheldon yelled, clapping his hands, making sure his voice was the only one on the field that Blake heard.

Little Blake's legs took him fast as they could, as he chased after one particularly overbearing bigger boy that bothered Sheldon. He held his breath as the young buck locked feet in position, eyes in place, stretched his arm, tossed the water balloon and snapped it back. He hit the target. Little Blake's fists pumped, and a huge smile spread across his face, before he took off running again while the boys resumed chasing.

Sheldon beamed to watch the boy relax some.

"He has made some really big improvements these past few months, since he moved here from L.A.," a woman's gentle voice said at his side.

Sheldon turned to see Blake's school teacher. Arms folded across his chest, he kept eying Blake to make sure he interacted well with the bigger boys, as they'd worked on. "Yes, he has. He's a little rockstar."

"I'd like to think you had more than a little something to do with that," Mrs. Gray replied. "He hasn't had a fight, or even a confrontation, in two months. His grades are stellar. And look at that smile."

"It's mostly him. He's been putting in all the heavy lifting. I'm just here to support what's already in him." Sheldon turned to Mrs. Gray. "But thank you for that."

"Thank *you*. And please congratulate Mrs. Mason for me as well. He is a very fortunate young man to have you both in his life. I look forward to watching all his amazing growth from afar next year," she said, before moving on.

Sheldon cringed at that title— *Mrs. Mason.*

As if he needed to be reminded that Chrissy still wasn't quite divorced. And as such, their romance remained secret, known among only a small few, namely his brothers, Chrissy's closest friends, and their parents.

Their children didn't know officially, but he suspected Little Blake was onto them. As far as the world was concerned, they were just friends and Sheldon was a mentor to Little Blake. So Sheldon never spent a single night at Chrissy's brownstone in the city until they went to their grandmother's. And it had been a long three weeks since the kids last visited their grandparents.

But this weekend, after five months of dating, and with Chrissy's divorce almost in her rear view, they would make their relationship public. All the families— including the Pages, Rouses, and Townsends— were headed to Sag Harbor, and the kids would take time with the grands. While the adults played. Sheldon's heart thudded for the alone time he and Chrissy would finally get tonight in a penthouse he'd rented, right on the beach.

After he joined Little Blake for dodge ball, the day's big finale was a father-son tug of war over a mud pit, which they won. Yet the mud found them anyway, caked around their calves, shoes and clothes.

"Your mother will not be happy about all this dirt," Sheldon commented as they got in his Maybach that he'd already covered with towels and plastic to lessen some of the mess on his seats.

"Can we get pizza before we go home?" Blake asked.

"I supposed I can squeeze that in, before we get on the road to the Sag."

After Blake said goodbye to his friends, and Sheldon exchanged numbers and information with parents for summer gatherings, they headed to Pete's Pizza Parlor. Sheldon filled the kid's gut with whatever he wanted, because the boy had earned it.

As they walked back to the car, they passed up a jewelry store. On a whim, he took Blake inside. Together, they looked over jewelry and gifts for Chrissy's birthday in August, while Sheldon got Blake's thoughts on what he liked.

"What about red?" Blake asked, pointing at a ruby necklace.

"How about light blue? What's her favorite color?"

"Umm," Blake said, his eyes darting around as he tried to guess.

Sheldon squeezed his head. "Oh, no, man. Don't tell me you don't know. Your girl game is slipping. Your mom is your main chick, and you don't know her favorite color. Dude, that's rule number one in the playbook."

Blake let out a sheepish laugh as Sheldon tickled him.

"Yes, could you pull out the FL-quality rings, please?" Sheldon asked the store manager. His eyes peered at Blake. "What do you think of those?"

"Whoa." Blake's eyes grew large when he saw the price tags. "That's a big number. I wonder how many video games I could buy for that much."

The ring that had caught Sheldon's eye was $216,760.00 for a five carat oval SI1-FL cut.

Sheldon laughed. "Don't worry. I'll teach you how to figure it out in your head. When I'm done with you, you will be a math aficionado."

"A math *what?*" Blake giggled, as his eyes meandered with a confused expression. "Sooo… are you going to ask my mom to… marry you?"

Sheldon swallowed. "No, I am not. Not right now."

"So maybe later?"

He shrugged. "I don't know. I'm kind of scared." They left the store.

The kid smirked. "But I thought you said we fear no one."

Sheldon chuckled. "Is that what I said?"

Blake laughed with him, a matter-of-fact expression crossing his face. "Yes, that's what you always say."

"Well, the rules are different for your mom. We always fear her."

They both burst into laughter while getting into Sheldon's car.

"So, if you do ever ask my mom to marry you, would that make you my dad?"

He inhaled. "I'm always going to be whatever you want me to be. Uncle, friend, basketball coach, water balloon instructor, anything you need. Okay? And that's no matter what. If your mother and I stay friends or not, you can always call me."

Blake nodded his head. "Okay."

"I'm real proud of you, Blake. You worked hard this year. After a lot was put on you. Leaving your house and friends in L.A. Coming way out here to cold New York, where you didn't know anybody." Sheldon left out Little Blake's father not being around. "Starting a whole new school. And you tackled it all like a strong man would. I'm proud. Be proud of yourself."

Blake smiled, and sat back in the seat, owning his moment. With that, Sheldon started the car.

"I love you, Sheldon."

The words moved him. This had come after months of rushing to Blake's school when Chrissy was too busy with her new job, and Sheldon's more flexible schedule allowed him to leave work as he pleased. After nights of helping with homework, taking Blake to therapy sessions, and playing video games. All so that Blake would trust him, and see a different example of men than the boy's father had shown him.

Overcome by the wave of emotion, he grabbed Little Blake's head, bringing it to him and kissing it. He spoke the words as he choked. "Thank you for that, man. I love you too."

After he released him, they took off, and headed toward Chrissy's brownstone to get clean, and pick up Chrissy and Blake's little sister Kara. Their first family outing. Chrissy had wanted to be the one to break the news of her and Sheldon being boyfriend and girlfriend that weekend. Sheldon was trying his best not to spoil it.

"Alright, we need to hurry upstairs and get this dirt off, before your mom comes home and sees." Sheldon began to get out.

"If you do ask my mom to marry you," Blake started, swallowing, "you won't make her cry the way my dad did. Will you?"

Sheldon's insides shuddered. "No, big man, I would never hurt a hair on your mother's head. Or ever make her feel anything but absolute joy. I will certainly do my best."

"You promise? From one man to another?" Blake asked, repeating a phrase Sheldon often used, his eyes penetrating Sheldon's heart.

Sheldon nodded, rubbing the face of Chrissy's son again. "From one man to another, I promise."

CAN Sheldon survive an overheated summer without breaking his promise?

THANKS FROM LULA

Thank you for reading *Flinging All Spring*! If you enjoyed this story, please leave a review at your favorite retailer.

If you were feeling the Rouse family and the characters in Sag Harbor, here's how you can stay connected.

Lula's Store: lulawhitebooks.myshopify.com

Lula's Web site: www.lulawhitebooks.com

Email: lula@lulawhitebooks.com

Lula's Luxe Suite Reading Group:

https://www.facebook.com/groups/lulawhite/

Read the stories before they go on sale:

https://www.patreon.com/lulawhite

Lula's Youtube:

https://www.youtube.com/@lulawhitebooks/featured

You can find Lula mostly on her Patreon, where she writes her stories and shares her research first, as well as her Facebook reading group and Youtube page, Lula's Footnotes. 🤍

The *Sag Harbor Black Romances*

Brown Sugar This Christmas - Maddy & Jerrell

Hot Chocolate This Winter - Chrissy & Sheldon Part 1

Flinging All Spring - Adella & Desmond

Overheated for Summer - Chrissy & Sheldon Part 2

Rouse Family Christmas - All Couples

Books in the spin-off *Explore Men of the Hamptons* series

One Tasty Night FREE Novella - Solomon & Chaitra

Explore You - Kevin & Cher

Christmas Down Under Novella - Keenan & Eugenia - (FREE Download on website only)

Taste You - Solomon & Chaitra

Drink You - Lion & Kamila

See Through You - Keenan & Eugenia

Find You - Roland & Neeraja

Books Related to the Sag Harbor Stories

A New Life for Christmas — Tazima & Odell

The Young & Luxurious

Love & Fire — Korienne & Easton